Persephone's Curse

ALSO BY KATRINA LENO

The Half Life of Molly Pierce

The Lost & Found

Everything All at Once

Summer of Salt

You Must Not Miss

Horrid

Sometime in Summer

The Umbrella Maker's Son

Persephone's Curse

KATRINA LENO

WEDNESDAY BOOKS
NEW YORK

This is a work of fiction. All of the characters, organizations, and events portrayed in this novel are either products of the author's imagination or are used fictitiously.

First published in the United States by Wednesday Books, an imprint of St. Martin's Publishing Group

EU Representative: Macmillan Publishers Ireland Ltd, 1st Floor, The Liffey Trust Centre, 117–126 Sheriff Street Upper, Dublin 1, DO1 YC43

For information, address St. Martin's Publishing Group, 120 Broadway, New York, NY 10271.

www.wednesdaybooks.com

Interior and case stamp designed by Devan Norman
Pomegranate art © Tatiana Goncharuk/Shutterstock

The Library of Congress Cataloging-in-Publication Data is available upon request.

ISBN 978-1-250-34290-4 (hardcover)
ISBN 978-1-250-34291-1 (ebook)

First Edition: 2025

10 9 8 7 6 5 4 3 2 1

to all the Farthing girls out there
and all the magic you contain

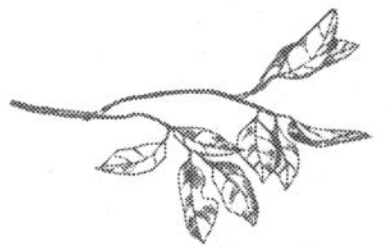

Persephone's Curse

I

Every family has their myths, their stories passed down from generation to generation, a game of telephone that subtly shifts from one mouth to another, from one mother to her daughter, until the message has changed almost entirely. It is hard to tell the truth of something, hard to tell what your aunt means when she whispers a favorite bedtime story into your ear: the Farthing girls are descended from Persephone, are the children of the in-between, one foot in this world and one foot in another . . .

It is hard to tell the truth of something, and yet . . . it feels *real, doesn't it?*

My mother has only seen the ghost once.

And that was fourteen years ago.

If we asked her about it now, she'd dismiss it as a labor-induced hallucination, the result of immense pain and no drugs, a home birth she'd decided to have for her fourth and final daughter, since she'd done the hospital three times before, considered herself something of a pro, wanted to try something different.

But we knew the truth.

Of course she'd seen the ghost.

We all had.

The night our youngest sister was born, we waited on the third floor with Aunt Bea. There were three of us then—Bernadette, six; Evelyn, four; me, two. Clara would make four. Four Farthing sisters, each two years apart.

The labor was happening on the fourth floor, which had once been the attic in our family's Upper West Side brownstone but had been converted by our parents into two rather cramped bedrooms with a larger playroom attached. The birthing pool was set up in the playroom, and every now and then we heard a low, mournful wail drift down the stairs.

The fourth floor was where the ghost lived, in the smaller bedroom, which was now empty but, with the arrival of the baby, would soon be Evelyn's room. She didn't mind sharing a bedroom with a ghost. He'd always been nice to her, to all of us. He wasn't a scary ghost at all. He was a largely shy, mostly quiet, very gentle ghost. If he thought he had spooked us accidentally, turning a corner in the middle of the night as we made our way to the bathroom or down to the kitchen for a glass of water, he grew agitated and insisted—*oh, I didn't do it on purpose!* And we knew that. Of course we knew that.

While my mother gave birth to Clara upstairs, the three of us already-born Farthing sisters and Aunt Bea camped out in what was now Evelyn's room but would soon be the new nursery. We all loved whenever Aunt Bea came to visit because she told the best stories and she always smelled like mint and vanilla and you could often find strange and wonderful things in the pockets of her linen skirts (a partial catalogue: matchbox cars, tiny notebooks, propelling pencils that opened with a tug, satchels of tea, pages torn from her favorite books, hard caramel candies, soft caramel candies).

"Did you girls know . . ." she'd begin, and we'd snuggle into her sides, all of us piled on the twin bed, running our hands through her hair, down her arms, pinching her knees and her elbows, squeezing as close to her as possible, "that us Farthing girls are descended from Persephone?"

Our mother hadn't taken our father's last name, so we were all Farthing girls, and so was she, and so was Aunt Bea, and so was little Esme, the sister they'd had who died when she was just a child.

"Is that true, Auntie?" Bernadette prompted, and the three of us held our breaths, desperate for her to continue.

"Yes," she said, pausing to bop each of us gently on our perpetually sticky noses. "You girls are the great-great-great-great-great-great-grandchildren of Persephone. The children of the in-between, just like she was. Persephone, daughter of Zeus and Demeter, wife of Hades, mother of Melinoë and Zagreus."

Melinoë, Persephone's daughter, would always be our favorite.

She was the goddess of nightmares and madness, and in a houseful of women, there was plenty of that to go around.

Were we *really* descended from Persephone?

Did we believe it then, snuggled up together, the lilt of Aunt Bea's voice putting us half to sleep, the lollipops our father had given us sticking to the sheets as we let them fall from our hands, distracted?

All I will say is this:

We believed everything Aunt Bea told us. Without reservation, without hesitation, without verification.

So, yes.

Even that, we believed.

"How do you feel?" Bernadette asked our mother, when we were allowed to see her. She held a naked, pink baby to her chest—the stranger Clara, who none of us really loved yet but would, quickly, because she was a bubbly, sweet baby with an easy laugh, unlike me, who, at two years old, still cried an awful lot.

"I feel wonderful," my mother said.

"Did it hurt?" Evelyn asked.

"A bit."

"Who that?" I asked, and pointed at the baby. Everyone laughed.

(Of course, in practicality, I don't remember saying this, I don't remember anything about the night Clara was born; I was too young, everything I know came from Bernadette, a collective memory of sisters now.)

"This is your sister. Clara."

"Clara." We all practiced saying her name.

Then my mom took Bernadette by the hand. She rubbed her

knuckles and pulled her in a bit closer. My mother whispered, so no one else would hear, "Have you ever met Henry?"

And Bernadette's eyes grew wide, wide, wide.

And she nodded.

Of course she'd met Henry.

We'd all met Henry.

Henry was our ghost.

I know what you're thinking. Shared hysteria, maybe, what Bernadette called *folie à deux* after one year of French in high school made her act like she'd grown up in the bell towers of Notre-Dame.

That's certainly what our mother believed, what she convinced herself, even though she'd seen and talked to the little boy when my father had taken a quick pee-break and left her alone with the midwife, who'd been momentarily distracted by some rare type of bird out the window. ("One second, just keep breathing, holy *shit,*" she'd said to our mother, "it's a western fucking tanager, wait until Eileen hears about this.")

"Who are *you*?" our mother had asked the little boy poking his head out from the as-yet-unoccupied fourth-story bedroom that would soon belong to Evelyn.

"I'm Henry," Henry said.

"What are you doing here?"

"I live here."

"But *we* live here."

"Well, I live here, too," he insisted. "Actually, I lived here first."

"Are you real?" my mother asked, cutting to the chase as she usually did, trying to decide, maybe, if Henry was a figment of her imagination or a squatter or a friend of Bernadette's who'd squirreled away when nobody was looking. I don't think *or a ghost* would have crossed her mind.

"Are *you* real?" Henry responded.

And then he'd disappeared.

This conversation was relayed to Bernadette by our mother in whispers, while she held both the naked, new Clara and Bernadette's hand. "Have you ever met Henry?" she'd asked, and Bernadette's eyes had grown wide, wide, wide, and she'd nodded, and Clara had fussed, and our mother had grown distracted and, it seemed, when she next looked up at Bernadette, she had made the decision to forget about the ghost entirely. Her expression softened and she let go of Bernadette's hand to cup her cheek instead.

"You're an older sister again, Bernie," our mother said. "You have a new little sister to watch out for. I'm so proud of you."

And in true Bernadette fashion, she had taken a step backward, shrugged ambivalently, and said, "I'm descended from gods, so, I won't be changing any diapers."

Once, when I was nine and Bernadette was thirteen and going through the worst of her *I hate everyone* phase, she'd slapped me, *hard,* for going into her room and looking at her journals without her permission. I hadn't read them, I *hadn't,* I'd just wanted to hold each one in my hands, feel the smoothness of the leather or the way another one's cardboard cover was so worn and soft that it was pliable, like water in my hands. Bernadette had always written in her journals incessantly, every day, filling up page after page with her innermost thoughts and secrets. It was an irresistible treasure trove for a younger sister.

Evelyn had been out at her weekly piano lesson, so after Bernadette slapped me, I'd gone into Evie's room and flung myself across her bed, sobbing into her pillow. Evie would never yell at me for going into her room without permission. Evie would never slap me for touching her things. Evie would sit next to me and stroke my hair and tell me, quite clearly, how she could see both sides of the story and how, no matter what I'd done, Bernadette shouldn't have hit me.

And even though Evie *wasn't* there, suddenly Henry *was*, standing by the foot of the bed, looking translucent and ephemeral and (if I had to admit it), quite dreamy in his deadness.

"Are you all right?" he asked.

I stopped crying right away and sat up on the bed. It was always Evie who'd been the closest with Henry, but that was inevitable, they shared rooms, after all, and Evie was the quiet, sensitive, sweet one, the patient, kind, and friendly one. Of course her best friend would be a ghost.

"Bernadette hit me," I said, my voice hiccupping, my breath catching in my throat. In her bedroom next door, Bernadette had put on some toneless, loud, angry music and was singing along in a toneless, loud, angry voice.

Henry nodded.

He was about fifteen, if I had to give him an age, but he was also sort of ageless, and if you caught him at the right moment, he could be seven or eight, and if you caught him an hour later, he might be almost seventeen.

He'd made us promise to never look for information about him. Never to see how he'd died. Never to see *when* he'd died. *It's private,* he'd said.

And although it wasn't explicitly stated, it also felt like a promise that we never told anyone, not Dad or Mom or even Aunt Bea, the most likely to nod her head and think for a moment and say, "Well, that makes sense, that you've befriended a ghost. You have a direct connection to the Underworld, after all. One foot here, one foot there, the children of the in-between, you know."

But we didn't tell Aunt Bea. We didn't tell anyone. And we never looked for information about Henry. We kept our promises, even Bernadette, whose angry stage had never completely faded and Clara, who was an artist and therefore rarely did anything she was told.

"I saw her hit you," Henry said. "That wasn't very nice."

"I went into her room without asking," I said, leaving out the part about her journals, because I didn't want him to know, because I knew the trespassing was enough of a crime on its own, because I doubted Henry would even understand the importance of a journal to a teenage girl.

Henry nodded. He was always thoughtful with his words, slow to speak, as if he really considered everything he was going to say before he let it free. Evelyn was a bit like that, too, and sometimes I'd wondered if she'd learned it from him, growing up alongside him as she had, in a much closer way than any of the rest of us.

"Would you want her to go in your room without asking?"

Henry said finally, and I huffed and bit my lower lip and then finally admitted I wouldn't.

"Well," he said. "She shouldn't have hit you. But I think you should be the bigger person and apologize first. And she better apologize back to you, or I'll put worms in her bed."

"You wouldn't!" I said, my eyes growing wider.

"I wouldn't," Henry admitted, smiling sweetly. He was a little fadey now, which happened right before he was going to disappear for a while. "Is Evelyn home?" he asked.

"Piano."

"Oh, right."

He was barely visible anymore, just the outline of a boy. The room smelled faintly of flowers. The sweet, subtle fragrance of jasmine. I breathed it in deeply. It made my eyes prickle.

When Evelyn woke me up an hour later, you could still smell it—the jasmine—and for some reason, I couldn't quite look her in the eyes.

Bernadette dropped out of college a week into her sophomore year. It was almost midnight on a Friday night and Evie, Clara, and I were awake playing a game of Monopoly on the living room floor when we heard the key scrambling around for the lock, the click and twist when it caught.

"It's Bernie," Clara said, the only one of us who didn't look startled by the midnight visitor, and we believed her, because every so often Clara just knew something, and we all understood that we shouldn't question it.

I was sixteen then, Evie had just turned eighteen, Clara was fourteen, and Bernadette, soaking wet from the rain that was pouring down outside, was twenty, breathless, coatless, and wide-eyed as she flung herself into the entranceway.

"Bernadette!" Evie exclaimed, getting to her feet.

"Nobody say anything," she pleaded, dropping her suitcase by the door, kicking off her shoes (because even in the middle of a mental breakdown, you took off your shoes in this house, or our mother would find out somehow).

Of course Clara ignored her, jumping up and shouting, "Bernie, what *happened*?"

I was the only one still sitting. I wrapped my arms around my knees because I felt afraid for some reason I couldn't immediately figure out.

Bernadette locked the door behind her. "Will you shut up? I don't want Mom and Dad to hear."

"Mom and Dad are away for the weekend," Evie said. "The Berkshires."

"Oh, God," Bernadette said, putting her face into her hands. "Thank *God*."

"Put the kettle on," Clara said to me, and I scuttled out of the room, relieved I wouldn't have to think of anything to say to my oldest sister, who was so wet and looked so *wild*. The three of them stayed in the entranceway, talking in low voices, and I got four mugs and four bags of peppermint tea and tried not to look toward the back of the house, where the wide, dark windows would only reflect my scared face looking back at me.

Then Bernadette was beside me, and she was hugging me and

dripping all over the floor and all over my clothes and for some reason I was starting to cry.

"You smell like a bus," I said into her shoulder.

"Greyhound, baby," she said, squeezing me tighter. "I missed you so much."

"I just saw you last week," I replied, which was true, she'd only left the house a week ago, but for some reason this made her laugh, and when she pulled away her face was contorted into some kind of joy.

"*Fuck,* Winnie," she said.

"What happened?"

"I couldn't do it anymore."

"Do *what* anymore?"

"College. Life. My part-time job at the fucking bookstore. Any of it. Mom and Dad are really gone? Jesus, that's a relief."

The water in the electric kettle boiled and I poured some into each of the mugs. Bernadette took the one I knew she'd take, the one with a chip on the rim and faded photos of puppies all around it. She held it in her hands and looked at me so deeply it made my stomach twitch.

"I missed you," she said again.

"Are you okay?"

"I'll be okay now. I just . . . I had to come home."

"Are you going back?"

"No," she said, blowing into her mug. "Fuck no."

She took a sip, but it was still too hot, so she made a face and put the mug down on the counter again. I wondered where Evelyn and Clara had gone; either of them would have been better at knowing the right thing to say. I never knew the right thing to say; the best I could do was hope for poignant silences.

Bernadette pulled her sopping-wet shirt over her head and dropped it into the kitchen sink. She was wearing a light pink, lacy bra. My own chest was as flat as the kitchen counter.

"Did something happen?" I asked.

She shrugged. She twisted her long brown hair over one shoulder, held it over the sink, and wrung it out like a towel. I had brown hair, like her. Evelyn and Clara were blondes. All of our hair was long and snarly because our mother had an irrational fear of hairdressers and had never taken us to get trims. We cut our own hair in the attic bathroom when it got too knotted to comb anymore. I reached out now and took a piece of Bernadette's hair in my hand. I knew I was crying and I didn't know why and I couldn't stop. If Bernadette had gone through an angry, wild phase, I was firmly in the middle of a phase of deep, impenetrable sadness. I couldn't remember the last time I'd felt happy. It occurred to me then, standing in the kitchen with Bernadette, that the answer might have been *never.*

"I missed you," she said again, the third time now, an incantation, and I melted into her arms, my tears falling against her already soaking, bus-and rain-scented skin.

We all slept in the fourth-floor playroom that night, which wasn't really a playroom anymore, but instead held Clara's easel and a small upright piano Evelyn had gotten for her fifteenth birthday.

They'd brought it in through the windows with a crane; it had been quite the operation. We dragged Evelyn's and Bernie's mattresses out of their rooms and pushed them together, all sleeping in a big clump of arms and legs and hair. I don't think we fell asleep until dawn, and the last thing I remembered was a quiet whisper from beside me: Evelyn, on the end, saying something to Henry, who'd stayed mostly invisible that whole night, maybe not wanting to intrude as we each took turns crying and laughing and refilling our mugs of tea, the long walk from the fourth floor to the ground floor and back. It was just the five of us, all back together again: girl, girl, girl, girl, ghost.

I put my arm over Evie's stomach and she got very quiet and very still, and then finally, a moment later, relaxed and curled up next to me.

I always woke up last, and when I woke up that next morning, the mattresses were bare beside me and someone, probably Evelyn, had left a now-tepid mug of coffee on the floor beside me. It was after ten and the house was quiet and still, which meant they'd all gone out. I sipped the coffee and got dressed in my uniform of late, jeans and a sweatshirt. Evie wore skirts and turtlenecks, Clara favored short dresses with tights, and Bernadette always looked so, so androgynous and hip, like she'd stepped out of the pages of a fashion magazine. I mostly wore her hand-me-downs but could never make a pair of high-waisted jeans look quite as good as she did.

They'd left me a note on the kitchen counter: *Todd's.*

It was the diner on the corner of our street. The rain had stopped but the skies were still a threatening, steely gray. When I turned around on the sidewalk, there was Henry, in the fourth-floor bedroom he shared with Evie, waving to me. I waved back and he grinned, really wide, and it made me grin, and it made the knot of anxiety inside my stomach loosen, just a little. I carried an umbrella but left it closed up and tucked under my arm, and when I got to the diner, my sisters had already ordered for me and I realized that Bernadette had a black eye. How had I not noticed that last night?

"It's not what you think," she said as I slid into the seat. "It was barely there last night and just—fuck, it totally exploded overnight. I look like I've been punched, I know, but I *haven't*. It was a fucking volleyball right in the fucking face."

Bernadette always swore more in the mornings. She wasn't a morning person but she also couldn't sleep in, and this was a poor combination for her mood. She gulped coffee while Clara, sitting next to me, dropped a piece of her sourdough toast on my plate and exchanged it for a piece of my rye.

"Nobody is doubting you," Evelyn said gently, even though we were literally all doubting her. "It just seems so . . . I mean . . . Well, Bernie, you don't even *play* volleyball."

"That's probably why I took a volleyball to the face," Bernadette said brightly, and we all had to admit she had a point. She was wearing a vintage leather jacket with shiny silver buckles, and she'd smudged black eyeliner over the eye that wasn't currently half-closed with swelling. Clara, to my left, wore a pale blue dress with a Peter Pan collar. She'd had Evelyn do her hair in two braids. She was fourteen and still looked a bit like a baby. On my diagonal,

Evelyn spread a very even, neat layer of marmalade on a piece of wheat toast. She wore her favorite evergreen-hued turtleneck, and when she saw me looking at her, she smiled warmly.

"Are you going back to school?" Clara asked, even though Bernadette had sworn up and down all night that she would not be stepping foot back on that campus. But we all knew the morning light often changed people's minds.

Not Bernadette's, apparently.

She rolled her one good eye and said, "Can you all stop fucking asking me that?"

"But you *love* that school," Evelyn said gently. Evelyn said everything gently.

We'd gone over all of this last night. Bernadette looked at me, for help, but I stuffed my mouth with toast and gave her a weak smile. She rolled her eye again.

"I have changed my goddamn opinion of school, Evelyn," she said.

Todd's packed tables in like sardines, and a gray-haired lady next to us sighed loudly at that, and said to Bernadette, "Can you *please* mind your language?"

"I don't mind my language at all," Bernie replied, and she flashed a smile so big and catching that the woman actually laughed.

"So you're just going to live with us again?" Clara asked.

"Do you not want me to, Cece?" Only Bernadette ever called Clara *Cece*.

"Of course I want you to," Clara said, her cheeks reddening with delight. I thought she was probably the one who missed Bernadette the most, because despite initially claiming she would never change a diaper, Bernadette had ended up being very fond of her third younger sister, and vice versa.

"Are you going to get a job?" I asked.

Bernadette raised an eyebrow. "I've been home for twelve hours and you want me to get a job? What are you, *Dad*?"

"She's just asking," Evelyn said. The peacemaker. But Bernadette wasn't really annoyed; I could tell because she was still eating, and she never ate when she was annoyed, she always rested her fork down on the side of her plate and just waited.

"Well, I'm glad you're back," Clara said.

"I'm glad you're back, too," I said.

"Of *course* I'm glad you're back," Evelyn said.

"I'm glad I'm back, too. When are Mom and Dad getting home?"

"Tomorrow," I said. They were in the Berkshires, a place they went often because they had friends with a house there and didn't have to pay for a hotel. Our family wasn't particularly wealthy, more luck-touched. Our brownstone had been in the family for generations (and was, of course, paid off), and we all went to private schools on funds set aside by our father's parents (except for Clara, who hadn't wanted to).

Everything else was aggressively budgeted by our parents, and some months I caught them giving some *very* skeptical looks to a stack of pale red bills.

("Persephone didn't have to pay bills," my mother would sometimes mumble, petulant and snooty, and my father would nod his head in a mollifying way and say, "Yes, darling, it's so hard to be cast off Mount Olympus, isn't it?" in a tone that implied that perhaps he didn't believe that particular old Farthing yarn.)

"I miss the Berkshires," Clara said. "So green. There isn't any green in the city."

"We live two blocks from Central Park," Bernie pointed out. "How much green do you want?"

"It's not the same," Clara said. "You know it's not the same. There isn't anywhere in Central Park you can go where you don't hear cars."

Clara was the only one of us who hadn't gone to a private all-girls school on the other side of the park. She was oddly practical, for a fourteen-year-old, and she'd negotiated a deal with our parents—she took the money they would have spent on private school and had them put it in a trust fund she could access when she was twenty-five. I had a feeling, in about ten years, we'd all be pissed with ourselves for not going to her for financial advice.

Evelyn and I left the house every morning at seven and walked across the park together to get to our school on the Upper East Side. Evelyn was a senior now. She'd been offered a spot at a prestigious music conservatory next year. She hadn't given them an answer yet.

I was sixteen and thought I would go to college for something unexpected and strange—like a classics course at a small liberal arts school in Vermont (I'd read *The Secret History* recently and won't admit just how much it had altered my brain chemistry).

The art Clara made was dark and violent and strange. Disembodied heads and fifty shades of black piled meticulously on top of each other and open, bleeding wounds leaking from the canvas like someone had cut it open from the outside. It wasn't anything like what you thought she would make, if you heard she was an artist. Our parents had hung an enormous piece over the fireplace on the ground floor. It kind of creeped us all out to look at it, but also, we loved her, and it was beautiful, if you didn't have a weak stomach.

Bernadette had gone to school for an undecided major. We all knew she'd have to declare soon, and we were wondering if that was why she was here now, and it was what we were all thinking about as we ate our breakfast and realized, with a start, that she was suddenly sobbing. Deep heaving sobs that wracked her shoulders and made the woman next to her, the one who'd scolded her about her language, jump with fright.

Evelyn didn't say anything. She wrapped her arms around Bernadette and Bernadette turned her body and melted into Evie's side. Clara and I looked at each other. Neither of us were good at nurturing; open displays of emotion made the insides of my wrists itch. I could feel the other diners looking at us, some of them neighborhood people, faces I had seen all my life but couldn't put names to, and some of them strangers, visiting the American Museum of Natural History, tourists who'd taken the subway up from Union Square and stumbled into the first place they saw that said BREAKFAST in the window.

Clara took my hand, and I knew when I looked at her that she'd done something she shouldn't have; her eyes had gotten very wide and she wasn't looking at me, she was looking *past* me, and when I turned around my breath caught in my throat, because there were Mom and Dad, looking frazzled and car rumpled. For a moment they didn't see us, and then their eyes landed on me, and Mom practically launched herself across the room, pushing Bernadette's butt over in her seat as she sat next to her and hugged her.

"I called Mom and Dad," Clara whispered into my ear, as our

father hung back awkwardly, even now, after all these years of practice, never quite knowing what to do with a table full of women.

"No shit," I replied.

"She has a *black eye,*" Clara said.

"No shit."

"What was I supposed to do!" Her voice was getting high-pitched, like it did when she was worried she'd done something wrong, so I gave a half-hearted wave to Dad and turned around to face her.

"It's fine, Clara," I said. "They're here. It's fine. It's going to be fine."

"Traitor," Bernadette mumbled from underneath Mom's left arm, but we could tell from the sound of her voice that she was mostly joking, and Clara relaxed a little and stabbed at her egg scramble, because she never left a meal unfinished, as a rule.

Dad was still sort of hanging out around the entrance, but Todd spotted him and brought a chair over next to me, apologizing to the woman who'd admonished us for our language but who was now looking quite thrilled at the soap opera of our family. Dad came and sat down next to me. I'd always been closest with him, just by a little, and he put his hand on my knee and squeezed, relieved to finally be sitting.

"Hi, kiddo," he said.

"Hi, Dad."

He was facing me but his eyes were trained on Bernadette and Mom, who were still hugging. But at least it seemed like Bernie had stopped crying by then.

I slid my plate toward Dad, suddenly not very hungry, and he started eating without a moment's hesitation, I think happy for the distraction. Across the table, Evelyn met my eyes and she looked a little sad and far away. With Evelyn, though, it was hard to tell what that meant. Was she actually sad and faraway or was she composing a sonata in her mind?

I smiled at her and she smiled back and I noticed that her smile didn't touch her eyes. She started eating again. Mom and Bernadette were still hugging. Everybody was either eating or hugging, except me and the woman next to us, who was eagerly awaiting the next move in our little family drama.

"Luckily there was no traffic," Dad said, apropos of absolutely nothing. "Made it in about two and a half hours, if you can believe it."

That meant Clara had been up at least three hours before anyone else, calling them from another floor, speaking in hushed tones so we wouldn't overhear. Clara didn't seem to need as much sleep as the average person. She was always the last to close her eyes and the first to open them. She must have seen Bernadette's black eye and sneaked downstairs to call our parents.

"Sleep is a waste of time," she'd said once, lying across my bed, her long, blond hair waterfalling over the side of my mattress. It was exactly like her to be a petulant, slightly bratty kid in one moment, and a waxing philosopher in the next, with barely a breath between the two extremes.

Nobody had answered Dad's traffic comment, but he didn't seem dismayed. He was very used to people not answering him, and he simply tried again, taking a sip of my coffee and sighing happily. "The best coffee in the city, and it's right on our block. How lucky are we, kids?"

How lucky are we, kids? was a true Dadism, and we all nodded our agreement while, again, not answering.

The woman next to us was getting bored. She went back to her food.

Mom finally pulled away from Bernadette and I saw that they'd traded places—Mom was crying and Bernadette was looking worried. Then Dad looked up and for the first time caught the full extent of Bernie's battered face, and he paused, a statue, with a bite of egg halfway raised between his plate and mouth.

Bernadette pulled her phone out of her pocket and tapped it a few times, then handed it over to Dad. I leaned in to watch over his shoulder, and to my surprise, it was an actual video of said volleyball getting spiked into my sister's face. I didn't think my sister had made any friends in college, at least she'd never spoken of anyone, so I found myself focusing on who exactly had taken the video, although I recognized that wasn't the point.

"Yikes," Dad said, after he'd played the video three times, once holding the phone at a bit of an angle, so the woman next to us could get a better view. "That looks like it hurt."

"The whole world erupted into a beautiful cacophony of color," Bernadette said loftily, taking the phone back and winking at me with her good eye. "And then, yes, it did hurt, a fucking lot."

Mom called the server over and ordered poached eggs and toast and "A lot more coffee, please," and Bernadette watched the video of herself getting volleyballed in the eye with a weird smile on her face.

"You can't say *cacophony of color,*" Clara said thoughtfully, to no one in particular. "*Cacophony* refers to *sounds.*"

"This was yesterday morning," Bernadette clarified. "But it's not why I came home."

"You can tell us when you're ready," Mom said.

"I might not ever be ready," Bernadette replied.

Mom wiped at her eyes. Out of all of us, she looked the most like Evelyn, especially when she was sad.

"Well, if you're going to be home for a while, I do think you should get a job," Dad said, and Bernadette gave me a look of such dramatic annoyance that I actually laughed.

"Let's go to the museum today," she said suddenly.

"I have to practice," Evelyn replied.

"I have an assignment to finish," Clara said.

"I'll come," I said.

"I know," Bernie said, smiling at me, eye squinted closed, and I felt very, very happy she was there, no matter what the reason was.

We walked to the museum right from the diner, waving bye to the rest of our family and heading east. It was only a block away, and the skies had brightened; you could just see some blue coming out from behind the clouds. I felt sort of empty, since I hadn't eaten much, but also sort of full, because Bernadette was home. She took off her leather jacket and swung it over her shoulder and then put her arm around me, squeezing, and then kissed the side of my head.

"Fuck, I love this neighborhood," she said. We'd reached a corner with a little flower shop on it, and I caught the long leaf of a tulip between two of my fingers. "It always smells so good."

"Right now it smells good," I agreed. "Because we're standing next to a floral explosion."

She snorted. The light changed and we crossed the street and dove forward into the park and despite what Clara had said, the sound of the cars actually did die away quite quickly. If you squinted and looked a certain way and suspended a little bit of disbelief, you could pretend you were in a deep, dark forest. A forest of another world. I tried to do that, but Bernadette seemed to be in a bit of a hurry and took my hand and pulled me along before I could really get into it. She dragged me deeper into the park.

"Oh, you mean the Met?" I asked, because I'd thought we were going to the Natural History Museum, Bernadette's favorite.

"Unless you have something better to do."

"The Met is fine, but can you stop pulling me?"

She stopped pulling me abruptly, stopped walking altogether, and stepped off the path, her hands on either side of her head, her fingers tugging gently at the ends of her hair.

"Bernie? What's going on?" I asked, taking a step toward her.

"I can't *tell you,*" she said. Crying again. She rubbed at her chest with the butt of one hand. "I can't."

"Why can't you tell me? You can tell me anything."

"I just *can't,* Winnie," she sobbed.

"Does your chest hurt?"

"Everything hurts."

"What does it feel like?"

"Like claws," she said, and she made her own hands into hooked, pointy things, and dragged her fingernails down my chest, scratching against my sweatshirt.

"I know exactly what you mean," I said.

She nodded. She had already stopped crying. Like a faucet. Tears starting and stopping with the blink of an eye. She looked at my sweatshirt, where she'd scratched me. There were marks in the fabric. She buffed them out with the palm of her hand.

"Why do you like this?" she asked.

It was a sweatshirt with the name of her college on it. She'd brought it home with her after her first semester, but she never wore it, so I took it.

I shrugged. "I don't know. It reminds me of you."

"I hate it. I hate looking at it."

"I won't wear it again."

"Take it off. Burn it."

"I don't have any matches."

"At least take it off. It's fucking . . . I don't want to see it right now."

I took the sweatshirt off, pulling it over my head and tying it around my waist. The shirt I was wearing also belonged to Bernadette. She squinted at it for a minute.

"Hey. I was looking for that."

"Do you want me to take it off, too?"

She smiled. "No, you can keep it. It looks better on you. With your hair."

We had the exact same hair. The exact same shade of brown. The exact same curl on the left side. Just one single curl in a whole head of hair. She touched mine now, and I touched hers. Inverted mirror images. Long and tumbling down our backs.

"I know," she said. "I know exactly what we're going to do."

When we got home, three hours later, Evelyn was standing on the stairs holding a mug of tea she'd been bringing up to her room. When she saw us come in, her jaw dropped down to her chest.

"Holy *shit,*" she said.

"I donated it to kids with cancer," Bernadette replied proudly. She gave a little twirl. Even though I'd been there when it had all come off, I still couldn't really believe it was gone. A messy, short pixie cut was all that remained. Her black eye was shiny and raw and still swollen mostly shut. She'd put the leather jacket back on for our walk from the hair salon, and I didn't think she'd ever looked cooler than she had in that moment.

Then Dad came around the corner holding a bag of recycling and he actually dropped it when he saw her.

"Okay," he said. "Okay. I can do this. I can handle this."

"Dad," Evelyn said.

"It looks. Very. Lovely," he said.

"Thanks," Bernadette said.

"Bernadette, it really looks so nice," Evie said.

"I love it," I said.

"I love it," Bernadette repeated.

But then the faucet opened up again, and she was crying so suddenly that I didn't even have time to react before Dad folded her up in his arms.

"Go upstairs, girls," he said to Evie and me.

He didn't have to tell us twice.

"What were you thinking?" Evie hissed to me when we reached the second-floor landing.

"What was *I* thinking? I didn't do anything!"

"That's exactly my point," she said.

"What was I supposed to do? She said she wanted a haircut."

"This has nothing to do with hair," Evie said when we reached the third floor. She paused there, waiting to see if I would go into my room or come up to the attic with her. We sometimes still called it that. A ghost in the attic sounded cooler than a ghost on the fourth floor.

"If this has nothing to do with hair, why are you upset with me?" I asked.

"You were supposed to go to the museum," she complained, and I followed her upstairs. "You weren't supposed to facilitate any major life decisions."

Clara was at her easel and Henry was sitting on the love seat we'd brought up a few summers ago when Mom and Dad had replaced the ground-floor living room set.

"What major life decision did she facilitate?" Clara asked, not turning around from her easel. Henry was mostly transparent and kept winking out altogether. He was much better at manifesting at nighttime, and I was surprised to see him at all, except I knew how much he liked to watch Clara paint. They'd always had a bit of a special bond because he'd been there when she was born. (The rest of us had been born at the hospital and Henry had met us only a day or two later; I'm sure Clara had been very exciting for him.)

"Bernadette cut off all her hair," Evelyn said. She wasn't looking at me, for some reason I honestly couldn't understand, and she was pacing back and forth now, fuming.

"Really?" Clara said. "Huh. I didn't see that coming."

"She looks beautiful," I offered.

"Of course she looks beautiful."

"Something is obviously really wrong with her," Evelyn said. "She doesn't need to be cutting all her hair off, she *needs* to be resting and processing."

"Hair grows back, Evie," Clara said. "I think you're being a bit dramatic."

"A bit? A bit? *A bit?*" Evelyn sounded like a broken record, and she was still pacing, and the whole thing was kind of funny. I sat down on the love seat next to Henry, and he looked at me like *you better not laugh.*

"Duh," I whispered.

"And processing *what* exactly?" Clara asked.

"That's a great question," Evie said. "I would love to know the answer to that question."

"Why are you being so punchy?" I asked, and Evie didn't respond, just let out a huge huff of air and went into her room. She slammed the door behind her.

Clara and I looked at the door, then at each other, then at Henry. He shrugged.

"I don't know," he said, to our unanswered question of, *what is her problem?*

"You always know," Clara said.

"Not always," he said.

I could tell he was lying.

"I can tell you're lying," Clara said.

Henry disappeared then, completely, which for a ghost was a pretty passive-aggressive way of getting out of a conversation.

"How does it look?" Clara asked, even though I'd already answered that.

"Really, really, good."

"Ugh. Of course. Bernadette is the hot one."

It was true—Bernie *was* the hot one, although Clara was fast on her heels. Evelyn was pretty in a subdued, understated, sneaks-up-on-you sort of way and I was what my mother had once annoyingly referred to as a *late bloomer.*

"Do you think something really bad happened to her?" Clara asked, in a small kind of voice. She put down her paintbrush and came and sat next to me, in the space Henry had just vacated. "I mean, aside from the volleyball to the face."

"I don't know. She hasn't said. Maybe it was something big that happened or maybe it was more of . . ."

"A lot of little things?"

"Maybe, yeah."

"She should have taken a gap year," Clara said. Now that she was one year away from high school, she'd become very obsessed with the idea of taking a gap year. She had a map on her bedroom wall of all the places she'd go. She wanted me to go with her.

"You can't take a gap year in the middle of college," I said.

"Who is making these rules?" she asked. "Who is deciding all of these things for us?" Then she took a bunch of hair in her hand and arranged it so it covered her forehead. "Should I get bangs?" she asked.

"Yes. You'd look adorable."

"I don't want to look adorable," she said.

"You'd look very pretty with bangs," I amended.

"I *do* want to look pretty," she admitted. "And if Bernie cut off all her hair, maybe it's time for me to try something different."

"It's just hair," I said, echoing her earlier words. "It grows back."

She flashed a quick smile. Her blue eyes were bluer than Mom's, bluer than Evelyn's. A crystal blue. The color of a lake in summer, the sky reflected off the surface, deep and vast. I had brown eyes, like Dad's. Bernadette's were green. Like Aunt Bea.

"I miss Aunt Bea," I said.

"Hey," Clara said. "I was just thinking that." She put her head against my shoulder. "Let's go watch TV."

But I didn't feel like watching TV; I felt like getting out of the house before dinner, walking around the neighborhood, pounding the familiar pavement of the Upper West Side. If *getting a bit of fresh air* could count as a personality trait, that was my father and me to a T. He often said the cure for most of life's woes was a brisk stroll around the block, and I'd picked up his penchant for sensible walking shoes and always double-checking that you'd grabbed your house keys.

The faster I walked, the less processing speed my brain had; my troubles simply couldn't keep up. I couldn't wonder whether I should have talked Bernadette out of the haircut or tried to convince her to go back to school or dragged her to the museum come hell or high water. I couldn't think about how high school was already half over and most of my classmates were already working on their college admission essays. I couldn't compare myself to my sisters, endlessly wondering if I was the least interesting Farthing girl among us. And I definitely couldn't let the feelings of panic and despair catch up to me. Panic and despair were notoriously slow walkers; I left them in the dust on Eighty-First Street and kept right on moving. After fifteen minutes, I was feeling hot and slightly sticky and blissfully blank, my brain a clean, white space with high, high walls around it.

I loved this city. I loved being *out* in this city. I loved the way the walkers of New York had a rhythm and a cadence, and if you bumped into someone on the sidewalk, they were almost certainly a tourist, just trying their best to fit into the slots we had provided for them.

I loved this city, and I loved the way my father had filled up my head with random facts about this city, facts that had now become lodged in my own brain, resurfacing at relevant moments.

Like: no one, aside from a few very special pastors and the cardinal of the Archdiocese of New York, was allowed to be buried here anymore.

In the early 1800s, new burials were forbidden south of Canal Street. A few years after that, the rule was extended to anything south of Eighty-Sixth Street. You couldn't make a new cemetery anywhere on the island.

But before that?

Before that Manhattan was a veritable free-for-all. Cemeteries were plentiful. You could barely walk for all the graves.

And were we ever-so-careful when we closed up all those little burial sites and told people to take their dead elsewhere? Or did we leave a lot of bodies in the ground and build Duane Reades on top of them?

I'll let you guess.

For most people, this doesn't pose much of an issue.

It's superstitious faff that walking over a grave is bad luck, ditto holding your breath past a cemetery. There's nothing technically dangerous or worrisome about living so close to so many long-dead people.

But I bring it up now, because . . .

Well, if you were like *me*—potentially descended from Persephone, Queen of the Underworld and all the ghosts in it—you occasionally ran into them.

The ghost in front of me now was nowhere near as distinct as Henry.

It was a woman—the ghosts I saw were always women, always Farthing women, distant relations who'd inhabited a version of New York much older than the one I currently lived in. Her body was buried somewhere close, probably underneath this very sidewalk, and she was tied to it like an anchor.

She was a wisp of a thing, all shadow and suggestion, really, the *idea* of a ghost. She wouldn't be able to talk or communicate with me or do much of anything. The only ghosts I could actually speak to were Henry, of course, and my dead Aunt Esme in Vermont—another Farthing woman only I could see.

My sisters knew I could see other ghosts, and would sometimes ask me about them, but mostly I didn't have anything interesting to report. Aunt Esme only wanted me to sit and watch her play with her ghost dolls ("I like that she comes with accessories," Clara had said once), and most of the others, like this one in front of me, were pretty boring. ("Interesting to call a ghost *boring*," Bernadette had noted before. "As if she should perform for you.")

Where did this second sight come from, and why was I the only one of us who had it? Why could my sisters see Henry but not this ghost before me, who I swore seemed to smile a little, incline her heard toward me, then move aside to let me pass?

Was it a gift from Persephone, Queen of the Underworld, or was it a gift from her daughter, queen of the mad?

I thought it could go either way.

I nodded my head slightly to this Farthing woman now, giving her a moment of acknowledgment, unable to help myself from wondering—was she happy? Was she aware? Had she had a nice life? Was she having a nice death?

Then I put my head down and pointed myself toward home.

Bernadette didn't come down for dinner.

"She's fine," Mom said. "She just needs a little rest."

"What do you think of her hair?" Clara said, who somehow still hadn't seen either Bernie or her hair.

"It suits her," Mom said. "She has the face for it."

"It's a big change," Dad said, who didn't like change and reacted poorly whenever Mom suggested any home renovations. The new living room set from a few summers ago had really thrown him for a loop and I still caught him occasionally turning around in a circle, eyeing everything with what I could only describe as the most extreme distrust.

"I think I'll get bangs," Clara said.

I actually saw Dad flinch.

"You'd look wonderful with bangs," Mom said.

Evelyn stabbed at her mashed potatoes with unnecessary force. She was still not really speaking to Clara or me, and in general acting like a huge brat.

"I want to look French," Clara said. "Or at least more French than I currently look. Will bangs do that?"

"Definitely," Mom said. "Curtain bangs. Brigitte Bardot."

"French?" Dad said.

"Everybody wants to look French," I explained.

"I hate France," he said.

"You don't hate France," Mom replied. "You're thinking of Brussels. You had a nice time in France."

He squinted, then nodded. "I hate Brussels."

"You also don't really hate Brussels. You just have a sour memory," Mom said.

Dad tried to work out what that meant exactly, to have a sour memory, and Evelyn stabbed at her plate again. It must have been very unsatisfying, to stab at mashed potatoes, but we didn't point that out.

"Evelyn, darling," Mom said. "You haven't had a bite to eat."

"I'm not hungry," she said.

"Am I sensing some . . ." Dad waved his fork back and forth between the three-out-of-four kids in front of him.

"I'm fine," Clara said brightly.

"I'm great," I said.

"I'm peachy," Evelyn said.

Nobody in the history of the world has ever said they're peachy and meant it, but Dad winked at me and said, "*I* don't want to look French," and Evelyn managed the smallest of smiles at that.

We were all quiet when Bernadette entered the kitchen. There was a more formal dining room, but we always ate in the kitchen nook surrounded by windows. Bernadette was wearing old flannel pants and a white T-shirt with pinprick holes all over the sleeves and collar. With her pixie cut, her black eye, her one visible green iris—now *she* looked French.

"Bernadette, sweetheart," Mom said.

"I got hungry," she replied.

None of us knew what she'd talked to Mom and Dad about, just that she'd been in her room ever since.

"Fuck," Clara said. "It looks *amazing.*"

"Language," Dad said, without any real gumption.

"You like it?" Bernie asked, touching the ends of her hair.

"I *love* it," Clara said. "You look so motherfucking—sorry, Dad—*cool.*"

"I've always wanted to do it," Bernie said, then looked at me. "You talked me into it."

"I didn't do anything!" I said quickly, seeing Evelyn's eyes widen.

Evelyn lifted her head and studied Bernadette quietly, then nodded. "It does. It really suits you."

"Thanks, Evie," Bernadette said, shrugging. "It's just hair."

She got herself a plate and took her empty seat between Clara and me. She pulled one of Clara's braids.

"Should I get bangs?" Clara asked.

"Absolutely," Bernadette said, at the same time Evie said, "No!"

"What is it with hair?" Dad murmured to no one in particular.

"You wouldn't really understand," Mom said. She herself had long, long hair that she mostly wore in a sloppy bun on the top of her head, unless she was going to a fancy event for her job, in which case she switched to an easy, elegant chignon. I loved that word. *Chignon*. It sounded so French.

"*Is* chignon French?" I asked.

Bernadette nodded enthusiastically (French in high school). "It means *nape of the neck*."

"What's a chignon?" Dad asked.

"You wouldn't really understand," Mom repeated. "Evelyn, darling, are you going to eat your potatoes or just continue to subject them to the wrath of your fork?"

Evelyn pushed her plate away, stood up from the table, and left the room. It happened very quickly. We were all sort of surprised, because even though it wasn't uncommon for someone to storm away from a Farthing dinner, it usually wasn't Evelyn.

"Did I miss something?" Dad asked.

"You wouldn't really understand," Clara said, beating Mom to it.

"Can't I have just *one night* to be the upset one?" Bernadette said.

"Nobody can ever just be *happy* in this household," Dad mused.

"You were upset last night, too, so," Clara said.

Bernadette nodded. "Fair point, Cece."

"Do I need to go and talk to her or do you think I can finish my dinner first?" Mom asked, an actual question that we took a moment to think about first.

"I think she's upset about Bernadette's hair," I said. "No offense, Bernie. I don't think she likes it."

"None taken," Bernadette said. "Evelyn doesn't love change. She gets that from you, Dad."

He pointed to himself, exaggeratedly admonished, like, *me?*

We all nodded.

He shrugged.

We went back to our dinners.

I knocked on Evelyn's bedroom door after dinner and when she didn't answer, I let myself in. I could tell she'd been crying because her windows were open. She didn't like to cry unless her windows were open. And I could tell Henry had been there because it smelled like jasmine, although he wasn't there now.

"Where's Henry?" I asked.

"What is that supposed to mean?"

"I'm just asking. Jesus, Evelyn, what is going on with you?"

She was sitting on her bed with her back against the wall, between the two windows. There was a strong breeze and her hair blew around her face. She sighed deeply and I watched her chest expand and contract.

"I'm sorry," she said finally. "I know I've been cranky."

"Are you really this mad at me about the hair thing?"

"I'm not mad at you at all," she said.

"Well? What's going on then?"

I sat down on the bed and leaned against the headboard, snuggling my feet under her feet. She always had warm feet.

"It's hard to explain," she said.

"Something to do with Bernadette?"

She looked at me sharply. "Why do you say that?"

"Well, it started last night. Are you upset that she's home?"

She blinked, blinked, blinked, the rapid-fire blinking that usually meant someone was trying not to cry.

"No," she said finally. "Of course not. I mean . . . It's not like that."

"What's it like, then?"

"It's just. Seeing her . . . If *she* can't do it . . ."

"Do what, Evie?"

"College. School. Life."

"I don't know what you mean."

"She's the strongest one of us, and she came home."

"Right, but it's not . . . It's not going to be, like, permanent. She went back before, remember?"

Halfway through her freshman year, Bernadette had come back for Christmas break and then flatly refused to return to school. She'd missed the first two weeks of her second semester. She'd thrown a full glass of water at Clara's head when Clara asked her to pass the salt at Christmas dinner. Like, not just the water. The glass, too. Dad had stood up from his chair, very calmly, walked over to Bernadette, pulled her up by her arm, and gently led her upstairs. Clara had cried. Mom had comforted her. Evelyn and I had stayed very still, very quiet, listening to Bernadette's echoing sobs as Dad brought her to her room. We didn't see her again until New Year's Day. She came downstairs wearing a crushed green velvet dress. Clara kept one eye on Bernadette's water glass throughout that dinner, and afterward, when Mom brought out dessert, Bernadette had apologized to everyone, but mostly to Clara, even though she insisted, and she just wanted to make this clear, that she hadn't actually meant or tried to hit her.

"This feels different," Evelyn said.

"Different because she hasn't attempted to murder one of us yet?"

"Don't be mean," she said, but smiled.

"I still don't understand."

"Next year. Graduating high school. Moving on, moving out. I'm not *ready,*" she said.

"Take a gap year," I said, mimicking the wide-eyed innocence Clara managed to have every single time she gave one of us that suggestion.

But Evie didn't smile. She just closed her eyes and took a long, thin sip of air. When she opened her eyes again, they were wet.

"I don't want to leave," she said in a very small voice.

"You don't have to leave, Evie," I said.

"No, I mean. *Ever.*"

"Well . . . You don't want to live with Mom and Dad forever."

"This house," she insisted. "I don't want to leave this *house.*"

"This house? I mean, it's nice, sure, but won't it be a relief when you don't have to climb three flights of stairs to get a pair of socks?"

"You're being so obtuse," she said, almost smiling.

It clicked for me then. The smell of jasmine. "Henry?"

She bit her bottom lip so hard that when she stopped biting it, I could see her teeth marks in the red flesh.

"He doesn't have anyone else," she said, her voice quivering, the tears welling up in her eyes.

"Well, he has me," I said. "And Clara."

"And when you leave? When you both leave?"

I honestly hadn't thought about it. It had never really occurred to me, what Henry's life (well, death) had been like before the four of us. Or what it would be like after we'd gone.

"I mean . . . We can't just *not* live our lives. Because of Henry," I said, feeling like a huge asshole even as I said it. "I don't mean . . . I mean, I'm *sorry*. I know that's terrible, but . . . You can't just . . ."

It clicked for me again. Puzzle pieces falling into place.

"Oh," I said. "You love him."

The tears were spilling out of her eyes now, running down her cheeks, and it occurred to me then just how much our house full of girls cried.

"I don't . . . I don't *know*," she said. "I just know that I don't want to leave him, okay? I'm not ready to leave him."

"Well you have . . . some time," I said. Not the greatest advice in the world, but to be fair, I felt very put on the spot. Evelyn had a crush on Henry? My sister was in love with a ghost? I needed a few minutes to process that information before I came up with any advice worth giving.

She didn't say anything. She just nodded her head a little.

"Maybe you'll . . ." I didn't finish that sentence. What was I going to say? Maybe you'll fall out of love with the ghost that haunts our house? Maybe you'll fall in love with someone else? To be honest, I was surprised I had never picked up on the fact that my sister was having a secret love affair with the spirit that haunted our four-story brownstone. But maybe I shouldn't have been that surprised. Evelyn was the only one of us who could actually touch Henry. I'd always thought it had something to do with their proximity, the bedroom that was now hers but had once been his. The rest of us, if we brushed against him, felt only a slight thickening in the air. A coldness. To Evelyn, he had always been as solid as anyone else.

"I'm sorry," I said. I couldn't think of anything else to say. She took my hand and then crawled slowly toward me, so we ended up hip to hip. She put her head on my shoulder.

"Please don't tell them," she said.

"I won't."

I saw ghosts and my sister was in love with one.

If only Persephone could see us now.

II

They say Persephone came to Manhattan before it was even Manhattan. That she planted a jasmine bush on a plot of bare land. They say her descendants would forever be drawn to it, like moths to a flame. They say that her footsteps left fragile places in the earth, places you could crawl from one world to another . . .

Having secrets from my sisters made me itchy, and for a few days I simply avoided them altogether, waiting until Clara had finished breakfast and left for school before darting downstairs and grabbing a piece of toast and walking across the park with Evelyn. Bernadette slept late, so I didn't have to worry about her much, and when I got home, I complained loudly about all the homework I had to do and nobody really questioned it when I spent hours locked in my room, running downstairs to shovel dinner into my mouth and retreating as soon as I was done. I was worried I'd develop a UTI from holding my bladder, waiting until everyone else had gone to sleep before I crept to the bathroom. Sometimes I'd catch a glimpse of Henry, shining and bright in the moonlight, wandering the halls of our brownstone, moody and morose, like a caricature of a ghost, and my stomach would twist uncomfortably as I'd pray he didn't see me.

My walks across the park with Evelyn were quiet, although I could tell now, in the silence, how little I'd been paying attention to my older sister. It was painstakingly, achingly obvious that she was in love. It was obvious in the way she left the house as if against her will, turning back every ten or twenty feet to gaze longingly at her own bedroom window. It was obvious in the way she pressed rose petals between her fingertips when we passed the florist on the corner. It was obvious in the way she sighed heavily at absolutely fucking nothing, every five or six minutes. And it was obvious in the way we were late to school every single morning, because she'd started insisting we walk along the southern edge of the reservoir, even though it was absurdly out of our way, going north only to come back south again once we'd reached Fifth Avenue. Finally, on Thursday morning, I whirled around to face her after she'd stopped walking to gaze mooningly over the water.

"I am going to fail history if I keep being late, Evie, *please* throw me a bone here."

She blinked, then glanced at the time on her watch (she always wore a dainty gold watch that had belonged to our grandmother) and swore under her breath.

"I'm sorry," she said. "I'm just . . . This weather. You know?"

I didn't know.

The weather was great, sure, and autumn in New York was almost as good as spring in New York, and I was happy to not be sweating buckets anymore, but still. We both knew this was not about the temperature of the air, but the temperature of my sister's raw and aching heart.

"If you want to keep walking by the reservoir, we're going to have to leave earlier, okay?"

"No, it's stupid," she said, her shoulders falling slightly.

"It's not stupid. It's nice. I get it."

"We can go back to the usual way. I just . . ."

"What?"

"I like looking at the water."

Her voice was thick. I gently took her by the hand and guided her forward. She could cry, but she had to walk and cry, or else I was going to miss history altogether.

"Water is nice," I said after a few minutes, feeling guilty for rushing the moment.

"He used to go to the reservoir. When he was alive. To sit and read."

Because our father was a true history nerd, I knew that the Central Park Reservoir—renamed in 1994 to the Jacqueline Kennedy Onassis Reservoir—had been completed in 1862.

Because I was a possible descendant of Persephone and slightly obsessed with morbid facts, I knew that Central Park had been built over several cemeteries.

"You think it's ridiculous," she said. "That I love a . . ."

The word *ghost,* if left unsaid, is a bit like a ghost itself. You can't see it, but you know it's there.

"It's not ridiculous, Evie," I said, and squeezed her hand, which I was still holding, worried, maybe, that if I let go, she would drift away from me. "That's not what I was thinking."

"What *were* you thinking, then?"

Since *I was thinking about dead bodies* would potentially ruin the mood, I softened my voice and said, "I was wondering how long it's been going on."

"Oh," she said, sighing. "A year."

"A year?"

"My seventeenth birthday. Do you remember?"

Evie had never been one for celebrations. We had a quiet family dinner. I had baked a carrot cake, her favorite. Bernadette had videoed in from school, where she was knee-deep in finals and couldn't get away. Clara had upset a piece of cake onto the table and Dad had eaten it anyway, forkful by forkful.

"That was a good cake," I said.

She smiled, a zillion miles away. "He was seventeen when he died."

My heart gave a little flutter. New information I tucked away for later. "Really?" I'd always thought he was younger.

She nodded. "When we were all kids, he could kind of make himself a little younger. He didn't want to be too much older than us. That would have been creepy."

Oh yes, *that* would have been creepy, says the ghost in the attic.

"But he can't make himself older than seventeen," she continued. "After cake, when I'd brushed my teeth and gotten into bed, he knocked on my closet door—"

"He knocked?"

"That's how we do it," she said. "He stays in the closet and knocks, and if I say it's okay, he comes into the room. That way he doesn't see me, you know . . . changing or something."

I'd never really thought about Henry visiting my sister afterhours, but I felt very grateful for that little system. It felt incredibly decent to me. I nodded.

"Anyway, he came out and sat on the edge of my bed, and I was really tired, but I could tell something was wrong. He wasn't saying much, he was sad. So I kept asking and asking, and finally . . . He said, 'Happy birthday, Evie.' And I said, 'This is about my birthday?' And he said, 'You're seventeen now.'"

"And he was sad because you were finally leaving him behind," I finished. "Getting older while he stayed the same, forever."

"It had honestly never occurred to me until that moment," she continued. "I had never looked at him and realized . . . But of course, I loved him. And he loved me."

"Love," I said. "Wow." Which wasn't the most elegant contribution I'd ever made, but this was all still very new to me.

The northern façade of the Metropolitan Museum of Art was just coming into view. Evie saw it and quickened her pace, leading us along the great wall of slanted windows. Through the glass we could see the Temple of Dendur, taken apart brick by brick in Egypt and painstakingly pieced back together here. It was imposing and slightly weird in its urban setting; we were in the middle of Central Park in New York City, and this was the most-visited Egyptian temple in the entire world.

Evie stopped walking abruptly. We were as close to the glass as we could get.

"The ancient Egyptians knew a lot more about death than we do," she said.

"Okay . . ."

"They understood the changeability of death. The thin veil that separates our world from their world. The processes a human might go through, to . . ."

"To . . . ?"

She turned to me. Her eyes were wide.

"He found a way to stay here," she said. "To live forever."

I was definitely going to miss history.

"Well . . . to be *dead* forever . . . if we're being technical."

"Don't be crass, Winnie."

"I think I'm being realistic," I said. All that talk about death was making my teeth hurt.

Evelyn smiled, and truth be told, her smile looked a little bit terrifying.

"Persephone came to New York once," Evelyn said, beginning to walk again. I knew all the same Persephone stories that my sister did, could recite them line for line, but I let her talk, a little bit afraid of her in that moment. "She used to wander the earth in spring, ushering in the new growth, shaking off the cobwebs of the Underworld."

We reached Fifth Avenue and turned right. The expansive front steps of the Met were mostly empty, save for a few small clusters of people eating breakfast or drinking coffee.

"They say she came to Manhattan before it was even Manhattan. That she planted a jasmine bush on a plot of bare land. They say her descendants would forever be drawn to it, like moths to a flame. They say that her footsteps left fragile places in the earth, places you could crawl from one world to another . . ."

"Although I've never actually found myself tripping into Hell while walking around the brownstone, you know?"

Evelyn shot me a perfectly withering look, then reached over and took my hand.

"I understand that you're not in a place to receive this information," she said quietly, infuriatingly.

"Exactly what information are you hoping I'd receive?"

"Forget it," she said. She let go of my hand, and it couldn't help but feel like a metaphor I wasn't quite smart enough to understand.

Evelyn was quiet on the walk home from school, and when we got back to the brownstone, she went right upstairs to her room.

I went into the kitchen to get an apple and paused only slightly when I saw Bernadette already there, at the kitchen table, writing in her journal.

"I know you're avoiding me," she said. "It's very obvious when you avoid me because you eat your food quickly so you can get up to your room sooner, and I'm always afraid you're going to choke."

"I don't know what you're talking about," I said, and even I could hear the lack of conviction in my voice. I grabbed an apple from the fruit bowl on the counter and took a very slow, purposeful bite, chewing it extra slowly. Bernadette rolled her eyes so far back in her head that I could only see white, then she shut her journal and got up from the table.

"It's clear what's going on here," she said.

I swallowed the apple and a piece of it lodged in my throat, despite my excellent chewing. I gagged for a moment and when I finally got it loose, I didn't really feel like eating the apple anymore. Bernadette plucked it from my hand and took a bite.

"It is?" I asked.

"Yes. And frankly, it's so unfair."

"It is?"

"Stop acting like you don't know exactly what I'm talking about," she demanded.

I was trying to figure out how Bernadette had discovered the secret love affair between Evie and Henry when she set the apple down on the counter and crossed her arms over her chest.

"You think I'm going to snap again," she said.

"Ohhh," I said. That made much more sense. "No, I don't."

"You do. Of course you do. You won't even look at me!"

"I do not think you are going to snap again. Look, you even put the apple down instead of throwing it at my head."

I smiled. She snarled.

"Well then *why* have you been avoiding me?"

I wasn't a good liar. In the few seconds after she asked me that question, I came up with absolutely nothing that she might believe. So I decided to lean into the excuse she'd already hand-delivered to me.

"Fine," I said. "I've been a little worried, yes. Not that you'll snap, Bernie. But just worried about you, okay? I don't know how to say the right thing or do the right thing, so I guess I was subconsciously avoiding you to avoid saying something wrong."

Finally, after what seemed like an endless amount of time, she nodded. Hook, line, and sinker. "I wish you had just told me that," she said, softening. She picked up the apple again and took a bite. "You always make everything more complicated than it needs to be."

"I do not," I said.

"I'm *fine,*" she continued. "It would have been nice if you had asked me that at any point during this week."

"I know. I'm sorry."

"But I *am* fine. It's not like last time. This isn't *The Bell Jar.*"

"I've never read *The Bell Jar.*"

"Then my perfect reference is lost on you." She sighed and set the apple down again. I could tell she was gearing up for some truth speaking. She rubbed at her eyes. "It's not like last time," she repeated. "I just knew. If I spent one more night there . . . I just knew."

"You knew what?" I asked, when she didn't elaborate.

"I just knew it *would* end up like *The Bell Jar.*"

"I'll look up the SparkNotes later," I said.

She laughed. "It's really, really nice to be home. It feels like the right place for me. I think we underestimate, sometimes, or we don't stop to pause and really think . . . Is this where I'm supposed to be?"

"And this is where you're supposed to be?" I asked.

"For now, yes," she said, her voice confident and sure.

"But did something happen? It feels like maybe something happened."

"I don't want to talk about this anymore," she said, and picked up the apple and her journal and left me alone in the room.

I stopped ignoring Bernadette and, for good measure, I stopped ignoring Clara, too—although to be fair, it hadn't appeared that my avoidance had even been detected by my youngest sister. Clara had recently begun a new painting, and when she was in the early stages of her art, she didn't really notice anything that was going on around her.

"It came to me in a dream," she said on Friday night. It had been a full week since Bernadette had arrived home and she had been strange that morning, at breakfast. Bernadette, not Clara. Although Clara had been a little strange, too. And Evelyn. I must have been the only normal one, actually, because Dad peered into each of my sisters' faces, then settled on mine, and, liking what he saw there, smiled and asked me to pass the jam.

It was after dinner now and I was sitting on the love seat in the attic. Evelyn sat on the floor in front of me while I tried and failed to braid her hair into a crown. Clara painted. Bernadette was in her room, the door closed, some quiet audiobook playing from her computer's speakers.

"Well really, it was a nightmare," Clara amended. All of her best paintings came to her in nightmares; we Farthing girls were prone to them. We called them Melinoë's messages, her secret whispers to us, trying to frame them in a more positive light. But of course there wasn't anything positive about waking up in a cold sweat, about being six years old and terrified to go to sleep because your great-great-goddess aunt was a vessel of nightmares and now, ages later, you were, too.

"Is it a person?" Evie asked, squinting, cocking her head, ruining the braid I was working on (no, I'll be honest, it was already ruined).

"I don't think so," Clara said. "The dream was fuzzy. Like . . . out of focus."

The painting was out of focus, too, but I didn't say that out loud. Plus I knew it would come together if we gave it some time to develop.

"What happened in the dream?" I asked.

"I don't remember," Clara said. "But it felt like maybe someone had died."

"Woof," Evelyn said. "Bummer."

It was a little bit unlike her, the *woof,* but the energy in the room was weird, slightly sparky, like someone had stuck their finger in an electrical socket. I kept braiding, undoing what I'd done, starting over. At some point, Henry showed up, sitting cross-legged on the floor and staring very thoughtfully at Clara's painting. He was fully-formed tonight. If you looked quickly, you might mistake him for a real boy.

"A building?" he said after a while, still looking at the painting.

"I don't know," Clara said. "Does it look like a building?"

She stepped back, and we all studied the painting.

"Yes," Henry said.

"No," I said.

"Yes," Evie said.

"Who knows," Clara said.

She dipped her brush in paint and stepped toward the canvas.

Clara painted in precise, rhythmic strokes. She reminded me of a ballerina, when she painted, but instead of *pliés* with her body, they were concentrated in her fingers, which were nimble and long and elegant. She had our Aunt Bea's hands.

"Devant," I said. *"Derrière. Croisé.* Um . . ."

"Seconde," Henry supplied.

"How do you *know* that?" Evelyn asked him.

"Ècarté. Effacé. Epaulé," I finished. How did *I* know that? It was information wedged somewhere in my brain from the two years I'd spent, ages nine to eleven, absolutely convinced I'd become a ballerina. I'd taken lessons. Our father had installed a short bar on one wall in this very room (gone now). Henry used to watch me practice. It made me happy, that I knew why he knew the French word for the fourth position. I knew something about Henry that Evelyn didn't, and I didn't know why that made me feel so . . . *superior* wasn't the right word. (And was I *jealous* of Evelyn? Of course. I was jealous of all of my sisters, each so perfect and full in their own ways. And was I jealous of Henry? Of course. I'd often wondered what it might feel like to be dead.)

The next day, we drove to Washington Heights, to the Cloisters, the six of us piling into Mom's SUV and heading north, up and up and up, the Hudson River on our left and the windows cracked to let in the sweet autumn breeze. Mom drove, Dad sat in the passenger seat, Evie and Bernie took the second row, and Clara and I, the youngest, were eternally relegated to the third row. Clara worked on a friendship bracelet she'd started about a month ago, only pulling it out during car rides and leaving it in the SUV the rest of the time, untouched.

"I don't think I even like this," she said now, holding it out to examine it. "I keep unraveling it and starting over. I'm like Penelope, but with friendship bracelets, not tapestries."

"Excellent reference," Bernadette called over her shoulder.

"Are you making it for yourself?" I asked.

"I thought I was. But now I'm not so sure. Do you want it?"

"Okay," I said. She was still less than halfway done, but she nodded and kept working at it, lazily, her fingers finding the knots and then pausing as she zoned out, staring out the window at the water. She wasn't fast at anything, painting or friendship bracelets, but the end product was always worth the wait.

"*Nothing* like the Cloisters in the fall," Dad kept saying, a broken record of optimism. "How lucky are we, kids?"

Bernadette grunted. Evelyn made a small noise of agreement. Clara hadn't heard him.

"It's gonna be really nice, Dad," I said.

He turned around and smiled at me gratefully.

In truth, the Cloisters was my favorite museum. We all had our favorites: Bernadette's was the Natural History, Evelyn's was the Met, and Clara's was the Frick. I liked the Cloisters because it was so old and because it was out of the way; we only went once a year, always in the fall, and that made it more special to me.

In the seat in front of me, Evelyn fidgeted, uncrossing her legs and crossing them the other way. She'd slept in the braided crown I'd eventually managed to give her and it was perfectly messy and undone today. Next to her, Bernie's black eye was finally fading and she was quiet and still, staring out the window, her hair mostly hidden by a stylish French beret only she could get away with. I'd tried it on once; it looked like I was wearing a pancake on my head.

(*"Les bérets ne sont pas pour tout le monde, mon ami,"* she had said. In response, I had rolled my eyes so far back in my head that they had ached for minutes afterward.)

We parked on a tree-lined street in Fort Tryon Park. It was as if we'd been plunged into a perfect oil painting of autumn. Leaves crunched underneath my feet as I got out of the car, and it smelled so deeply of earth and green that I actually sneezed.

"Bless you," Clara said, squeezing past me.

"Wow," Evelyn breathed as she slid out of the car. "It's so beautiful."

Again it struck me how unobservant I'd been over the past year, to not realize my sister was in love. She said *it's so beautiful* like her heart was about eight sizes too big for her chest, and when I looked over at her, I saw her eyes were filling up with tears, her bottom lip gently quivering. I took her into my arms, ignoring the sudden itch on the insides of my wrists, and we crossed the street holding on to each other.

"Get it together," I whispered into her hair.

"But it *is* so beautiful," she protested, her voice shaking.

"I know. But try to remember that you don't actually like it here that much."

"That's not true," she said, but out of the corner of my eye I saw her smile.

She'd never been a fan of medieval art. It ended up being a lot of religious pieces, and none of us were religious. I wasn't particularly drawn to it, either, it was more the Cloisters itself, how old it felt, how dark and quiet the rooms were, how the stone walls and floors and courtyards felt like you'd stepped out of New York and into some nameless, ancient European city. If you squinted and held your breath and tilted your head and suspended disbelief for just a few moments, it felt like you were somewhere else entirely. A fantasy novel. Cair Paravel. The room far, far underground where Alice landed after plummeting down the rabbit hole.

"What's wrong with you?" Bernadette said, appearing suddenly on Evie's other side, ruining the mood. Her voice was flat and lacked any real concern. Evelyn looked at me quickly, raising her eyebrows before replying.

"Oh, just thinking about how there's nothing like the Cloisters in the fall." She mimicked Dad's eager-beaver voice perfectly, but Bernadette didn't so much as crack a smile. I didn't even think she'd heard her, forgetting that she'd asked her a question as soon as the words had left her lips. She broke apart from us and walked on her own, just behind Mom and Dad. Clara was bringing up the rear, her eyes wide and happy as she soaked everything in, recharging her artist's brain with miles of green leaves.

"What's her problem?" Evelyn asked, pointing her jaw at Bernadette.

"I don't know," I said.

"You must know," Evie countered. "You always know."

Inside the lobby, we waited as Dad showed our membership card. Clara was in a playful, kiddish mood, and she kept twirling, her knee-length dress spinning out in a very satisfying way. She wore gray tights and Mary Janes that had once belonged to Evelyn. And she wore our grandmother's watch, which was weird. Evelyn usually never took it off.

"She gave it to me," Clara said when I asked about it. We were standing in front of an enormous wooden triptych.

“She did not give it to you,” I said.

“She did,” Clara said, and pouted a little. “She said I could have it.”

“But she loves this watch.”

“Geez, chill, it’s not like she pawned it,” she said, and stuck her tongue out at me before loping away.

I turned to watch her go and saw our father wander in from an adjacent doorway. He spotted me and bounded over, tugging my arm excitedly. “I’m going to the Treasury. Did you know they have the only complete set of illuminated playing cards from the fifteenth century? The *fifteenth century,* are you freaking kidding me!”

“Cool, Dad,” I said, but he had already skipped away, shaking with anticipation to see these cards I was sure he’d already seen a dozen times.

“Did you give your watch to Clara?” I asked Evelyn when I found her a few minutes later, in the Bonnefont Cloister.

“Hmm?” She didn’t turn to look at me. She was staring at a plant with two signs next to it.

The first said:

DEADLY NIGHTSHADE

ATROPA BELLADONNA

(SOLANACEAE)

The second said:

POISON PLANT

“Grandma’s watch. Did you say Clara could have it?”

“Isn’t it odd that they have that sign,” she said, pointing to the one that labeled the plant as poison. “I mean, it’s in the name, you know? Deadly Nightshade? You would think that would be enough of a warning for people.”

"Evelyn. Clara. The watch."

"Yes," Evelyn said, still not looking at me. "I gave it to her. She's always wanted it."

"But you love that watch."

"And I also love Clara," she said, and that was such a compelling argument that I didn't know what else to say.

She went inside. I stood in the cloister, surrounded on all sides by impressive stone archways. Above me, the sky was a pale gray-blue. The air was crisp and smelled very clean. It smelled like my mother's perfume. I lowered my gaze and there she was, in front of me.

"Status report, please?" she said, touching a hand to the braided tie of my hooded sweatshirt.

"Clara's fine," I said. "Evelyn's fine. Bernadette is . . . mostly fine, I think."

"And you?"

"Oh. I'm fine," I said.

"Not a very thorough status report, I have to say."

"Things are a little . . . weird."

"I've picked up on that."

"But I think it's mostly okay."

"Okay," she repeated. "I trust you." I had pulled my hood over my head; she gently pushed it down. "I wish you would stop wearing the same sweatshirt every day."

"Well, I wash it," I said.

"But still. You have so many beautiful clothes."

And she wandered away without waiting for a response.

I found Evelyn an hour later, after spending some time with the Farthing ghost who always hung around the Merode Room, staring somewhat morosely at the Annunciation Triptych, nodding in my general direction as if to indicate she didn't mind my company. This was nice because sometimes they *did* mind my company, and they'd disappear or walk through a wall or sink dramatically into the floorboards to get away from me. That always made me feel a little weird, like I'm the only person left alive who can see you and you still can't tolerate me?

Evelyn's hands, when I found her, were stuffed into the pockets of her ochre-colored corduroy skirt, her head slightly tilted to one side as she stared, unblinking, at what had always been our favorite piece of art in pretty much the entire world—*The Unicorn in Captivity*. I didn't have to look at my sister's face to know that she was on the verge of tears again, in that in-between place where your nose is tingling and your eyes are burning but you could come back from it, if you wanted to.

"Evie?"

"He could get out," she said, not taking her eyes off the tapestry. It showed a snow-white unicorn, legs folded, reclined in the middle of a beautiful, overgrown garden. The unicorn was chained to a pomegranate tree that was encircled by a wooden fence with no gate. But the fence was low, to Evelyn's point. The tree was thin and weak. The unicorn could get out if she wanted to.

"I've always thought of it as a *she,*" I said.

"There's blood on its coat," Evie continued.

"Pomegranate juice," I said, and Evie looked startled, like she was surprised to find me next to her. I said it again, and pointed to the ripe fruit hanging in the tree over the unicorn. "Pomegranate juice."

"Do you really think so?" she asked.

"Look at her face. She's not in pain. She's serene, calm. *Waiting.* She's not a captive. She's in charge of her own fate."

"But she's *chained.*"

"But she's not mad about it."

"Who in the world is chained and not mad about it?"

"A dog, maybe?"

We'd never had a dog. Dad was allergic and Mom was pretty blanketly against pets. There had been talk of a guinea pig, once, but nobody wanted to be the one to clean its cage.

"Can you believe this was made over five hundred years ago?" Clara, suddenly, on Evie's other side. "It could just hop right over that fence, too."

"Break the tree in half with one good yank." Bernadette, suddenly, on my other side.

"But it doesn't *want* to get out," I said. "Clearly."

"It's a metaphor," Bernie announced.

"How do you figure?" I asked.

"The unicorn can't see past its own situation. It's like a person who thinks they're drowning in water when really, it's shallow enough for them to stand."

"Deep," Clara said. "No pun intended."

"It's about all of us being trapped in these situations, these societal constructs, holding ourselves to impossible standards, money is king, working yourself to death is admirable, your prison is your own *mind.*"

"It sounds like you're writing a thesis statement for a freshman-level English class," I said, and Bernadette punched me on the arm, a little harder than she meant to, I hoped.

"Have you seen the other tapestries?" Clara asked. "Your theory doesn't really hold up when you walk over there and see the one where four men are surrounding it with spears."

"There's always another side to the story," Evelyn said quietly.

"There are always men with spears," Bernadette retorted.

"Poor guy," Clara said sadly. "Are you all ready to go? I'm very hungry."

"Are you crying, Evie?" Bernadette asked.

"I'm moved by the art," Evie said, a little dramatically.

"We've seen it a thousand times."

"I've also seen you a thousand times and I still like looking at your face."

"Fair. Meet you back at the car."

And it was just the two of us again, Evelyn and me, and I saw her suck in an enormous amount of air and hold it for so long my own lungs ached. When she let it out again, all trace of sadness was gone from her face. She turned to me and smiled.

"Ready to go?"

"Ready," I said.

She turned and walked away, not waiting for me.

That night, in bed, stuck in the in-between place, both sleep and awakeness so close and equally so far away at the same time, I kept dreaming I was the unicorn. I could feel the collar around my neck, the grass underneath my hooves, the way the long, skinny horn on my forehead weighed down my neck. I could smell the pomegranates, thick and ripe just above me. Did I want to stay here, in this walled garden, or did I want to be free again? What did I want? Why was my own mind so hard to read? You would think that would be the one thing you'd always know, what your own heart *wanted*.

"What the hell?" Clara said from the foot of my bed. I hadn't heard the door open. "You keep, like, *neighing*." Her voice was thick with sleep.

I tried to rub my eyes, but my hand was still a hoof. I smacked myself in the face.

"Ouch." Not a hoof. Just a hand, but asleep. Coming awake now with a million pricks.

"Neighing," Clara repeated.

"I wasn't."

"You *were*. I had just fallen asleep, too."

"I'm sorry."

"It's fine." She sat on the edge of my bed. "It's almost two in the morning, you know."

"Two?" I'd gone to bed at eleven, which meant I'd been stuck in the in-between for *hours,* fighting off the strange unicorn nightmare.

"I was working on my painting," Clara said. "Henry was there. He looked so sad." She looked upward, as if she could see through the ceiling, then she shrugged and sighed. "I almost know what it is now."

"Your painting?"

"Almost."

"Can you remember your dream any better?"

"Not at all. I just let my hand go." She swiped her hand through the air, like she was conducting an invisible orchestra with an invisible paintbrush. "I don't know. It will come to me."

"It always does."

"Mostly, yeah," she agreed.

"I'm sorry I woke you up."

"It's fine. Are you okay now? No more horse dreams?"

"I was the unicorn," I said.

"Ahh," she said, nodding. "That makes more sense." She hopped up from the bed. "Night."

"Night, Clara."

"Hey," she said, turning around at my door. "You can always come back."

"What?"

"If you're the unicorn in the tapestry, and you *do* decide to break free, you can always come back. If you decide freedom isn't your bag, you know. Hop right back over that fence and go back to resting in the garden."

"What *is* freedom, anyway?" I asked, fake-dramatic.

"Exactly," she said, and left the room, closing my door behind me.

"You can always come back," I whispered to my empty room.

I didn't dream of the unicorn again, but instead of the courtyard in the Cloisters, and all its rows of solid, steadfast archways and my mother's perfume, and my mother herself, just out of reach.

Despite what I had told Bernadette in the kitchen that one afternoon, we had all been sort of waiting for it to happen, and it happened on Monday night, after dinner.

She was helping Dad wash the dishes and her hand slipped and she dropped a wineglass on the kitchen floor. It shattered everywhere, shards of glass flying clear across the room, one large piece landing so close to my foot that I bent down and picked it up carefully between my thumb and index finger.

"I'll get the vacuum," Evelyn said.

"Oopsie daisy," Dad said. "Don't move, Bernadette."

And Bernadette didn't move, but she *did* scream, a sudden, sharp, angry, gunshot-loud scream that made Clara jump and me freeze and Evelyn, just coming back with the vacuum, stop dead in her tracks.

Mom was working late. Dad looked like a deer in headlights for just two or three seconds. Bernadette kept *screaming* and finally Dad grabbed her, pulled her close to him, and hugged her hard to his chest, like he was a straitjacket. She melted into him and buried her face in his T-shirt and he looked over the top of her head to each of us, landing on me, raising his eyebrows as if to ask me, *What the fuck is going on?*

Bernadette stopped screaming and started wailing—a sad, animal noise that was more guttural than anything, starting in the pit of her stomach, escaping her mouth unbidden.

"Evelyn, can you . . ." Dad trailed off but pointed his chin at the vacuum, and Evelyn nodded, turning it on, sucking up a trail of glass from the kitchen sink to the doorway, so they could get out.

When she was done, she turned off the vacuum again and pressed herself against the fridge door. Dad gently turned his body and led Bernadette out of the room, step by cautious step, his eyes searching the floor for glass.

When they were gone, we all stood motionless for a long time, maybe thirty seconds, and then Clara said, in a small voice, "Do you think it will be like last time?"

"I don't know," I said. "I don't think we can know."

Evelyn turned on the vacuum again and I brought the chunk of glass I was holding over to the garbage, opening my hand and letting it fall into the bag.

"Why did she *scream*?" Clara pressed. She still hadn't moved. She had to raise her voice, to be heard over the vacuum.

"I don't know," I repeated. I spotted another shard of glass and picked it up, depositing it in the trash.

Evelyn was methodical in her cleaning. She spent at least ten minutes going over every inch of the floor. Occasionally Clara or I would point to a smaller piece she'd missed, and she'd diligently suck it up.

"Did she do it on purpose?" Clara asked when Evelyn had finally turned off the vacuum. "Drop the glass?"

"Of course not," Evie said.

"No, I was looking right at her," I added. "It slipped."

There were still a few plates on the table; Evelyn gathered them up and washed them off in the sink, then loaded the dishwasher.

"Shit," she said. "There's glass in here, too."

So we spent another five minutes cleaning the dishwasher, picking glass out of its nooks and crannies, Clara standing over us with a flashlight, me holding the bottom rack up as Evelyn dug around.

"What is happening here?" Mom said when she found us like that. She looked tired and worn around the edges, and almost amused to find the three of us hunched over the dishwasher.

"Bernadette broke a glass," Clara said.

"Accidentally," I added quickly.

"Where is she now?" Mom asked.

"Upstairs, with Dad," Evie said.

"She screamed," Clara added. "A lot."

I smacked her on the leg. Mom looked alarmed.

"Okay. Okay. I better go up and see."

She left the kitchen. I set the rack back down and we closed the dishwasher door.

"Why do you have to be like that?" I asked Clara.

"Like what?" she asked.

"So forthcoming."

"I didn't do anything!"

"It's fine," I said. "Forget it."

She was pouting.

"Let's all take a deep breath," Evelyn said.

Clara took an exaggerated, rude inhale, and Evelyn actually laughed, which broke the tension. What brought the tension right back was a loud, shrill wail from the fourth floor.

"It sounds like she's in pain," Clara said, her eyes wide.

"She's okay," Evie said. "She'll be okay."

Another wail, followed by choked sobs. She had to have been crying really loudly for us to hear her all the way down here.

"Henry," Evelyn said in a quiet voice.

And there he was, hardly more than an outline of a boy, standing in the middle of the kitchen.

"It's so loud," he said. Even his voice was thinner this far away from the attic.

In my sixteen and a half years of communing with ghosts, I'd learned that they really were quite tied to their own specific places, whether that was where they had died, where they were buried, or near something they had really, really loved in life (in the Met, there was a long-ago Farthing woman who stayed very close to a particular gold ring). But there were no other ghosts quite like Henry, not even my Aunt Esme, who could hold pretty reasonable conversations but never looked more solid than a wet paper towel.

"What's happening?" Evelyn asked now. "Is she okay?"

Henry looked utterly out of his element, both being on the ground floor and trying to describe the familial drama that was now unfolding on the fourth floor.

"I don't know," he said. "She's so upset. What happened?"

"She accidentally dropped a glass," Clara explained, shooting me a quick look.

"And she just lost it," Evelyn added. "She started screaming."

"She's still kind of screaming," Henry said, looking upward, winking in and out of existence in a way that made me think he was popping back upstairs to check in on things. When he reappeared again, he took a staggered step backward and then sat down in one of the kitchen chairs. It struck me as odd, seeing him there, looking pale and strange under the bright light of the kitchen lights, fidgeting a bit, finally looking up and letting his eyes land on Evelyn. How had I missed it before, the way he always found her in a crowd of Farthing sisters? How had I missed the way he never looked quite as alive as he looked when Evelyn was in the room?

She was leaning against the kitchen counter now, and as both Henry and I looked, she reached up and absentmindedly began unraveling her hair, which she had French braided that morning. Her fingers worked quickly, automatically, and soon her long hair hung in crimped curtains over her shoulders.

"I'm exhausted," she said, but Clara was the only one who heard her words. Henry and I were both transfixed by the waves of dirty blond. Evelyn's hair was darker than Clara's and somehow right now, it seemed darker still. She was almost a stranger to us. We couldn't take our eyes off her, and I noticed then, by the way the kitchen light hit her face, that she'd developed dark, purplish shadows underneath her eyes. How long had those been there? How unobservant had I become that I kept seeing things now that I'd never seen before?

"Me, too," Clara said.

"What?" Henry asked.

"Me, too," Clara repeated. "Evelyn said she was tired. I said, 'Me, too.'"

"Right," Henry said. "Right."

We went into the living room. Evelyn got a board game out from the cupboard that all of us knew we weren't going to play. It was just a prop of some sorts; if someone came downstairs, we could pretend that we weren't devoting every ounce of our energy to the act of eavesdropping.

Clara sat on the floor next to Evie and the two of them set it up. Monopoly. They divvied out the money. They assigned each of us a pawn. They laid out the property cards by color. They set out the Community Chest and Chance cards in two neat piles. They put the two die in the middle of the board. With nothing else to do, Clara fidgeted, taking the pewter dog pawn and prancing him around the edges of the board. Evelyn was perfectly still. A statue with wavy hair.

"This is miserable," I said.

"Yes," Evelyn agreed.

"When she threw the glass at my head, do you think she really meant to hit me, or she didn't, like she said?" Clara asked quietly. It wasn't the first time she'd asked that question, and nobody knew how to answer her, because nobody knew.

"She's just adjusting," Evelyn said. We weren't sure what she was adjusting *to,* but still. It sounded like a nice excuse, so we didn't press it.

Footsteps on the stairs and then Dad was in the doorway, squinting, rubbing at his temple. He surveyed the room, the Monopoly board, the fourth spot that he must have assumed was for Bernadette but had really been for Henry, who of course by that point had disappeared (he had never shown himself to my father, and I wasn't sure my father would even be able to see him, had he done so).

"I don't think Bernadette is going to be up for any games tonight, girls," he said sadly.

He went into the kitchen and came back a few moments later with a glass of water, which he took upstairs.

"Let's just play," Henry said, there again. "We might as well just play."

"Oldest goes first," Clara said brightly, and handed the dice to Evelyn.

She stared at them in her hand for a long time before letting them tumble to the floor.

III

Persephone had two children, Melinoë and Zagreus. Zagreus, the prince of the Underworld, was the god of hunting and rebirth. Melinoë, his sister, was the goddess of madness and nightmares, but also of ghosts and spirits. She could speak to them, converse with them, guide them, command them. She loved them, just as her father, Hades, loved them. People debate endlessly over whether Melinoë was a good *goddess or a* bad *goddess but that is ultimately irrelevant, because in the end she loved her favored subjects endlessly: the mad, the dead, the sleepless. . . .*

September gave way to October, and it grew chilly and gray in the city. The days were getting shorter. It was dark when Evelyn and I walked to school in the mornings and it was dark when we walked home. Sometimes we'd meet up with Clara at Todd's and do homework together at one of the back tables, pressed against a wall with endless hot chocolate delivered by Todd himself, who was a friend of Dad's and who had obviously, judging by the expression on his face, heard about Bernadette. Otherwise we'd never have gotten away with the homework thing; there were signs everywhere—NO LAPTOPS!!!

We made quite the trio. Evelyn: sad and morose. Me: lonely and irritable. And Clara: frustrated with her painting, withdrawn and sullen. You knew things were really bad when Clara descended into a dark mood. Her painting wasn't progressing how she wanted; she had covered up half the canvas with a wash of white paint. I had found her late one night with a brush in her hand, murmuring to herself angrily.

After that night with the broken glass, we hadn't seen Bernadette for four days, and then she was gone in the middle of the night; I'd woken up and just knew, could feel that four had become three, that one Farthing sister was missing from the nest. I went upstairs early and peeked into her room. The bed was made, the clothes that usually littered the floor had been folded and put away, the dirty glasses and candy wrappers had been disposed of.

"She left," Evelyn had said from the doorway of her room. She'd had a blank expression on her face.

"Gone where?" I'd asked.

She'd shrugged.

To Aunt Bea's, it had turned out.

"In *Vermont*?" Clara had shrieked at breakfast when our parents told us.

"A little bit of country air will do her good," Dad had said, keeping his voice bright and calm. Mom hadn't been there; we'd assumed she'd driven Bernadette north. She'd returned a few days later, sans Bernadette, and none of us had asked any of the questions we'd wanted to, like *How long is this going to be?* and *What is wrong with her?* and *Do we need to be seriously concerned here?*

Now, at Todd's, we trudged through our school assignments and diligently plodded along with essays and Clara held an enormous English textbook in front of her face, reading some short story that made her knit her eyebrows together in maybe confusion or maybe dislike; I didn't ask.

After my second mug of hot chocolate I felt bloated and a little too warm. Todd's was filling up with its early dinner crowd and I was having trouble concentrating over the increasing volume, the dull murmur of voices.

"I think I'm going to go home," I said.

"I'm in the middle of this," Evelyn said, not taking her eyes away from her laptop screen.

"Same," Clara said.

Neither of them looked up at me, so I gathered my things and left them behind, stepping out into the sharp chill of the night, grateful it was almost the weekend, ready to sleep in on Saturday and put my schoolbooks away for a few days. We were split fairly down the middle for school—Bernadette and I had always been average students, Evelyn would likely be valedictorian, and Clara was constantly fielding scholarships for private high schools around the city. She took each letter she received, gave it a brief once-over, and tossed it in the trash.

"It's a grotesque waste of money," she always said, never minding the fact that said scholarships often offered full rides.

I was only wearing my usual sweatshirt and I raised the hood to try and stave off the chill of the night, even though it was less than a block to our house and I walked quickly, as if I could avoid the breeze.

Mom was coming down the stairs when I reached the sidewalk

in front of the house, and I stopped and waited for her. She didn't see me until she was almost on top of me, then she looked up and jumped a mile and grabbed at her chest dramatically.

"Jesus," she said. "What gives?"

"Where are you going?" I asked, because she had an overnight bag in one hand and she was wearing leggings and an oversize wool fisherman's sweater, two articles of clothing she wore exclusively on long car rides or if she didn't feel good and was planning on spending the day on the couch.

"I was attempting to sneak out so as not to answer any tough questions," she said, sighing.

"Is 'Where are you going?' a tough question?"

"Give me a break, will you, kid?"

"Where *are* you going? Vermont?"

Another sigh. "Yes. I am going to Vermont."

"Is she okay?"

"She's okay. I'm going to bring her home."

"Can I come with you?"

"You have school tomorrow, honey."

"Yeah, but I haven't missed a day all year."

"It's October," she said. "You've been in school a month."

"Almost a month and a half. I want to see Aunt Bea. I want to see Bernadette."

Mom took a very mom-like inhalation of breath and let it out slowly through her mouth. I could see it in the air, the faintest puff of white.

"Where are your sisters?" she asked.

"Well, one of them is in Vermont." She gave me a look. "The others are at Todd's."

She checked the time on her phone. "If you can get ready and be down here in eight minutes, you can come. If *anyone* catches you leaving, you tell them you were going to run away but have decided against it, and you go right back upstairs and unpack, and you stay here. Got it?"

"Got it."

"Meet me at the car," she said, and didn't wait for an answer before charging off down the street, in the opposite direction of Todd's.

I ran.

I ran upstairs and dumped the contents of my backpack on my bed, then shoved clean underwear into it, pajamas, another pair of jeans, some clean long-sleeved shirts and socks, my phone charger, and my laptop (under the delusion that I might actually work on school assignments). In the bathroom, I grabbed my toothbrush and my face wash and my moisturizer and then I was downstairs again, passing not a single soul as I burst out of the house and kept running all the way to the parking garage where we kept the SUV.

Mom was waiting in the driver's seat, the engine already running, her hands already on the steering wheel, and I climbed into the passenger seat, throwing my backpack behind me. I buckled my seat belt quickly, as if that could keep her from changing her mind.

"Your sisters are going to kill me," she said.

"I'll text them."

"Not until we're a few blocks away. I don't want anyone running after the car."

It took us awhile to get out of the city. I texted Evelyn and Clara as we crossed the George Washington Bridge, the Hudson River dark and ominous below us as we slipped from New York into New Jersey.

"Are they upset?" Mom asked after I'd stared at my phone for a while.

"Clara called me a traitor," I said. "Evelyn hasn't responded."

"Sounds about right."

Once we got out of New Jersey and back into New York (that part always tripped me up, how we left only to come back), the traffic got a lot better. Mom put on the cruise control and let out a big sigh that I thought she'd probably been holding since Eighty-First Street.

"You okay?" I asked.

She reached over and patted my leg. "I'm okay, honey. I'm glad you're with me."

"You were trying to sneak out," I reminded her.

"Yes," she agreed. "But this was a happy accident. I've found I'd much rather be with you than be alone."

It was about a six-hour drive to Burlington, Vermont, where Aunt Bea lived in the big old farmhouse where she'd grown up with my mother. There was a huge barn in the back where she made her art. Clara had gotten her love of painting from Aunt Bea, who was a few years my mother's junior and had never married or had kids herself. She was a professor of art history at the University of Vermont and although she traveled all the time and was constantly zipping off to faraway locales, she always returned to her childhood home. "It's my favorite place in the world," she often said. "Why would I ever leave it?"

Aside from art, she was also an accomplished musician (that's where Evelyn had gotten it) and had a very cool sense of style (Bernadette had inherited her love of vintage clothing).

It seemed like all of my sisters had gotten *something* from Aunt Bea, but what about me?

What did I have in common with my aunt?

"Status check?" Mom asked, glancing at me.

"Oh, just thinking."

"About what?"

"Do you think Aunt Bea and I have anything in common?"

"Hmm. What do you mean?"

"Like, you know. She and Clara are both artists . . ."

Mom tilted her neck left, tilted her neck right, flexed and unflexed her fingers on the steering wheel. Finally she said, "There is something, yes. You both show up exactly when you're needed. Like tonight. I walked down the stairs and *boom*—there you were."

"And I was needed?"

"You're always needed," Mom replied. "But yes, when it's most important, you're always there. And you always seem to know exactly what to do. Empathic. Maybe that's what I'd call it. A bit of empathy, coupled with a bit of 'right place, right time.'"

I scratched the insides of my wrists as I thought about what she'd said.

"You really think so?"

"You know I don't lie," she said. And it was true, she didn't.

She put on an audiobook a few minutes later, some very boring nonfiction thing about people who were absolutely batshit in love with orchids, and I leaned my head back and closed my eyes, not really meaning to fall asleep, but waking up with a jerk, surprised to find that two hours had passed.

"Are we there yet?" I mumbled, my mouth dry and sour.

"We probably won't get there until about one," Mom replied. "Rush hour slowed us down a bit."

Aunt Bea was a night owl, another thing she shared with Clara, and I knew she'd be awake and ready for us with cups of tea and a midnight snack.

And I knew Esme would be there, too.

The first time I'd seen her, I'd been younger, just around the age she'd been when she died. I'd asked her name, and then repeated it aloud, verifying. My mother had heard me, but luckily, just past the ghost-Esme, on the mantel over the fire, there was a photo of her. Mom had thought I was looking at the picture, and she laid a hand on the top of my head and said, "That's right. That's Esme."

Years later, I would learn that Esme had died in the house, after a short battle with a particularly aggressive cancer. She had been six years old, and she had never left.

Now, her favorite activities included playing with dolls and attempting to scare the absolute bejesus out of me (a skill at which she was most adept, though I couldn't tell if it was malicious or accidental).

Despite being constantly in fear of her sneak attacks, I was actually looking forward to seeing her again.

"Has Aunt Bea said how Bernadette is?" I asked now, my thoughts wandering back to my oldest sister.

"I've been talking to her every day," Mom said. "Your sister is doing much better."

"And why exactly did you banish her to Vermont?"

"When you say it like that, it makes it sound quite dramatic," Mom said.

"It felt a little dramatic, to be fair."

"I just wanted your sister to have some time alone. There are a lot of people in our house, and it can be hard to think. There's a lot more breathing room in Vermont."

"You think she needed breathing room?"

"I do," Mom said. "Plus, I wanted Bea to take her to a few classes. Let her sit in the back, audit, listen in. Maybe your sister picked the wrong college. It's very possible for her to transfer, you know. It might be nice for her to have family nearby. She could even live with your aunt. Bea would love that."

"What if she doesn't want to go to college at all?"

"That's another option," Mom said, nodding. "And that would be fine, too."

"But she's okay? She's going to be okay?"

Mom paused, and for a moment I wondered if she'd even heard me. Then she said, slowly, "Winnie, your sister struggles a bit. It seems like the older she gets, the more she struggles. And that was another reason we sent her up north. Your aunt has had her fair share of troubles, too. I thought maybe she was the right person for this job."

I thought of Bernadette in Vermont, hanging out with our aunt(s), convalescing. I couldn't help but think of Beth March, going to the seaside to beat the remnants of the fever that would eventually kill her. But everyone knew Bernadette was Jo, right down to the chopping of the hair.

Mom turned up her audiobook. Everyone was looking for some super rare kind of orchid.

The ghost orchid.

"Well, that's a coincidence," I said.

"Hmm?"

"Oh, nothing," I replied, and closed my eyes, suddenly there with them in Florida, for once smelling orchids instead of jasmine.

"Wake up, sleepyhead," Mom said, and I realized I had fallen asleep again. It was 12:45 and we were idling in Aunt Bea's driveway.

"Ugh," I said.

"Indeed," Mom said, opening her door to a blast of cold air.

I pulled my phone out of my pocket as I slid out of the car.

Evelyn had never texted me back.

Clara had texted me a string of different emojis, from sad faces to angry faces to dead faces. I knew she was still up, so I texted her before I got out of the car.

Is Evelyn mad?

Her response came almost immediately: *yup*.

I typed back: *are you mad?*

Her response: *YUP*

I put my phone in my pocket and helped Mom with her suitcase. Aunt Bea was waiting in the front doorway, dressed in paint-splattered overalls. She had her hair in a messy ponytail and her smile was so wide it looked like it hurt.

"I wasn't expecting *you,*" she exclaimed, throwing her arms around me and nuzzling her cheek into mine.

"She's a stowaway," Mom said, pushing past us into the house.

"It's *lovely* to see you," Aunt Bea said, pulling away and looking earnestly into my eyes. Everything she said was said earnestly. Everything she said, you got the feeling that she really meant, with every fiber of her being.

"It's nice to see you, too," I said. We stepped into the foyer and Aunt Bea shut the door. "Is Bernie awake?"

"No, sound asleep," she said. "Are you tired? Or will you have a cup of tea before bed?"

"I'll have some," I said.

"Great! Sissy, what about you?" Aunt Bea only ever called Mom *Sissy,* a remnant from their childhood, when she couldn't pronounce Mom's name—Anastasia.

"Sure, sure," Mom said. She was rummaging in her suitcase for something; she pulled out a cardigan and slipped it on. "It's *freezing* in here, Bea."

Aunt Bea rolled her eyes at me. "It's Vermont, Sissy. You grew up here. Surely your blood hasn't thinned *that* much."

"Just because it's freezing outside, doesn't mean it has to be freezing inside," Mom said, then *she* rolled her eyes at me, because when the two of them were together, they regressed about thirty years each.

I wanted to see Bernadette. I wanted to wake her up, crawl into bed with her, peer into her eyeballs and make sure she was okay, but I knew I shouldn't. She needed her sleep, and I needed to not give her a heart attack by jumping into her bed in the middle of the night. (Plus, you could *always* crawl in bed with Evelyn; you could *sometimes* crawl in bed with Clara; you could *never* crawl in bed with Bernadette.) I went and sat at Aunt Bea's kitchen table, repurposed wood from a barn that used to be on my grandparents' property. One of the professors at the school had made it for Bea. He taught woodworking or architecture or something.

"Why do men always bring you gifts?" Mom had asked her once.

And Bea had smiled and said, "Not just men."

There was a large painting hanging on the wall above an old record player, because of course Aunt Bea played actual vinyl records at one in the morning. The painting was one I'd always loved. It showed a naked woman reclining in a rural field, a river running alongside the left of her and a creepy old man peering around a tree on her right. The woman was Persephone; she wore a languid, sultry expression on her face and her body was all glowing skin and supple curves. The man was Hades, spying on Persephone right before he steals her away to the Underworld. The original painting was by Thomas Hart Benton and hung in the Nelson-Atkins Museum of Art. Bea's copy had been painted by one of Benton's students and was, in my opinion, just as good as the original.

I had seen Aunt Bea talking to this version of Persephone, telling her about the day, our plans, keeping her abreast of the goings-on of the Farthing girls.

"As long as she never talks back," Mom had said once.

"Of course she talks back, Sissy. You just have to know the right way to listen."

Aunt Bea caught me looking at the painting now, and she put an arm on my shoulder as Mom settled down at the kitchen table. "Did I ever tell you about the time I fell out of a tree?"

"Here we go," Mom said, but her eyes were twinkling, and she sat up a little, listening. You always listened to Aunt Bea's stories.

"I should have died, honestly. Must have been fifteen, twenty feet up. Broke my arm in two places. And I swear, I *swear,* as I was lying there on the grass waiting for your mother to run and get help, I saw this face . . ." She trailed off, her eyes unfocusing, letting the moment breathe, letting the image of her lying on the grass really take shape. She was an *excellent* storyteller.

"Persephone?" I asked, expertly delivering my line (I had of course heard this story a hundred times before; we all had).

Aunt Bea shook herself out of her trance and smiled at me, shrugging her shoulders. "I know it sounds like a tall tale, kid. But stranger things have happened."

Stranger things have happened could have been the slogan for a show about the Farthing girls, I thought to myself as Aunt Bea set mugs of peppermint tea in front of Mom and me and then slid into her seat.

One thing I loved about Aunt Bea is that she never asked boring questions like *how was the drive,* instead she went right from a story about how Persephone saved her from the clutches of death to looking at each of us for a moment, clearing her throat and saying, "Is there a reason you both sort of look like shit?"

I burst out laughing, but Mom just took a careful sip of her tea and said, "I'm sorry car travel doesn't agree with us as it does with you, Beatrice."

"No, that's not what I meant," she said. "There's something . . . going on." When she said *going on,* she waved her hand in a circle in front of my face. It felt vaguely ritualistic.

"What do you mean?" Mom asked.

"An energy," Bea said.

"Please don't bring out the crystals."

"I'm considering it."

"We're just tired," Mom insisted. "It's been a long day. A few long weeks."

"Isn't life just a series of a few long weeks, over and over and over until we die?" Aunt Bea mused, and she seemed almost chipper, even when talking about our inevitable deaths. It was hard to dampen Aunt Bea's spirits. That was one thing I didn't think any of us Farthing girls had gotten from her, unfortunately. One wrong look could pretty much dampen the spirits of any of us.

We fell into silence, and only then did I realize the music had stopped. Aunt Bea got up and switched the record, and I recognized the first few chords of Buddy Holly's "You're the One." Aunt Bea was a *big* Buddy Holly fan.

Mom let out a long yawn. "I think I'll finish the rest of this in bed," she said, picking up her mug. "Don't stay up too late, you two."

"I have you in the back room," Aunt Bea said, pointing vaguely upstairs and toward the back of the house. "Sleep tight, Sissy."

Mom cradled Aunt Bea's head in her arms and kissed her temple. "Love you. Night." Then she did the same to me. "Love you. Night."

"Love you. Night," we echoed, and she picked up her suitcase and trudged slowly up the stairs to the second floor.

Aunt Bea had closed her eyes and was listening intently to the music. Buddy Holly songs were short, and the next one was already starting. It was probably my favorite Buddy Holly song, only because it was Aunt Bea's favorite Buddy Holly song. It was called "(Ummm, Oh Yeah) Dearest." Like all Buddy Holly songs, the lyrics were simple, but the message was direct and clear: *I love you, I'm sorry, don't leave me.*

I looked at Aunt Bea; she was totally zoned out with that look she often got on her face. Like she wasn't even in the same room with you. Like she was somewhere else entirely.

I took a sip of my tea, which was sweetened with honey and absolutely delicious, then looked over to the right, into the living room. Aunt Bea had lit a fire at some point in the night, but it had almost gone out; the last few coals glowed with a delicate, orange warmth.

I blinked slowly, my eyelids growing heavy as the tea warmed me from the inside out. In one blink, the living room was empty. In another blink, my Aunt Esme sat in front of the fireplace, two small dolls in her hand. She didn't seem to notice I was there. A little ghost girl lost in her own endless childhood.

I knew Aunt Bea couldn't see Esme, but was there a part of her that was comforted by her younger sister's presence? Was there a part of Aunt Bea that had never left this house because she could never leave *her*? Was that so horrible a life? Aunt Bea still traveled, still worked, still went to countless art galleries and concerts, still hiked and swam at the local YMCA, still came to visit us in New York every chance she got. Was it really so bad, being tied to a ghost?

But Aunt Bea wasn't Evelyn.

And Aunt Esme wasn't Henry.

No, this was completely different.

Aunt Esme paused her game, let her dolls drop from her hands, closed her eyes for a moment before rising to her feet. She spread her little arms out and began to spin in a slow circle, swaying and dancing to the music.

In that moment, as she danced alone in front of the fireplace, I knew this had been Esme's favorite song, too.

Bernadette woke me up in the morning. She came into my dream first, wrapping her arms around me, squeezing me in a hug, and then she was there in real life, sitting on the edge of my bed, holding a mug of coffee, wearing flannel pajama pants and an old, holey T-shirt that had belonged to our father at one point. It was soft and threadbare in places.

"I can never keep a good T-shirt in this house!" he had said on more than one occasion. This one had a drawing of a sailboat on the left side, with the words PARK POINT MANOR written above it and SAILING WITH PROGRESS written below it.

"Bernie," I mumbled happily.

"I'm glad you came," she said. "I don't think I could have handled another six-hour drive with Mom listening to some boring audiobook."

"We listened to one about orchids."

"When she drove me up, it was mushrooms."

She set the coffee down on the nightstand and threw herself on top of me, smothering me, kissing my hair a million times before settling down and just laying her dead weight on top of me. She smelled nice, like Aunt Bea's fancy, organic, handmade soap, and her hair was slightly damp, like she'd showered before bed and it still hadn't dried all the way.

"I missed you," I said, my voice muffled and small.

"I missed you, too," she said. "I'm better now. I'm cured. I'll probably come to college here for the spring semester."

"Really?" I asked as she sat up, letting me breathe.

"It does make sense," she said. "Living with Aunt Bea is nice.

There's always fresh bread. She has it delivered from the bakery. And the college is really nice. I've been auditing some classes, just walking around. I like this town. It's pretty here."

"You had me at *bread*."

"Seriously, though. Shut up. I'm trying to open up to you," Bernadette said, but she was mostly joking, and I was mostly joking, and it felt easy and nice between us, like nothing strange had ever happened involving a dropped wineglass in the kitchen. "Do you ever feel like our house is kind of . . ." She paused, thinking. "I don't quite know how to phrase this. Like it's *trapped* us?"

"Trapped us," I repeated.

"Like it's hard to leave, maybe," she continued. "When I'm away from it, it's harder to keep everything straight in my head. My thoughts, my emotions. I get . . . angrier."

I thought back to the glass she'd thrown at the wall/Clara. That had been inside the house; I didn't want to imagine an *angrier* Bernadette outside of it.

"I *did* get hit in the face with a volleyball," she said.

"I know. We saw the video."

"But it wasn't what caused my black eye. It looked impressive on camera, but it wasn't really that hard."

"So then . . ."

"I was in a fight," she said. "In hindsight, I one hundred percent deserved it. I'd had too much to drink; I took the first swing and I missed and . . . I was way out of line."

"Why didn't you tell me?"

"I was so embarrassed. I've always had all this anger, I should have learned to control it by now." A pause, then: "It's why I threw that glass at Clara's head."

So you *did* throw the glass specifically *at* Clara's head—I wanted to say but didn't. Instead I said, "And what does this have to do with the house?"

"I don't know. I'm still working things out in my head. I just know that it's really hard for me, being away from the house. It feels like there's a constant pull. Like it wants me back. Or maybe it's *me,* being scared to be away from it. Being scared to be away from all of you, and from Henry."

Not you, too, I wanted to say, but didn't.

What I did say was, "I know what you mean."

Bernadette smiled. "I talk to Henry a lot, actually. About all this. It gets so jumbled in my head, but he's such a good listener."

"He is."

We were silent for a moment, both of us thinking about Henry, if I had to guess.

"Well, how has *this* house been treating you?" I asked.

"We go on a lot of hikes and I meditate and journal and stuff. I think I've filled up two journals since I've been here. Aunt Bea is really into, like, attacking my healing from every angle. I've been seeing a therapist up here. And a psychiatrist. And I'm so fucking sick of talking about my feelings. But I'm doing it." She paused, took a deep breath. "I'm stalling. I'm trying to just say it."

"Say it," I said, taking her hand. "Whatever it is."

"The psychiatrist diagnosed me with bipolar II disorder. She's referred me to a psychiatrist in New York so I can come home and continue my treatment there."

"Okay," I said. And because I didn't know what else to say, I squeezed her hand and repeated it. "Okay."

"You know what I thought when she told me? The first thing I thought?"

"What?"

"Fuck you, Melinoë."

"One point to the goddess of madness," I said.

"I will admit, I've gone a little bit down the rabbit hole with her," Bernadette said. "Did you know she was born by the river Cocytus? It's the River of Wailing in the Underworld. No wonder she went mad."

"Well, good thing we're fresh out of wailing rivers in New York."

"And she's also considered the goddess of ghosts. I didn't know that. *Ghosts,* Winnie. We might as well make an altar for her right now and start sacrificing baby sheep or something."

"I hope you're joking."

"Of course I'm joking. I'm a vegetarian."

I let go of her hand and tapped the side of her head. "I'm proud of you."

"Thanks. Although I didn't really do anything besides being descended from Persephone and her weird, weird daughter."

She got quiet then, and I looked at her face, remembering the black eye, how it had swollen and blossomed over a few days, then slowly faded again. There was no trace of it now, not even the faintest shadow or smudge. Bernadette's skin was porcelain, unblemished, framed by her very excellent pixie cut. I would have loved to say I couldn't imagine Bernadette in a fistfight but . . . I could.

"Good morning, girls," Mom said from the doorway. We hadn't realized she'd been there. "Bernadette, it's nice to see you."

"It's nice to see you, too," Bernadette said. "But are you here to take me even farther north? To, like, Canada or something?"

"I don't have any relatives in Canada, honey," Mom said. "You're safe."

I thought I should give them a few minutes alone, so I snuck out of the bed and went to the bathroom. The house smelled like coffee and warm bread. After I peed I went downstairs to the kitchen, where Aunt Bea was taking a baking sheet full of croissants out of the oven.

"Morning," she called over her shoulder, though she hadn't seen me and I didn't think I'd made any noise.

"Morning," I said. "Did you make those?"

"Oh, hell no. Just warming them up. Wait until you taste this, honey, you're gonna cry true tears of joy."

"Looking forward to it," I said. I poured myself a cup of coffee from the coffeemaker Aunt Bea had probably had for thirty years, then sat at the kitchen table as she transferred the croissants to a plate. She brought them over still steaming and set them in front of me, then got a jar of some locally made jam and stuck a spoon in it.

"You don't need anything on them, I'm telling you, they're phenomenal on their own," she said. "But I also love this jam. Blackberry. Who doesn't love blackberries? Show me a person who doesn't love blackberries."

"I can't think of anyone," I said.

"Exactly."

She grabbed her coffee and took a seat, putting her elbows on the table and staring me full in the face until I took one of the croissants, so warm it was almost too hot to hold, and had a bite.

"Howy thit," I said, my mouth full of flaky, buttery goodness.

"I know," she said. "I told you. Now try the jam."

The croissant was maybe the best thing I had ever tasted in my entire sixteen years on the planet. The jam was a close second. I was on my second one by the time Bernie and Mom came downstairs; Bernie's eyes lit up when she saw the croissants and she fell into the seat next to me, sighing dramatically.

"These croissants are why I forgive you for dropping me off in the middle of nowhere," Bernadette told Mom.

"This is hardly the middle of nowhere," Aunt Bea said.

"Yesterday I went for a run and I didn't see another person for three miles," Bernie said. She was slicing open her croissant for better jam application.

"You are absolutely full of it," Aunt Bea said.

"You run?" I asked.

"I run," Bernadette confirmed. "My captor said I must do one physical activity per day. So I run three miles, then collapse and cry on the front lawn until she comes and drags me into the shower."

"That's more or less accurate," Aunt Bea said. "Except, sometimes we go hiking."

"Wow, two weeks in Vermont and you're a regular athlete," I said.

"Has it been two weeks?" Bernie said with some surprise. "My captor also doesn't let me use my phone or watch the news, and she blacks out the date on the newspapers with Sharpie."

"None of that is true," Aunt Bea said, ripping a small piece off her croissant and throwing it at Bernadette's face. "Tell them about all the nice things we've done, you monster."

"Oh, there's a great vintage store," Bernadette said, perking up. "My captor has given me a small allowance, with which I've bought some seriously cool new swag."

"We'll pay you back," Mom said to Aunt Bea.

Aunt Bea waved her hand, like she was swatting a bug away. "Tish, tosh," she said. "Best two weeks of my life. You should send all the girls here, one by one. But send them on the bus next time. Less driving for you." She winked at Mom. Then, to me, she said, "Would you like to stay here? During the summer maybe?"

"Absolutely," I said. "Unless you make me run three miles a day."

"It's all about the give and take here," Bernie said. "You'll also have to *dust*." She fake-shuddered.

I surveyed the table. Mom looked really, really pleased. Aunt Bea looked content and happy. Bernadette looked glowing. If I had a mirror, I imagined I'd look a bit like all three of them combined.

Later that morning Mom went for a hike, Aunt Bea went to teach a class, and Bernie and I headed to Church Street, tucking ourselves into the corner of a small café and ordering two steaming hot chocolates.

"It's an art interpretation class," Bernie said. "I've gone to it a few times; it's really good. They're learning about John Singer Sargent. Aunt Bea calls him the 'eternal boy crush of art students everywhere.'"

"Should we have gone?"

"I considered it, but ultimately I thought our time would be better spent getting hot chocolate, vintage shopping, and wandering around aimlessly."

"I do love wandering around aimlessly."

"I know this about you."

I thought of Evelyn then, of walking across the park with her to get to school, of the way we could walk in silence the entire time, then each have the same thought at the same time, look at each other and smile, a moment of sister intuition, of sister ESP, of sister mind reading. I wondered what she was doing now. I felt terribly guilty for abandoning her.

"Don't be weird, Winnie," Bernadette said (another moment of sister ESP). "Everything's fine."

"What if it's not fine, though?" I responded. "What if it's really, really not fine?"

"What's not fine?" Bernie pressed. "Name one thing."

"Global warming."

"Name two things."

"Evelyn's in love with Henry."

I blurted it out before I meant to, the words taking on a life of their own, becoming slippery and wet and way too eager to make themselves known.

Weakly, I added, "She made me promise not to tell you."

Bernadette took a positively languid sip of her hot chocolate, set the mug back down on the saucer and said, "You're really not the most observant."

"You know?"

"Of course I know," Bernie said. "Clara and I both know. We've known for, like, six months."

"And you didn't tell me?"

"You didn't tell me, either."

"I'm telling you right now!"

"And what's your point exactly? What's the big terrible thing here?"

"She isn't going to leave," I said, my voice suddenly too loud, catching an unfortunate lull in the general din of the café. I cleared my throat, scooted my chair closer to Bernadette, and tried to give her a look that conveyed the severity of the situation. She looked rather blankly back at me, so I assumed my telecommunication wasn't working properly. "Like, ever. She isn't going to leave the house, ever. No college. No traveling. No life, no *anything*."

Bernie's brows furrowed just a smidge. "What do you mean? Did she tell you that?"

"She's in *love* love," I said. "Like *serious* love."

"Well, sure, but—"

"And if *you* were in love love, would you go away to college or get married to someone else or would you stay with the person you loved?"

"I never really considered . . ."

"That this would affect the rest of her life? That Evelyn would sacrifice everything just so she could stay in the attic of our brownstone forever?"

"I guess . . . no. No. I did not consider that."

"I'm worried about her, Bernie," I said. "She's not acting like herself. She's acting so strange and heartbroken and *lost*."

"I didn't realize, I thought it was just . . ."

"A phase?"

"No, you're right . . . Evelyn doesn't go through *phases*."

"So what do we do?"

"What *can* we do?"

"Can we do anything?"

"I'll think about it," Bernadette said. "I guess I have to think about it . . ."

"Are you feeling like . . ."

"A horrible sister?"

"Me, too."

"We're not, though," Bernie insisted. "At least, I don't think we are. This is just . . . a weird situation. Who could have predicted this?"

"Clara, maybe."

"But she didn't."

"She didn't."

"Fuck."

"Indeed."

For a moment we were quiet. I closed my eyes and let the sounds of the café block out any other thoughts. A man with an unnecessarily loud voice ordered a dirty chai latte. A woman sneezed. A baby whined. A table full of young girls giggled to themselves. The old-fashioned register made a satisfying *clink*. The world went on around us. Wasn't it weird how everything didn't just stop when you wanted it to? Just give me a *break,* for the love of—

"Are you almost done?" Bernadette said, reaching over and nudging my hand. "Let's go shopping. It's too hot in here. I'm going to claw my own skin off."

"Yeah," I said, and finished the rest of my hot chocolate in one long sip. "Ditto."

We walked to Bernadette's new favorite vintage store, a sprawling space that stretched back and back and back, going on forever, an entire wall just filled with different pairs of jeans.

I saw a gray tweed skirt and thought of Evelyn. Evelyn who still hadn't texted me back. Evelyn who hated me right now. Evelyn who was miserable and sad and in love.

I hated fighting with my sisters, especially the long, silent fights, the fights that felt like an empty chasm had grown up between us.

I pulled out my phone and texted her.

I miss you

Part of me wanted to say something ruder, something like *stop being a little baby; you would have gone in my place in a heartbeat.* But rudeness never worked with Evelyn.

I stared at the screen for a moment but she didn't type back, so I put my phone in my pocket again.

The vintage store had a smell. *All* vintage stores have a smell. It was a smell of wear, of use, of years and years and years of being in someone else's house, someone else's closet. It was the unknown, the unknowable. Another life entirely. The way each of my sisters somehow smelled just a little different, despite the fact that we all lived in the same house, used the same laundry detergent and the same soap and the same shampoo and conditioner. But, sound asleep in my bed, if one of them came into my room and laid down next to me, I'd know who it was without rolling over. I could pick each of them out in a crowd full of people without opening my eyes. Blindfolded, I would know them.

I rounded a corner and found Bernadette just slipping into a fitting room, an armful of clothes weighing her down.

I took a seat in an overstuffed armchair and waited. I got out my phone again. Nothing from Evelyn. I texted Clara instead.

Hi. Miss you

She sent back an emoji of a hand making a peace sign, which in Clara-speak meant she was at school and couldn't talk.

I texted Evelyn again.

I'm sorry I came to Vermont without you but Mom was literally running out the door, I just happened to catch her at the right time, and she wouldn't have waited for anyone else. If you want to blame anyone you can blame Mom but I am perfectly guiltless

Bernadette came out of the fitting room wearing acid-washed light denim jeans that somehow looked amazing on her and would have looked absolutely horrible on anyone else.

"Who are you texting? You look pained," she said, turning around to check out her butt in the mirror.

"Evie."

"Leave her be. She'll come around. What do you think of these?"

"They're perfect. Obviously."

"Don't be so fatalistic, Winnie," she said, throwing a pair of wool sailor pants at me. "And try these on."

Bernie made me wear the sailor pants out of the store, despite my concerns over when they might have last been washed. But she had guessed my size perfectly, and they looked and felt great. She even insisted on paying for them, so she could borrow them whenever she wanted (although she was a solid three inches taller than me and they wouldn't have fit right). When we got back to Aunt Bea's, both she and my mom made a big fuss over them.

"Honey, these are *cute,*" Mom said. I thought she was mostly just happy I was wearing something other than jeans.

"Stick with me, kid," Aunt Bea said. "Vermont has better vintage."

"Than New York?" Mom retorted. "You're out of your gourd, Bea."

"Not *better* vintage," Bernadette offered. "But definitely *cheaper* vintage. These pants would have been four times the price in the city."

"Well, they look great, honey," Mom said.

Bernie dumped her own tote bag on the floor to show off her goods, and I beelined for a cheese plate set up on the kitchen table. My stomach was rumbling as I smeared Brie on a cracker and ate it in one bite. Bernadette and I had been gone most of the day and it only just occurred to me that we'd forgotten to eat lunch.

"Salad and cheese plate," Aunt Bea said, putting an enormous serving bowl of salad on the table, along with four bowls and forks. "How long are you staying, anyway, Sissy?"

"Oh, we'll drive home Sunday, I think," Mom said.

"Perfect," Aunt Bea said. "We'll go for a big hike tomorrow. Pack a picnic."

"I didn't bring hiking boots," I said.

"Aunt Bea has a closet full of hiking boots," Bernie offered.

"It's true, I do," Aunt Bea said, sort of proudly.

"What about tonight?" Bernie asked. "We should play a game or something."

"Game sounds great," Mom said.

I served myself some salad and took a seat at the table as my phone buzzed. I pulled it out of my pocket and checked it eagerly—it was Clara, not Evelyn.

Can I borrow that Dior lipstick you got for your birthday and never wear

No. How mad is Evelyn now?

She has taken up smoking and used her cigarettes to burn your face out of every photo in the house

How's the painting coming?

It's coming. I still don't know what it is, but when I look at it, I get a very bad feeling in the pit of my stomach

Oh that's just great

In the interest of full disclosure, I
have already borrowed your lipstick
and it looks very good on me,
probably better than it looks on you

Jerk

I put my phone on the table and bit my bottom lip.

Now *I* had a very bad feeling in the pit of my stomach.

I made myself another cheese and cracker and tried to ignore what the pit was telling me—that something was coming, that something was here.

We played Aunt Bea's favorite game—Trivial Pursuit—which we were all hopelessly terrible at (including Aunt Bea). Mom opened a bottle of wine without asking and it turned out to be some incredibly expensive bottle Aunt Bea had been saving for a special occasion ("Although, I guess," she announced amiably, "what's a more special occasion than simply being alive and with people you love"), and Bernadette made us all ice cream sundaes at ten o'clock. We enjoyed short-lived sugar highs and then their inevitable crash, and everyone headed to bed by eleven. I'd just settled under the comforter when I realized I forgot water. Groaning, I dragged myself up again and plodded downstairs to get some.

Halfway down the stairs, I paused.

Aunt Esme was back, poised in her usual spot by the fire, playing with her dolls. Despite no lamps being on, the living room was bathed in a warm, comfortable glow. Esme herself was mostly transparent, and her eyes were glowing in a sort of creepy way. She looked up at me and smiled, and that was sort of creepy, too.

"Play with me?" she said, which is exactly what creepy little ghost girls say in movies before they drag you down to Hell. But I knew Esme didn't mean anything by it, and I was happy to oblige, folding myself into a cross-legged seat in front of her.

"It's nice to see you again," I said.

Esme shrugged and kept playing. When she asked you to play with her, this is what she meant: you sat and watched and were preferably quiet and didn't contribute much, while she moved her dolls around. She really just wanted a companion, someone to sit with her. She was more distinct than all of the ghosts I ran into in Manhattan, but I still knew it wasn't *really* Esme. This wasn't how she was when she was alive, this wasn't the full, complete Esme, but a pale copy of her, an imprint left on the earth. A ghost.

But Henry . . .

Henry was different.

Henry had always been different.

In the right light, in the right moment, from the right angle . . .

It was impossible to tell him apart from a real boy.

And that was why Evelyn had fallen in love with him. How could you *not* fall in love with a sweet, kind, handsome undead boy who lived in your bedroom and knocked at your closet door when he wanted to come out and court you? How could you not love Henry? We all loved Henry. But Evelyn had just taken it too far.

"She can't stay in that house forever," I said aloud now, to Esme, who actually cocked her head a little, like she was interested in the drama. "He'll ruin her life. He'll *stop* her life. I can't let that happen, right?"

"Who are you talking about?" Esme asked, pausing her game, looking up at me properly now.

"Evelyn."

"I like Evelyn," Esme said. "Our names start with the same letter."

"She's just . . . I'm worried she's making a terrible mistake."

"What kind of mistake?"

"Throwing her life away. For a . . ." I trailed off, not wanting to hurt Esme's feelings.

She let her dolls drop to the floor, then looked around her, as if seeing the living room properly for the first time. When she looked back at me, her eyes were bright. "I could see them, too, you know. Back when I wasn't dead."

A cold prickled down the center of my spine. "You mean you could see . . ."

"So it's not just you," she continued. "If you were thinking it was just you."

"You could see . . . *ghosts*?"

She nodded and picked up her dolls again. "You think you're the only one, but you're not."

"Did your sisters know?"

"No. It was just for me." Esme bopped her dolls up and down gently on the carpet in front of her.

"What do I do?" I asked her. Seeking advice from a six-year-old ghost might have been a low point for me, but I did my best to put that thought out of my head.

"What do you *want* to do?" Esme asked. She was barely paying attention now, fully invested in whatever tableau her dolls were currently involved in.

"I want to help her," I said.

"You should help her," Esme said with authority. "My sisters and I always help each other."

"I should help her," I repeated.

"Definitely."

To help her, I'd have to make her stop. Stop knocking. Stop loving him. Stop all of this.

But how could I make Evelyn do anything?

I sat and watched Esme for a few more minutes, then got up and got a glass of water. I drank it all at the kitchen sink, suddenly so, so thirsty. I filled it up again and drank a second glass.

My throat felt tight; my head ached. I couldn't stop thinking about Henry. I couldn't stop thinking about Evelyn.

I couldn't stop thinking about what Esme had said. *You should help her.*

In my pocket, I felt my phone buzz. I hadn't even realized I'd brought it down with me. I pulled it out and looked at the screen—finally, finally, a text from Evelyn:

I'm not mad at all. See you soon.

I didn't text her back.

I didn't know what I would have said.

I stared at her text until the screen went black.

We drove back to New York on Sunday morning, after a tearful goodbye with Aunt Bea and a lot of croissants for the road. Mom and I got to the car first (Bernie's tearful goodbye was lasting a little longer), so I slid into the front seat.

"You're a good sister," Mom said once our doors were closed.

"I didn't really do anything."

"That's not true at all." She reached over and squeezed my hand. "Status report?"

"Evelyn isn't really speaking to me. Clara is Clara."

"And you?"

"Oh. I'm fine," I said. "I'm always fine."

We got back to New York around five, taking our time, stopping for lunch in Saratoga Springs, a little town Upstate. It was already getting dark when we pulled into the parking garage and walked the block to home, and we were all quiet, for, I thought, entirely different reasons.

Our brownstone was dark and empty when we let ourselves in the front door. Bernadette went to take a shower, Mom went into the kitchen, and I went to the fourth floor and barged right into Evelyn's bedroom. She wasn't there. Nobody else was home, just the three of us, fresh from Vermont. But Henry was there. I could smell the faint fragrance of jasmine, and something darker on the air. And that was when I realized I hadn't really been looking for my sister at all. I'd been looking for Henry.

And that was when I realized I felt *angry,* really, really angry—an emotion I didn't usually feel and was very uncomfortable with.

Usually I felt sad or lost or vacant or strange. Anger was new. Anger was hot, crawling up the back of my neck, making my fingertips numb. It had been building since we left Vermont without me even realizing it. It had grown and grown and grown and now it was right on the surface. I could feel my skin rippling, creeping, crawling.

You should help her, Esme had said.

I couldn't make Evelyn stop loving Henry.

But maybe I could do something else . . .

"Why do you look so weird?" Henry said, there suddenly, sitting on Evelyn's bed.

"Aren't you supposed to knock," I said, not really a question so much as an accusation, a first blow.

He had a small (sad?) smile on his face. He looked like he had been waiting for something and the something had finally arrived. He looked almost relieved, maybe, like he could finally stop thinking about whatever it was he had been waiting for. I both did and didn't know what he had been waiting for. I both did and didn't know that somehow, he had been waiting for me, for this moment, for what I was about to do, for the inevitable conclusion I would come to, for this conclusion, here, now.

"How can I help you, Winnie?" he asked.

It was just a tad rude, the way he said it, but to be fair, I had started it.

"Where is she?" I said, and this, too, came out like a sort of accusation.

"She went out somewhere with Clara," he replied.

"And you're in love with her?"

He softened—visibly softened—and nodded. In a small voice, he said, "Yes."

"But that's ridiculous, Henry," I said. "You're dead."

I hadn't meant it to come out so mean, but maybe it was impossible to remind someone they were dead without it sounding very, very harsh, without it sounding almost a little braggy, like *I know you are but what am I.*

"Just say what you want to say, Winnie," Henry said, and he relaxed his stance a little, and I realized that before he had been tense, bracing, and now he was defeated, slumped.

"You can't be with her. You can't do this to her. You have to stop."

"I have to stop," he repeated.

"Stop," I confirmed. "Stop showing up, stop answering when she knocks, stop appearing, just STOP."

The last word came out as a shout. I could still hear the shower going, so I knew Bernadette hadn't heard me, and hopefully Mom was still downstairs or would assume I was yelling for Bernie.

"Good for you," Henry said, and he shifted again, back to tense, back to bracing. "You've finally found some gumption. Only took you sixteen years."

"Stop talking like it's the 1800s. Nobody says *gumption* anymore."

"I'm not going anywhere."

"You are," I argued. "You have to."

"I'm not leaving her. I would *never* leave her. That would kill her, Winnie! That would break her heart!"

"It will kill her if you *stay*!" I said, shouting again. "Don't you see that? Don't you see that if you don't leave, Evelyn won't leave? She won't *ever leave*. You've already been stuck in this house for far too long, do you really want Evelyn to be stuck here with you? Do you really want to watch her get older and older, do you really want to watch us all leave her, do you really want to watch her die *alone*?"

"She wouldn't be alone," Henry said, but his voice sounded uncertain now, his resolve was fading. "She'd be with me . . ."

"What a great comfort that will be. A half-here eternally seventeen-year-old boy who is so selfish, so self-centered, so *fucking greedy,* that he can't do what's right for the girl he *supposedly* loves."

"I do love her . . . Of course I love her."

"Then you have to leave, Henry. You know it's the right thing to do."

"I don't . . . I can't . . ."

His eyes were wet, like, if he could, he might start to cry—shiny, iridescent, sparkling tears. Ghost tears. I took a step closer to him, felt the temperature shift just the slightest amount, just a few degrees colder.

This was the moment. I could feel it. I could go through with it. I could convince Henry to leave. I was so close already. All it would take was just one final, crushing blow. The words were ready, on the tip of my tongue; my mouth *burned* with them. They held a power I didn't understand. It flowed through my body, a gentle pulse, my skin *thrummed*. I knew once I said them, I could never take them back.

I couldn't make Evelyn stop.

But I could make *him* stop.

I could make *this* stop.

"None of us want you here anymore," I said, not shouting now but almost whispering, my voice cold and horrible and not mine at all. "Can't you see that? We don't want you here. *GO AWAY, Henry.*"

He didn't say anything.

We looked at each other and I felt—

It was stupid, maybe. Because he hadn't had one in so long.

But I swear I could feel his heart stopping. Or breaking. Or shattering into a thousand pieces. I just swore I felt *something.*

And there was this look on his face, a look of confusion and pain and . . .

He cocked his head like he was listening to something I couldn't hear.

He said, in the quietest voice possible, "Oh."

And then he disappeared.

IV

Just as Persephone had the power to usher in the spring, to breathe new life into roots still and dormant, so might her descendants have powers of their own. The power to paint, perhaps. The power to make beautiful music. The power to see ghosts. The power to command them, the power to banish them . . .

That night I didn't sleep. I lay in my bed for endless hours, hearing phantom knocks above me; when I closed my eyes I saw Evelyn banging on the closet door, her knuckles split open, blood running down her arms, dripping onto her socks, the carpet. Evelyn always wore wool socks. Her feet were always cold. What had I done. What had I done. What had I done to her.

I dragged myself into the shower at five in the morning, leaving the water on cold, feeling absolutely nothing even as goose bumps rose up on my arms, covering every inch of my skin, making me itchy.

What had I done. What had I *done*.

What had I done to Henry.

I had meant to get him to leave, to send him away, but something had happened that I hadn't anticipated; my words weren't just words, they were a *command,* something Henry wouldn't have been able to disobey.

Did I have control over him? Over *them*? Over all of the ghosts?

Did I have power?

Because that's what it had felt like.

I had said those words—*go away*—and he had vanished. He had blinked out of existence.

I had banished him.

Had I banished him?

I was in the kitchen by five forty-five, my hair wet and dripping, my lips numb, why were my lips numb?

Dad was already there, making a pot of coffee in his flannel pajamas and an old ratty T-shirt he'd managed to save, so far, from my sisters. He raised an eyebrow when he saw me.

"Crack of dawn, there, daughter," he said.

"I couldn't sleep."

"Everything okay?"

"Nothing," I said. "Literally not a single thing."

"Can I offer you the first cup of coffee? A deep and meaningful hug? A penny for your thoughts?"

"One and two, please," I said, walking into his arms. He smelled like coffee beans, and he kissed the top of my head. I wanted to disappear, in that moment. I wanted to disappear like Henry had. I wanted to wink out of existence altogether.

By the time Evelyn and I set out for school I was so tired I was hallucinating; I couldn't tell if there were real ghosts outside or imaginary ones, hordes of them, an army of the undead. I kept blinking, trying to clear my vision, as if my eyes were the problem and not my sleep exhaustion, my guilt, my *guilt*. Somehow through my blinking, somewhere halfway across the park, I realized Evelyn had stopped walking; when I turned around to look at her, she was bright red and glaring at me, her eyes narrowed and her nostrils flaring.

"What?" I said.

It was the wrong thing to say, I quickly realized.

"Oh, like you don't fucking know *what,*" she hissed, her mouth barely open, the words forcing their way through clenched teeth, bared lips.

Evelyn didn't swear easily, and it was more powerful when she did, it was sharper, it made my heart speed up. I would just pretend I didn't know what she was talking about, I would just lie, it was fine, it would be fine. "Is this about Vermont?"

"You know this is not about Vermont," she said.

"Can you give me a hint here, Evie? Because I honestly don't know what you're talking about."

"WHERE IS HE?" she screamed—and her scream was so sudden, so unexpected, that I actually jumped backward, landing awkwardly on my ankle, catching myself before I fell. A man walking his very large standard poodle shot us both a dirty look and quickened his pace.

I couldn't do this, I was terrible at lying, I was drowning in my guilt, but then I remembered Henry, his face rising in my memory unbidden, the way he looked when he told me I had found some *gumption,* and the guilt was replaced by anger, and resolve (I had done the right thing *I had done the right thing*), and I swallowed and steeled myself against Evelyn.

"I have no clue what you're talking about, but can you stop screaming, please?"

She closed her eyes. Her hands were balled into fists so tight I could see her knuckles turning white.

"I swear to *god,* if you did something . . ."

"If I did something? If I did *what*? You're not making *any sense* and I'm going to be late *a-fucking-gain*!"

"You didn't care so much about missing school when you went to Vermont WITHOUT ME!"

"SO THIS *IS* ABOUT VERMONT?"

"NO IT'S NOT ABOUT VERMONT, I DON'T CARE ABOUT VERMONT."

Evelyn's face was so red I wouldn't have been surprised if she burst into flames.

But she didn't burst into flames.

She burst into tears.

And she collapsed on the ground, her legs buckling, her body plummeting like a stone.

I ran to her, kneeling in front of her, cradling her face in my hands.

"Evelyn, Evie, Evie, what's wrong? What's happening? Please tell me what's going on."

I felt like a monster.

I *was* a monster.

If she knew . . .

Never in a million, billion years would she have forgiven me.

"He's gone," she said. She was rocking back and forth, her whole body quivering. "He's gone. He won't answer me. He won't come. He won't appear."

"Henry?" I asked, lying.

"Is it Henry?" I asked, lying.

"Henry won't come?" I asked, lying.

"Last night," she said, still sobbing, still rocking. "This morning. I knocked, and knocked, but he wasn't there . . . I didn't even . . . The jasmine . . . I didn't even smell it. He's not there. I don't know where he is."

"When was the last time you saw him?" I asked, lying.

"Yesterday morning," she said.

"And how often do you usually see him?" I asked, lying.

"Every day," she said, and she looked up then, directly into my eyes, an eye contact that made my retinas burn. "I see him *every day*."

"Okay, I hear you," I said. "I hear you, Evie. But you did see him yesterday. You just said you did. So let's just see what happens tonight, okay? Let's just see what happens tonight."

She buried her face in her hands. She rocked forward far enough that she was leaning into me, throwing her whole weight against me. I hardly heard her muffled retort.

"He has to come," she said. "He has to come."

"He will," I said, lying. "He will."

But he didn't.

He didn't come, no matter that Evelyn knocked on the closet door so frequently and so desperately that week that her knuckles really did turn bloody and fresh scabs were constantly breaking open, sending tiny rivulets of blood down her fingers, just like in my vision.

She didn't yell after that morning in the park.

She got very quiet.

Each night I went up to her bedroom and found her lying on her bed, bandages wrapped around her hands, her lips so chapped they were peeling.

"Maybe there's some *ghost* thing we don't know about," I said. Her stormy, ocean-blue eyes darted over to me, but she didn't say anything. I tried to keep my voice light. "Like a convention or something."

"He's never gone away for this long. He's never not answered me when I knocked," she said, and her voice itself was a ghost, a faint picture of the real thing.

I took her hand in mine and gently unwrapped the bandages. Her poor knuckles took my breath away. I was a terrible sister.

"Let me get you a fresh wrapping," I said. I kissed her forehead. She gave no indication that she'd either heard me or felt the kiss.

In the bathroom, I found Clara sitting on the edge of the tub and Bernadette sitting on the closed lid of the toilet. Over the past week, Bernadette had wiggled her way back into her old summer job at the florist down the street. She wore a green canvas apron now. She smelled like roses. She'd told Clara and Evelyn about her bipolar diagnosis one night after dinner that week. Evelyn had hugged her and said all the right things. Clara had been visibly frightened and had since treated Bernadette with a little more care than was probably needed. ("She'll get over it," Bernadette had told me when I'd asked if it bothered her. "We forget how young she is.")

I shut the bathroom door.

"What did you do to Henry?" Bernadette asked, her voice quiet so it wouldn't carry to Evelyn's bedroom.

"What do you mean?" I asked, my own voice shaky and strange.

"Winnie, knock it off," Bernie insisted, plowing right through my denial. "We need to know what's going on."

"We had a fight," I said.

"Okay, and?"

"And I asked him to . . . Or, I insisted he . . ." I took a breath. I closed my eyes, I opened them. My sisters were staring at me, waiting. "I sent him away. I made him go away."

"Made him?" Bernie repeated.

"I think . . . yes. I made him. I think I didn't know it, but I can . . . Maybe I can control them. The ghosts. Henry. I made him go away."

"You *banished* him?" Clara hissed. "Oh, Evelyn's going to kill you."

"Well obviously I'm not planning on her finding out," I replied.

"I don't know," Clara said, shaking her head. "It's hard to lie to her for too long. She really wears you down."

"Where did you send him, exactly?" Bernadette said, her voice calm and even, planning.

"Oh. I don't really know . . ."

"And for how long?"

"I don't really know that, either," I admitted. "It all just happened really quickly. I didn't really *mean* to . . . We had a fight, and I told him . . . I told him . . ."

I sat down on the cool tile floor, my legs suddenly shaky.

"What did you tell him?" Bernie pressed.

I covered my hands with my face and said through my closed fingers, "I told him we didn't want him here anymore."

"Oh, no," Clara said. "Winnie, that's *awful.*"

"When was this? I wish you had talked to us first."

"The night we got back from Vermont." I lifted my head. "I think I just . . . I don't know. It all just came out of me. And he can't do this to her, Bernadette. He can't *do* this to her. And I was talking to Aunt Esme and . . . I don't know. I thought I was doing the right thing . . ."

"You took advice from our six-year-old dead aunt?" Bernie said.

"Well, you'll just call him back," Clara said. "And you'll apologize, and it will all be fine. She loves him, Winnie, you can't just send him away."

"No," Bernadette said firmly. "No, you can't call him back. And you can't tell Evelyn. She can't know."

"What?" Clara asked, at the same time I said, *"What?"*

"She can't know, and you can't call him back, because you're right," Bernie continued. "It was the right thing to do."

"It was?" I said, at the same time Clara said, "It *was*?"

"What does she think is going to happen? Henry's a *ghost.* It's not like they can get married. It's not like they can have a long, happy life together. It's not like they can have kids."

"Evelyn doesn't want kids," Clara said.

"You get my drift," Bernadette said. "It's a road to nowhere."

"But it's *Henry,*" Clara whispered.

"I know, Cece, and we all love Henry, but what's done is done," Bernadette said, getting that I'm-the-eldest-child-and-my-word-is-final tone of voice that I was sure all eldest children were born instinctually knowing.

"So what do we do now?" Clara asked.

"We distract her," Bernadette said.

"We distract her?" I said.

"That's how you get over a broken heart," Bernie insisted. "Distractions and time."

"So what do we do?" Clara asked.

"I have tomorrow off. Let's do something fun. A bike ride or those boats in the park."

"You want to go for a boat ride in Central Park?" Clara asked.

"Yes," Bernie replied decisively. "That's exactly what I want to do."

"That's *far,*" Clara said.

"It's a twenty-minute walk," Bernadette replied.

"I don't like water," Clara persisted.

"We'll get you a life jacket," Bernie said.

We had lived in Manhattan for our entire lives and we had never once rented a boat from Loeb Boathouse.

"Yeah," I said. "Let's do it."

Clara rolled her eyes. Bernadette looked pleased.

"First thing in the morning," I continued. "Bernie, get Evelyn up. Clara, pack snacks. I'll get the cooler from the basement and steal a bottle of wine. It will be fun."

"I'm very irritated with both of you right now," Clara said.

"You'll get over it," Bernie said.

"But will *Evelyn* get over it?" Clara retorted.

A long silence. And then, my voice barely a whisper. "Did I fuck everything up? Did I do the worst thing in the world? Am I a horrible person?"

"Yes," Bernadette said. "Yes. *No.* We are going to fix this, Winnie. Everything is going to be fine."

But I don't think any of us—not even Bernadette herself—believed that.

The next morning was mild and sunny, with a light breeze and a scattering of white puffy clouds across the sky. Clara and I packed cheese and crackers and apples and pears into a backpack cooler, and I slipped a bottle of white wine into it and put it by the front door.

"Why are the three of you so insistent on going for a boat ride?" Evie said. She looked like shit. Dark circles under her eyes, unwashed hair, puffy face.

"It's a beautiful day," I said.

"We get plenty of beautiful days," Evie countered. "And never before have we spent one *boating*."

"She's crabby," Bernadette announced loudly, as if Clara and I had maybe not picked up on that.

"I brought sunscreen," Clara replied, as if maybe the sunscreen would do something for our sister's mood.

"Are we walking?" Evelyn asked.

"I thought we would!" I said. "I mean, it *is*—"

"A beautiful day," Evelyn interrupted. "Yes. We've covered that."

Outside, Evelyn walked with Bernadette and I walked with Clara. I had the backpack cooler on and after five minutes, my shoulders were already aching, so I clipped the chest strap on and hefted it higher on my back.

It really *was* a beautiful day, and we cut into the park before turning south, away from the reservoir, taking a path that would lead us past Belvedere Castle, past the Ramble, which, if I had to pick, was probably my favorite part of Central Park. Thirty-eight acres of woodlands in the middle of the city. Our father claimed he had once gotten lost in the Ramble for three hours and though that may sound like an exaggeration, it becomes very believable if you try to navigate it without the aid of a cell phone.

Southeast of the Ramble was the Loeb Boathouse, and it was early enough that the line of people waiting to rent the four-person rowboats was small. We let Bernadette wait in the line and pay as the three of us hung back.

"Maybe after, we can go visit Alice," Clara said. The *Alice in Wonderland* sculpture was east of here, and Clara had always been fond of it.

"Sure," I said. "And the model boats, maybe."

"Bethesda Fountain is close," Evie added.

"Oh, we can reenact some movies!" Clara said, because Bethesda Fountain was featured in probably every movie that had ever been set in the city.

Evie smiled then, an actual smile, something I hadn't seen for at least a week. She looped her arm through mine and laid her head on my shoulder and I smelled her hair, which needed to be washed, but still smelled so undeniably like her, like lukewarm coffee and old books and vintage wool, that my stomach gave a little flip. Everything was going to be all right. Evelyn was going to be fine.

A few minutes later and we had donned our life jackets and set off into the great blue waters of the Lake, the backpack by our feet, Bernie and me manning the oars, paddling west. It felt like sailing into a painting. The trees surrounding the lake were on fire with fall colors—oranges, reds, yellows—and the calm surface of the water reflected everything perfectly.

"Okay," Evelyn said after a minute. "This *is* pretty beautiful."

It broke the tension that had been building between the four of us. Clara laughed and dipped her hand into the water, Bernadette rested her oar against the side of the boat and took an enormous breath of air, and I unzipped the backpack and triumphantly pulled out the bottle of wine.

"What time is it?" Evie said.

"I know, I know," I said. "But it's *white* wine. You know what Grandma says about white wine."

"'It's never too early for a nice glass of chardonnay,'" Bernadette recited, in a very accurate impersonation of our father's mother.

I poured three glasses and handed one to Bernie and Evie, then glanced at Clara and said, at her exaggerated frown, "Absolutely not."

"None of you are twenty-one," she whined.

"Right, but you're fourteen," Bernadette countered. "You can have one sip of mine."

"One sip?"

"One sip or nothing."

Clara, managing to still scowl during the whole process, took a sip of wine from Bernadette's glass and then handed it back.

Bernadette, Evelyn, and I clinked glasses and took a sip. I didn't really get the fuss about wine, but this didn't taste so bad, and it felt really fun, drinking with my sisters in a rowboat in the middle of Central Park.

Clara stopped scowling after another minute or so and pulled a pear out of the backpack. She took a bite, sighed happily, and leaned back against the side of the boat.

"How lucky are we, kids?" Bernadette said.

Clara laughed so hard she snorted, which made me laugh, and made Evelyn smile again, a wide, happy smile that caused my heart to balloon in size. She reached forward and dug around in the backpack, pulling out a wrapped wedge of Brie and a box of crackers. She kept smiling as she made each of us a cracker with a neat slice of Brie on it, passing them around before finally making one for herself.

"I can't believe we've never done this before," I said.

"I can," Bernadette said. "We don't really do touristy things."

"Sometimes we do," Clara corrected. "We've gone to Ellis Island."

"That was a school trip," Bernie said. "And you weren't with us."

"Oh, right."

"This should be a new leaf for us," I said. "Doing the things we've never done before. One new thing a week."

"We could go ice skating at Rockefeller Center!" Clara exclaimed.

"I've always wanted to try Magnolia Bakery," Bernie added thoughtfully.

We all looked to Evelyn for her input. She had a funny expression on her face.

"What's going on here?" she asked.

"What do you mean?" Bernie responded, because she was the best liar out of the three of us.

"I *mean,*" Evelyn said, tightening her grip on her wineglass, "this who-can-out-happy-the-hardest thing that's happening."

"I'm just happy," Clara said. "Mostly. I mean, I'd like another sip of wine."

Evelyn handed Clara her wineglass without looking at her. She was alternating between Bernadette and me, swiveling her eyes back and forth like she was scared of letting either one of us out of her sight.

"We all live in the same house," Bernadette said. "We know something's going on with Henry. We know something's going on with *you* and Henry. We're trying to take your mind off it. It's not some big conspiracy, Evie. We're your *sisters*. And we care about you. We don't know *what* happened to Henry, but we love you, okay?"

Evelyn was blinking rapidly, in the way a person blinks when they're trying desperately not to cry. It made my heart ache to watch her, so I looked down at my hands, at the wineglass, at a piece of cracker that had fallen to the bottom of the boat.

"I don't know where he went," she said finally, her shoulders collapsing, her tiny frame folding in on itself. "He won't come back."

"It's going to be okay," Bernadette said, her voice decisive and strong. She handed me her wineglass and pulled Evelyn close to her. Evelyn collapsed into her lap and Bernadette wrapped her arms around her, holding her. "It's going to be okay," Bernadette said, but she was looking at me, and I got the impression that she was talking to me, too, staring directly into my eyes as I felt my bottom lip start to tremble. "It's going to be okay," she said again, for the third time, and it began to feel like an incantation, like a mantra, like a spell.

Next to me, Clara took a big gulp of Evelyn's wine and then silently poured the rest of it over the side of the boat. She wasn't looking at any of us; she was looking out of the boat, away into the city, north over the lake and back in the direction of our home. She was squinting her eyes so hard that her brow was wrinkled and I knew what she was thinking about because we were sisters and I always knew what all of us were thinking about.

"Do you know what it is?" I asked, as Bernadette continued to hold Evelyn and Clara continued to stare out at the city.

The painting.

Clara blinked a few times, then looked back at me. Her expression was thoughtful, patient. She nodded slightly and said, "Almost."

We tried again.

We went skating at Rockefeller Center, drank frozen hot chocolates at Serendipity, waited in line to get up to the top of the Empire State Building. We saw our city through the eyes of tourists; we ate lunch in Chinatown and Little Italy and got desperately lost in SoHo trying to find Balthazar, where we ate the most expensive omelets I had ever encountered in my life. We took tours of St. Patrick's Cathedral and Radio City Music Hall and the Apollo Theater.

And it seemed to be working.

October melted away into November and the days got colder and bitter and we went to Central Park the first time it snowed, standing in the middle of the Great Lawn (none of our favorite places, but nice for this purpose) and watching the grass turn white around us.

Aunt Bea came down for Thanksgiving, a holiday none of us really liked and didn't celebrate in the traditional way, instead always opting to visit a local Chinese restaurant so we didn't have to deal with the hassle of cooking and cleaning.

By then, Evelyn was mostly back to normal. It had been about a month since we'd last seen Henry and we'd kept every waking moment of her life busy with activities.

"She's stopped knocking," Bernadette said to me in the bathroom of the Chinese restaurant as she waited for me to finish washing my hands.

"She has?" I asked.

"Just this week," Bernadette said quietly.

I shut off the water and stared into the mirror.

"We did the right thing?" I asked.

"I wasn't sure," she replied after a few moments. "For a long time, I wasn't sure. But I think we might have."

Bernadette grabbed a paper towel from the dispenser and handed it to me. I dried my hands and we walked back to the table. Two servers were just arriving, carrying trays laden with food. I slipped back into my seat between Clara and Aunt Bea, who reached over and patted my leg, giving me a knowing smile I couldn't guess the meaning behind.

Dad was in the middle of a long story about the TV remote (I'd missed the beginning and although I briefly tried tuning in, I had absolutely no idea what the point was), so I focused on filling my plate with a little bit of everything. Across the table, Evelyn was doing the same, and at one point we knocked hands reaching for the same serving spoon. She looked up at me and smiled happily, and for some reason it made me want to cry.

I mean, I knew the reason.

Because I had betrayed her, and she didn't know, and even

though it all seemed to be working out, I knew, deep down in my bloody, red, betraying heart, that I shouldn't have done it. I should have found another way.

I shoveled a forkful of fried rice into my mouth. It tasted like torn-up cardboard on my tongue. I washed it down with water and tried not to look miserable.

"You're coming undone," Bernadette said to me that night. The three of us were crowded on my bed—Bernie, Clara, and me—and it was true, I *was* coming undone. As it turned out, I wasn't entirely good with guilt. It was eating me alive. It seemed like the happier Evelyn got, the more I fell apart. Like she was sucking the life force out of me.

"She's stealing my life force," I said, but even as I said it, I realized it didn't make any sense and it wasn't going to be something I was able to explain.

"She's doing better," Bernadette countered. "As shitty a decision as it was, it's actually working out."

Clara was quiet, distant, staring at a mark on my wall, her eyes unfocused and unseeing.

"I'm a terrible sister," I said.

There was a knock at the door and we all swiveled to look at it.

"Come in," Bernie said.

Aunt Bea poked her head in. "We're missing one," she said.

"Evelyn went to bed," Bernie replied.

"Smart girl. I'm exhausted. Clara, thank you again for letting me steal your room."

"Oh, it's no problem, Aunt Bea," Clara said. "Do you need anything?"

"Nothing at all." Aunt Bea smiled and looked at each of us in turn and I couldn't help but feel like she was looking *into* us, like somehow she knew our sins—*my* sins—and she was deciding for herself just what punishment would suffice. The beating heart in the floorboards. I could hear it even now, pounding away like a siren. "Dismal mood in here," she said after a moment.

"We all have our periods," Bernadette replied.

"No," she said thoughtfully. "That isn't it."

"I don't have *my* period," Clara said, oblivious, and I smacked her on the arm.

"All right, kiddos," Aunt Bea said. "Night, night."

She left the room, pulling the door closed behind her. It didn't quite latch. We all stared at it, and finally Bernadette got up and went and pushed it closed.

"I'm tired," Clara said. "Aunt Bea wants to leave early."

We were going to look at all the Christmas display windows on Fifth Avenue. It was sort of a tradition, but one upheld only because for some reason, Aunt Bea loved them. And she had a point, I guessed; in all their consumeristic opulence, there was true beauty and artistry to be found behind those blocks of shiny glass.

Bernadette said good night and left the room, and Clara made herself comfortable in my bed. It wasn't that bad sleeping with Clara; she was small and didn't take up a lot of space, plus she slept like an actual rock, hardly moving at all throughout the night.

"Do you mind if I read?" I asked. For once I was tired before her.

"Knock yourself out," she said, her voice muffled by the covers, which she'd pulled up over her face.

But I knew I wouldn't be able to read anyway, and when I opened to the bookmarked page, the lines swirled and blurred in front of me. I couldn't make out a single word. I rested the book on my chest and stared up at the ceiling instead, imagining it going clear, transparent, seeing Evelyn in her own bed, staring up at her own ceiling, perhaps, or at her closet door, even now waiting, waiting, waiting . . .

I put the book on the bedside table and got up.

It was too late and too cold to go for a walk, but I couldn't stay still anymore; I couldn't even think about going to sleep.

Ever since Henry had left, I'd had trouble sleeping.

Ever since I had made Henry leave.

When I thought about it too directly, when I remembered Henry's face in Evelyn's bedroom, when I remembered the words that came out of my mouth, the vitriol, the hate . . .

I thought I would die from the guilt.

I thought it would tear me into pieces.

I let myself out of the bedroom and went downstairs. Everything was dark. Sometimes Mom stayed up later, hunched over the kitchen table, paying bills or doing a crossword or just watching her tea grow cold, but today it was only me. The wide windows at the back of the house were dark and creepy and haloed by cold; even double paned, they couldn't completely keep out the chill of a New York winter. I stood close to the glass, all the lights off inside so I could actually see to the backyard, the outline of the high wooden fence at the back of the property, the scraggly branches of the jasmine bushes, dormant now until spring, when they would grow back with reckless abandon, needing multiple rounds of trimming over the course of the year. Jasmine grew quickly, wildly, it was impossible to kill.

He smelled like jasmine. He always smelled like jasmine.

I put my hand on the glass. ("I swear to god I can never keep these things clean," Dad would say, had said a hundred times before, and Mom would reply, "Maybe swear to goddess next time and you'll have more luck," and wink at me if we caught each other's eyes.)

"I'm so sorry, Henry," I whispered.

Did I still think I had done the right thing?

She's doing better, Bernadette had said.

But at what cost?

At what cost was Evelyn doing better?

Where was Henry? Where had I sent him and was he okay and why did he always smell like jasmine and why did I miss that smell more than anything in the world? I felt the absence of that smell like a physical thing that had been ripped away from me. Like I had given up a kidney.

I took my hand from the window. Five perfect fingerprints.

The proof that I had been here, that I missed him, that I would hate myself for the rest of my life for the things that I had said to him.

The next morning was absolutely freezing, the first really, really cold day we'd had, the kind of cold that made your bones stiff before you even opened your eyes in the morning, the kind of cold that didn't pay attention to how many layers you were wearing or how snuggly you wrapped your scarf around your neck. I wore jeans, wool socks, a long-sleeved T-shirt underneath my sweatshirt, an ankle-length winter coat, a hat and scarf and gloves. By the time I stepped out our front door I looked more like a bundle of laundry than a human being, and the cold found the only exposed skin it could—around my eyes—and crawled immediately downward, leaving me feeling completely naked.

Bernadette linked her arm through mine and snuggled close to me as we walked to the subway. "Winter," she said dramatically, and kissed me quickly on the cheek. "It comes earlier every year, doesn't it?"

"I guess so," I said even as my wrists, inside my gloves, started to itch.

"Although I *have* figured out the only thing I miss about having long hair."

"What?"

"It's warmer."

We reached the subway entrance and as every New Yorker in the winter has experienced, I went from freezing to standing in a pile of my own sweat as we waited for the train to come.

We took the 2 to Columbus Circle and walked east along the southern edge of Central Park. Bernadette took my arm again and Evelyn and Clara walked together and Mom and Aunt Bea held hands and Dad looked like the odd one out, but happily oblivious to that fact as he stopped at a cart to buy a cup of black coffee.

Fifth Avenue was already swarming with tourists and shoppers—it *was* Black Friday, after all—but there was a certain order to the chaos, and a specific movement to the crowds of people itching to see the holiday windows. Bergdorf Goodman's always had the best displays, and this year did not disappoint. They had gone with a mythology theme, and each window told a different story, all exploding with color and detail and over-the-top theatrics—Circe dripping in gold, mid-spell; Hermes with gold-winged ankles; Persephone covered in flowers.

"Did you know," Aunt Bea said, suddenly next to me, wrapping her arm around my waist, "that we Farthing girls are descended from Persephone? That we live here and there, the children of the in-between . . ."

"How do you know if that's *true* though?" I asked.

"Oh, can't you feel it? Can't you just feel it? A warm certainty just here—"

She put her hand at the base of my breastplate, somehow finding it through all the layers.

"I don't feel certain about anything," I responded darkly.

"Oh, Winnie," she said. "You have to let it all in. You have to open up. You have to find it, know it, seek it."

"Are you calling me closed off?"

"Gosh, darling, *yes*. You're a locked hope chest. A closed book. A flower before it blooms. But you'll get there. I've no doubt of that."

We spent two hours on Fifth Avenue, peering into each window and getting jostled by strangers and losing feeling in our extremities. Clara's nose was so pink at one point that I cupped my hands around her face and huffed hot air at her.

"Sort of gross," she said. "Sort of nice."

We ate a late brunch at Sarabeth's, a super-fancy diner on

Fifty-Ninth Street that was a solid part of our window-looking tradition. As usual, Dad grumbled about the prices. As usual, the food was actually pretty good. As usual, Mom and Aunt Bea got a little tipsy on mimosas and giggled so loudly together that surrounding tables shot us dirty looks and mumbled under their breaths about *tourists*.

Evelyn sat next to me and stole french fries off my plate and we laughed about how much coffee Dad drank and Clara leaned back in her chair so far she toppled over backward and Bernadette laughed so much I thought she might actually have peed her pants a little.

Honestly, it was kind of the perfect day.

It would have been the perfect day.

And I didn't know why I said it.

I didn't know why I chose that moment.

But I leaned over to Evelyn and said, "I knew you'd be happy again."

I didn't even really think that was what I had meant to say, when I'd first leaned toward her. I really thought I'd say something about Dad, about Clara rubbing the back of her head dramatically, about Aunt Bea laughing so hard an enormous booger dripped out of her nose, about Mom's cheeks turning the brightest shade of pink.

But I didn't say any of those things.

I opened my mouth, and those six words came out—*I knew you'd be happy again.*

And Evelyn turned to me, her smile undisturbed and unfaltering, her eyes wide and clear, and said, "It *was* you, wasn't it?"

And I didn't respond.

I didn't have to.

Because I was a terrible liar, and I knew the truth was written all over my face.

Although I knew Evelyn was avoiding me, it was an incredibly subtle avoidance, a gentle evasion that absolutely no one else was able to detect.

"I don't know what you're talking about," Bernie said a few days later, when Aunt Bea had gone back to Vermont and we'd gone back to school and life had returned to its usual rhythms.

I didn't want to tell her what Evelyn had said to me at brunch that day. It felt like the biggest admission of guilt, the truest conviction of my sins.

So I dropped it.

Evelyn and I walked to school each morning. We exchanged idle chitchat. We talked about the dreams we'd had the night before, the assignments we were working on for school, the dead rat that someone had left on the principal's desk. Even I began to question my own mind—had I imagined it all? Was everything fine?

But a week passed in this way.

And then we woke up one morning.

A Saturday in early December.

And Evelyn was gone.

V

Persephone's footsteps were said to cause plants to bloom, trees to blossom, flowers to open wider. But they were also said to cause weak spots in the fabric of the universe, becoming their own tiny little portals to another world. Persephone loved her husband, and she loved the Underworld but she also loved our *world, and when she was there, she longed for* here, *and when she was here, she longed for* there. *You might say she was destined to never be completely satisfied; you might say she lived so firmly in the in-between as to have no real home. You might say that women who grew up in these footsteps lived in the in-between, too. So close to two worlds they might somehow find a way to travel between them . . .*

I found her empty bed, of course. It was ten o'clock in the morning and our parents had gone to the Berkshires for a four-day trip with friends; they'd left the night before. Bernadette and Clara and I had decided to go to Todd's for breakfast and I'd volunteered to wake Evelyn. So of course it was me who pushed open her bedroom door and found her bed, perfectly made, perfectly smooth, and her room, neat and clean, with not a piece of clothing or scrap of paper out of its proper place.

I didn't move for a long time.

I didn't move for so long that I heard Clara stomping up the stairs, grumbling, emerging on the fourth floor, and huffing impatiently behind me.

"Hel-*lo,*" she said.

I turned around stiffly. My joints felt unlubricated. I felt like a wooden board, unbendable and frozen.

"She's . . . not here," I said.

I almost said *She's gone,* but I stopped myself, because Clara was sometimes so young to me, even though there were only two years between us, it felt like the space between fourteen and sixteen was expansive and huge, a massive ocean I was even now still wading through. And in that moment, with her winter coat on and her hair a mess underneath her pale pink knitted hat and her eyes narrowed at me and annoyed, I felt this sudden need to protect her. To not cause her unnecessary worry and harm.

"What do you mean she's not here?" Clara asked, still annoyed.

"I think she told me she was staying over Danielle's house last night," I lied.

It was the first name that popped into my head. Truth be told, none of us Farthing sisters were the best at having or keeping friends (a side effect, perhaps, of having three ready-made ones), but Evelyn and Danielle had met in kindergarten and were close enough that it wouldn't be unheard of, if Evie spent the night there.

Of course no one ever spent the night *here.*

But that felt obvious. We had a ghost.

"Oh," Clara said. "Why didn't you just say so?"

"I forgot."

"Okay. Well, I'm hungry. Can we go now?"

"Yeah, of course. Hey, can you send Bernadette up here? I want to ask her if I can borrow something."

"I'm *hungry,*" Clara repeated, annoyed again. "Just take whatever it is you want to take."

"I'll be quick," I said. "It's important."

Clara rolled her eyes and stomped back down the stairs. I counted the stomps as they grew quieter and quieter, then I counted the seconds before Bernadette started walking upstairs, then I counted her footsteps, and by the time she reached the fourth-floor landing, my head was full of numbers and when she spoke, I didn't hear what she said, just a sort of *whomp whomp whomp,* like the sound the grown-ups made in *Peanuts.*

Bernadette's expression darkened, she frowned, she pushed me aside and stormed into Evelyn's room, then rounded on me again, put her hands on my shoulders. It felt nice, having her hands there. It made me confident that I was standing on the ground instead of floating into outer space.

"Where is she?" Bernadette asked.

"I don't know. She's gone."

"Fuck. Fuck. Did you call her?"

"My phone's downstairs."

Bernadette pulled her phone out of the pocket of her corduroys and tapped the screen. She held it to her ear and we both heard it immediately—the buzzing.

Our heads swiveled into the room, toward Evelyn's nightstand. I couldn't move yet, but Bernadette crossed over to it and pulled the drawer open and there, of course, was Evelyn's phone.

"Okay," Bernadette said. "Something isn't right."

"Something isn't right," I repeated dimly.

"We have to call him back."

"We have to call . . . What? Who? Henry?"

"Yes. Call him back, Winnie. It's time to call him back."

My body filled with an achy, throbbing panic.

I didn't want to call Henry back. I didn't want to see Henry ever again, not after the things I had said to him. Not after what I had done to him . . .

But I nodded stiffly. My body didn't really belong to me, it felt like it was my first day getting used to new controls, and it took a minute to figure out which lever made my legs work, and another minute to figure out how to get my arm to raise.

I knocked on the closet door.

"Henry? Henry, it's me . . . Can you come out? If you're there?"

I never wanted to see Henry again but also, I was desperate to see him. I was desperate to apologize, to beg him for his forgiveness. I didn't realize, until that moment, how much I'd missed him, this ghost-boy who was like a brother to us, this constant in our lives, this seventh member of the Farthing household. I held my breath while I waited for him to appear, and he kept not appearing, and I kept holding my breath, and—

"Make him, Winnie," Bernadette said, interrupting my thought spiral. "If you made him go away, you can make him come back again."

"Henry," I said, trying again. "Henry, come back, come *back* . . ."

But my words wouldn't have commanded anything, there was nothing behind them, I could barely catch my breath. Finally Bernadette nudged me out of the way and knocked herself, louder, and a bit more aggressively, and it was a good thing she did, because the sound somehow reminded me to breathe again, and truth be told, I had come a little close to passing out.

"Henry! Come *back,*" she demanded, and in the silence that followed I heard Clara's stomping footsteps on the stairs again as she pounded her way back to us.

She appeared seconds later, my youngest sister, still in her winter coat, still annoyed, her eyes narrowed into two little slits. "I'm *hungry,*" she barked. "What is your actual *problem*?"

Neither of us replied. Probably Bernadette was trying just as hard as I was to figure out what the fuck to say.

Clara looked like she was going to say something else, but she paused with her mouth half open, and she said, after a long moment, evenly and quietly, "Wait, were you knocking? Why were you knocking?"

Henry had been gone for a month. Five weeks? Time was blurring together; I could barely keep the days of the week straight. I didn't so much sleep as have a long, constant rotation of nightmares. ("Melinoë's really working overtime," Bernadette had said one night when we'd met, both sleepless, in the kitchen at two or three in the morning.)

I had to say something, to respond to Clara, who was currently looking at me with wide, scared eyes. It was my responsibility because wherever Evelyn was, it was my fault. I had driven her there.

"We don't know where Evelyn is," I said, struggling to make my voice calm and even. Clara looked at me for a moment, then looked at Bernadette, then unzipped her coat and shrugged it off her shoulders and let it fall to the floor. She pulled her knit hat off and her hair stuck out at odd angles, staticky and alive, and she let the hat, too, drop to the ground.

Then she said, in a small voice, "You said she was at Danielle's house."

"That was a lie. We don't know where she is."

"Well, just call her," Clara said, and although the change was subtle, I could detect the panic in her voice, the rising swell of it.

"She left her phone here," Bernadette said, holding it up as proof. "Cece, did she tell you *anything,* say *anything*?"

"I didn't talk to her last night," Clara said, biting her lip, her hand moving to the watch that had once belonged to our grandmother and had then belonged to Evelyn and that now looked out of place on Clara's small wrist.

"Where would she *go*?" I asked.

Henry obviously wasn't answering us, so I brushed past Bernadette and threw open the closet door to look inside. "All of her stuff is here. I don't think anything is missing. Her suitcase, her backpack . . . It doesn't look like she packed anything."

"We have no idea *when* she left," Bernadette said.

"The camera!" Clara exclaimed.

"What camera?"

"That doorbell camera thing Dad bought last year!" Clara had already pulled her phone out; she was tapping the screen furiously.

"You have the app?" I asked.

"I taught Dad how to use it," she said, still tapping. "I kept it on my phone. What time did they leave for the Berkshires?"

"It was around eight," Bernadette said. "After dinner. After rush hour."

“Okay, got them,” Clara said. “There are a few motion alerts during the night, let me check . . . Nothing . . . Enormous rat, gross . . . Nothing . . . Nothing . . . I don’t . . . I don’t understand.”

“What is it?” Bernadette asked.

“She doesn’t leave. She never leaves.”

“Back door?” I asked. “Is there a camera there, too?”

“Yeah, hold on.” Clara tapped the screen a few times, concentrating so hard I could practically feel her biting her own tongue, then shook her head. “Nothing. She doesn’t leave the house.”

“Evelyn?” Bernadette said suddenly, raising her voice. “Evie?”

She stepped out of Evelyn’s room and Clara and I followed right behind her. We went through the house from top to bottom, moving like a search party, fanning out on each floor, heading back upstairs again when we didn’t find her, ending up back in her bedroom, all of us breathing harder.

“Let me see that app,” Bernadette said, and Clara handed her phone over.

We were quiet as Bernie double-checked the cameras, first the front door, then the back door.

“Did she go out a fucking window?” Bernie mumbled, mostly to herself. “This doesn’t make any sense.”

“She’s not here,” Clara said slowly, puzzling it out. “But she didn’t leave . . .”

“Could the cameras have glitched?” I asked. “The cameras must have glitched. That’s the only solution.”

“I guess,” Clara said. “They’re pretty expensive cameras, though . . .”

“But she couldn’t have just disappeared,” I said.

"We looked everywhere," Bernadette reasoned. "Winnie is right; the cameras must have glitched."

"But then where did she *go*?" Clara asked. "Where *is* she?"

I sat down on the bed, holding the sides of my skull with my hands, holding myself together. Where would Evelyn go if she was betrayed by the very people who were supposed to protect her the hardest? Where would she go if she couldn't trust *us,* her sisters, anymore?

"Maybe she really did go to Danielle's?" I said finally. "Maybe? Just to . . . get away?"

"Aunt Bea's?" Bernadette said.

"But she didn't pack a bag," I asked. "If she was going to Vermont, she would have packed a bag."

"And she would have taken her phone," Bernadette agreed.

I covered my face with my hands. I wanted to dig a hole in the ground and crawl into it, bury myself alive in penance for the terrible thing I'd done to my sister. I had driven her away. I had driven Henry away and now I had driven my sister away, too.

Bernadette slapped my hands down. "Get it together," she hissed, and I saw how worried she looked, how nervous and scared, and I shook my head.

"It's all my fault," I said.

"It doesn't really matter whose fault it is," Clara said matter-of-factly. "What matters is that Evelyn is gone, we have no way to contact her, and Henry isn't answering us. So what do we do?"

"Maybe she left something," I said.

"Something?" Clara repeated. "Like a clue?"

"I don't know, like . . . Just *something*."

"No, that's a good idea," Bernadette said. "We should look for something. Anything."

It gave us something to do.

We searched Evelyn's room, top to bottom, then moved into the shared attic space, methodically overturning couch cushions, peering into bathroom cupboards, shining a phone flashlight into the crevices of Evelyn's piano, eschewing all logic to look in the most unlikely of hiding places.

And then we actually found something.

It was buried in the bathroom trash, which Clara had overturned on the tile floor and gone through meticulously, piece by disgusting piece.

"What does this mean?" Clara asked in a small voice, flattening out the crumpled piece of notebook paper on the floor, pressing the creases out as best she could.

There was one single line here, written in Evelyn's unmistakably neat, careful handwriting:

I know why you did it and I

The line was crossed out, the paper torn and balled up, discarded.

"Wherever she is, she might check her email," Bernadette said, and walked into her own room, emerging a moment later with her laptop, so covered in band stickers that not a speck of its metal case was still showing. We sat down on the couch, Bernie in the middle, Clara and I on either side.

The note was in Clara's pocket but it was burning a hole into my skin; I could feel it as clearly as if it were pressed against my leg.

Bernie opened a new email message and began typing feverishly. Clara and I were both grateful she didn't ask us for input. I

didn't think, at that moment, I would have been able to come up with anything remotely like a sentence.

We found the note you put in the trash can and we know you left sometime last night. We know you're upset with us and you have every right to be. We just want to know that you are safe. We won't tell Mom and Dad you're gone okay, just let us know you're safe and we'll give you all the time you need.

She didn't bother addressing it or signing it and she didn't ask for our approval before she hit *send*. A gentle *whoosh* flung the email into the void, and I pictured it bouncing off satellites, trying to find my sister in this cold and dismal city.

Bernadette closed her laptop and for a minute we just stared at it, stared at Bernadette's hands resting on it, her chipped black nail polish, the one signet ring she wore on her left pinky (it had been our grandfather's and it featured our worn family crest, the bust of a soldier in plate armor, head turned to the side).

"So what do we do now?" Clara asked, but what she meant was something like, *Would it be really terrible of us to still go out to breakfast because I'm genuinely very hungry.*

"Let's go," Bernadette said, standing up abruptly. All the worry that had been on her face before we'd sat down to write the email was gone, replaced with anger.

Going to Todd's was the last thing I felt like doing, but I followed my sisters downstairs and out the door. Out on the sidewalk, before I could stop myself, I turned around to glance up at Evelyn's bedroom window. For just one moment, my mind conjured up a shadow there, either a ghost boy or a living sister, but then the sun moved out from behind a cloud and there was nothing but an empty pane of glass.

We stuck together the entire day, the remaining Farthing sisters, as if letting one of us out of the others' sight was an invitation for another missing girl. After Todd's we came home and took showers and tried to pretend not to notice the obsessive way Bernadette was checking her phone, every five minutes taking it out of her pocket, refreshing her email once, twice, three times, pulling down with her thumb and letting the screen bounce back up, over and over and over. Around two o'clock the doorbell rang, and Clara almost fell down a flight of stairs trying to get to it, as if, had it been Evelyn, she might leave again if not immediately attended to, as if she might have rung the doorbell at all.

It was UPS.

"We have got to get out of this fucking house," Bernadette announced, and we agreed at once, unanimously, pulling on layers to combat the cold, heading outside with no clear idea of where we were going, ending up at the entrance of the American Museum of Natural History, wordlessly showing our membership cards and diving into the crowded exhibit halls (going to a major museum on a Saturday in Manhattan was not something I generally recommend, but if you've just misplaced a sister, it can be a welcome distraction).

We wandered into the Akeley Hall of African Mammals.

Carl Ethan Akeley, as my father had discovered from reading every single plaque available to him in the museum (multiple times), was known as the father of modern taxidermy, which meant he was not afraid of slaughtering animals to make a cute little diorama (he refused to call what he did *murder* or even *killing* and instead referred to it only as *collecting*) (he died of dysentery at the age of sixty-two so I guess he got his). And even though this was morbid and gross, it was also hard to imagine these animals as having once been alive. Staring into their unseeing glass eyeballs was a bit like disassociating, and that's exactly what each of us did, me blocking the entire display of okapis until a mother with a triple-wide stroller pointedly cleared her throat and glared at me until I moved.

"Sorry, um," I said, scooting to the left, "I just really love . . . okapis."

I found Clara in front of the greater koodoo display and we collected Bernadette by the ostriches.

"Do you think there are lesser koodoos?" Clara asked.

"There are," Bernadette said, pointing. "They're over there."

"What makes an animal greater than or lesser than?"

"I don't know," Bernadette replied. "I'm not a fucking zoologist."

We were all a bit tired and cranky by then and Bernadette was still moving with her phone permanently grasped in her hand, waiting for an email from Evelyn that I think we all knew wasn't coming.

"Let's get something to eat," I suggested (the newly appointed peacemaker in Evelyn's stead).

"The food here is gross," Clara said, but we course-corrected and headed downstairs to the food court, which was completely devoid of windows and felt a bit like eating in a dungeon. Bernadette got a slice of pizza, Clara got a veggie burger, and I stood in front of the grill for so long that Bernadette finally shoved a piece of pizza in my hands, along with a tepid bottle of lime seltzer. We found a table in a corner and sat down. The pizza tasted like cardboard. Clara picked pale, watery tomatoes off her burger. Bernadette ate with abandon. There was a fourth empty chair that was so metaphorical in nature that before I'd taken a bite of my meal, I'd had to get up and drag it to the next table, depositing it next to a small family that didn't even look up at me.

"Fucking hell," I said, upon my return.

"I don't have great service down here," Bernadette said, figure-eighting her phone through the air.

"The service is not the problem," Clara said.

If there were five stages of grief, there must be at least that many stages for losing one's sister, except I was bouncing around all out of order, swinging wildly from denial to anger to depression to bargaining (skipping acceptance altogether, of course, it would just never be my thing), and inventing some new ones for good measure: blaming-myself-horribly, disassociating, turning every girl vaguely Evelyn's age into a facsimile of her, doing double- and triple-takes until they shot me rude looks, turning back into themselves, becoming firmly not-Evelyn.

Why hadn't Henry answered?

I found myself wishing there was a ghost manual somewhere, a forum people could join where they could discuss the ghosts that lived in their own attics, where we could share tips and tricks and manifestation techniques and advice on what to do when your sister fell in love with a dead boy.

I tried to conjure up, if not Henry himself, then the last time I had seen him, five weeks ago when I'd banished him to who-knew-where. The way he had flickered in and out of existence, the way he had looked like he was about to cry. (On the forum I would have asked,—*Can ghosts cry?*) The way he had disappeared in front of me and then hadn't come back when I'd called. (On the forum:—*If I could make a ghost go away, surely there must be a way for me to make a ghost come back?*)

"Should we tell Mom and Dad?" Clara asked suddenly, halfway through her veggie burger, a bit of ketchup on her chin, and I remembered the way she had called our parents when Bernadette had appeared with the black eye. That felt like ages ago; that felt like years ago; that felt like another lifetime. At least she had asked this time, and Bernadette and I said, in unison, firmly, "No."

"She is being horrible," Bernadette said. "The fact that she didn't tell us where she was going, that she won't respond to my email, that she just left. Oh, fuck. I forgot to take my medication."

Bernie dug around in her bag for her prescription bottle, popped a pill in her mouth, and dry swallowed it.

I stared deep into Clara's soul. "You promise you won't call them, right?"

"I won't," Clara said sullenly.

"I'll smash your phone into a thousand pieces if you do," Bernie promised.

Clara bit her bottom lip and shrugged and Bernie winked at me. It felt almost normal, that moment. But of course it wasn't. It wasn't normal at all. Because Evelyn was gone, and even though I'd taken the fourth chair away, there was still a gaping space at the table where it had been. I hadn't fooled anybody.

I put the crumpled note from Evelyn on my bedside table.

I know why you did it and I

And you *what,* Evie? And you forgive me? And you hate me? And you're leaving home and never coming back? And you're brokenhearted and have renounced yourself as a Farthing sister?

And you *what*?

And you—

"I'm not going to be able to sleep," Bernadette said, interrupting my thoughts, bursting into my room without so much as a knock or a hello.

"Ditto," I said.

She had a journal with her, like she'd been upstairs, writing in it, and decided mid-sentence to come and find me.

"This is so fucked," I whispered.

"I'm so mad at her," Bernadette responded. "Usually I would find Henry and talk to him about it and he'd say something so infuriatingly level-headed."

"I can try." I cleared my throat. "'Bernadette, who are you *really* mad at here? Evelyn, or yourself?'"

She snorted. "That does sound like him."

"I'm mad at her, too," I admitted. "Although that's probably ridiculous, because I'm the one who—"

"No, thanks," Bernadette said. "We don't have to revisit all that sad-sack bullshit. Clara and I are going to watch *Practical Magic*."

"I think I might go for a walk."

"Bring pepper spray."

I did bring pepper spray, slipping it into my coat pocket even as I felt fairly confident that, should I actually attempt to use it, the only person I would be incapacitating was myself.

Outside, I exerted both physical and emotional effort not to look up at Evelyn's window, simply marching east down the street with my head down and my hands crammed in my pockets (there was about a 50 percent chance I would set off the pepper spray accidentally). I almost plowed into someone at the next intersection but thought it was safe to look up again, then, and as I crossed into the park I quickened my pace, because it was cold and dark and past nine o'clock and really I had no business going anywhere, but I needed to walk, I needed to *get out*.

I wasn't looking for my sister, not really, but I wasn't *not* looking for her, either, and I found myself studying every stranger I passed, looking for Evelyn's blue eyes, looking for Evelyn's slender nose, looking for Evelyn's face, a face I loved so much I didn't know what to do with myself.

I ended up at Bethesda Fountain. In the tunnel beyond it, someone was playing a violin (there was always someone playing a violin here—I mean, the acoustics, can you blame them?). It was eerily quiet other than the music. Of course it was New York, and it was a touristy spot, so there were plenty of people milling around, but they were all subdued, almost reverently hushed. I didn't know what piece the violinist was playing but they were very good. Evelyn would have known. Clara, too, maybe. Our father would have said, "Do you know the difference between a violin and a fiddle? Absolutely nothing! You just call it a different name depending on the music you're playing! How wild is that, girls?" Our mother would have tugged my arm and pulled me aside and said, "Status report?" and I wouldn't have had the faintest idea how to answer her. What would Henry have done? Gotten a faraway look on his face and remembered when he was alive, maybe. Bethesda Fountain was completed in 1873. That was eleven years after the reservoir. Had he ever seen this? Or was he dead by then, firmly stuck in our attic, forfeiting a life outside for a life firmly *in*.

But instead nobody said anything. Instead it was just me, and I sat down on the lip of the fountain and closed my eyes and let the music surround me, entering my body, traveling through my veins, replacing my blood with melody.

In Greek mythology, Orpheus played the lyre, a stringed instrument that predated the violin by thousands of years. He went all the way to the Underworld to bring back his beloved Eurydice, dead from the bite of a viper. Was that where Evelyn had gone? All the way to the Underworld to find her beloved Henry? *Our* beloved Henry?

But no. That was just silly.

Something nudged me, then, something almost real and very cold, and I opened my eyes to find a Farthing ghost sitting next to me.

She was as solid as they come, almost as real and *here* as Aunt Bea, and she wasn't looking at me, seemed almost not to even notice me, but she was sitting so close she was touching me (if ghosts could, you know, *touch*).

It was normal for them not to see me but to be drawn to me, something in our blood connecting us through years and slightly different planes of existences. I scootched a little, to give her some room, then watched the violinist until they stopped, sometime later, put their violin away, and began their journey home.

I stood and followed them out of the park, just until Central Park West, where they descended into the subway station and were presumably lost to me forever. I carried on until Columbus Avenue and turned north, starting toward home.

The ghost didn't follow me. They rarely did.

On Columbus Avenue, all the stores were closed or closing but there were restaurants and bars that were open and just like anywhere in the city, I wasn't alone. I walked a few blocks fingering the pepper spray in my pocket, imagining a complicated robbery scenario in which I fought off my attackers and left them reformed and apologetic, and then I crossed another street and found myself in front of a small store with a sign over the door that said DARK MAGIC.

It was one of those New York stores I'd probably walked by a thousand times (I was just a few blocks from home at that point) but had never really seen before. It was sort of corny looking, with lots of red velvet and black candles in the window, books on magic, lots and lots of crystals, and thick, heavy-looking journals Bernadette would have loved. From the looks of it, it was half actual magic store for practicing Wiccans and half tourist trap (a necessity: cast a wide net and try and make those exorbitant NYC rents). I'd almost moved on when I saw, in the back corner of the window, something I suddenly wanted.

I pushed into the store, slipping past a man and a woman browsing crystals (tourists) and a woman examining different Tarot decks (resident). Toward the back of the store I found them, a stack of slender cardboard boxes. I grabbed the one from the top and brought it straight to the counter, where the bored employee did her best to look mildly pleased to see me.

"This it?" she said.

"Yes, thanks," I said, pulling the pepper spray out of my pocket, putting it away hastily, pulling my wallet out of my other pocket.

"Need a bag?"

"No, thanks."

"You should be careful with this," she said then, her voice changing for dramatic effect, her eyes narrowing slightly as she took my credit card from between my outstretched fingers. "A lot of people think it's just a game, but . . ."

"To be fair, it literally says Hasbro Gaming on the side of it," I said, pointing.

"Commercialization of the spirit world, baby." She handed my card back to me.

"Do you really, like . . . believe in this stuff, though?" I asked. "Or are you just pretending? For the job?"

"I could have worked at Zara," she said. "They pay more. But here I am. And I think the better question is, do *you* believe in this stuff? You're the one buying it, after all."

"Do I believe in this stuff?" I repeated, sliding the Ouija board toward me, running my fingers over the photo, two hands posed jauntily over a cream plastic planchette, the tips of their fingers just barely grazing the vaguely heart-shaped piece. (On the forum I would have asked—*Can you commune with the dead? Do the dead want to be communed with? Are they peaceful and resting until we go ahead and ring their big undead telephone?*)

Do I believe in this stuff?

Well, I had grown up with a ghost in my attic. I had sat next to a ghost in Central Park just a few minutes ago. I had walked *through* ghosts on my way to get a seltzer water from the corner store (a horrible experience; it left you almost sticky with cold).

The answer might have been something like,—*Yes, whether I want to or not.*

"Or is it, you know, a gag gift?" she pressed, when half a minute had passed and I was still silent. She tore the receipt from the printer and handed me a pen. I signed my name and handed it back to her.

"Winnie," she said. "Cute."

"It's not a gag gift," I said finally. "I'm going to use it."

She nodded, her expression changing to almost . . . impressed? In that moment I found myself wanting her approval desperately, something I should probably speak to a therapist about.

"Cool," she said. "Just be careful, you know? The person we call isn't always the person who answers. Think of it like a big communal home. The phone rings, it's anyone's guess who's going to be on the other side."

"Okay," I said. "Thanks."

I picked up the box and tucked it under my arm.

I didn't want to leave the store, which was lowly lit and smelled like lavender candles and was quiet and cramped and cozy. But the employee was slipping quickly back into her state of gentle boredness and it *was* getting really late. My sisters would be worried. (My remaining sisters.) I probably had text messages from them. *Practical Magic* was long over. I hadn't checked my phone in a while.

"Okay, well. Bye," I said.

"Bye, little medium," she said, even though she was probably only a few years older than me and *little* was a stretch.

I left the shop, squeezing the Ouija board box to my side, pulling my phone out of my pocket and sending Bernadette and Clara a quick text, not bothering to read the twenty-eight they had sent me already.

If Henry wouldn't answer a knock on his closet door, we would simply try another way to reach him.

We spent Sunday wandering around the city.

It was a gray and bleak day and we welcomed it, and we welcomed the way our fingers grew numb with cold and our feet turned numb with walking and our brains turned numb from the repetitive movement of one foot in front of the other. We avoided the busiest streets, we zigzagged down alleys, we got back to the house around six and ate cereal for dinner, the three of us standing in the kitchen, I think simply forgetting to sit down or perhaps so used to being vertical.

It was already pitch dark outside by the time we washed the bowls out in the sink.

We set up the Ouija board on Evelyn's floor, pushing her bed against the wall, scooting her nightstand over, making room for the three of us to sit, all crowded around it. Clara lit cream taper candles. Bernadette closed the curtains and threw a square of black silk over Evelyn's lamp (where did Bernadette acquire a square of black silk? I simply didn't ask). The result was a room lit much like the magic shop itself. The shadows were alive and moving and I was thoroughly freaked out as I took my seat next to my sisters and stared at the board and planchette before me, made in China, probably, not connected to the afterlife or the underworld at all, probably, a waste of $39.99 (plus tax), but here we were, and I doubted Dark Magic had a return policy for slightly used occult products.

"Okay," Bernadette said, looking at me. "Take it away."

"Take it away?"

"This was your idea. Lead us."

"Lead us?"

Bernadette narrowed her eyes at me. "Come on. It's not rocket science. Ask a question."

"Ask a—"

"If you repeat what I just said again, I will be forced to summon up a demon and sacrifice your soul to Hell."

"I'm wondering if we shouldn't joke about things like that," Clara said gently. For the first time, I noticed there was a hardcover book in her lap. The title was visible on the front, written in embossed gold letters: *Mythology*.

"You brought a book to the séance?" Bernadette said.

"I thought it couldn't hurt, to do some light reading. If what Aunt Bea says is true . . . that the Farthing girls are . . . Well. You know . . . Persephone had a pretty strong connection to the Underworld . . . Maybe that's why . . ."

"Spit it out, Cece," Bernadette said, not unkindly.

"Maybe that's why we're able to see Henry in the first place," Clara finished, her words tumbling out before she could change her mind.

It was funny. Between us, we had three lifetimes of seeing a ghost in our attic and we had maybe never once considered the correlation Clara was now presenting.

"But then why can Winnie see *more*?" Bernadette asked after a moment.

"Against my will," I added weakly.

"I don't know," Clara said. "But she's the only one who can . . ."

"No," I said, suddenly remembering my conversation with Aunt Esme. "Aunt Esme could see them, too!"

"When did she tell you that?" Bernadette asked.

"In Vermont."

"And you kept it to yourself?"

"There's been a lot going on," I said, gesturing down at the Ouija board.

"Fair," Bernie allowed.

"So you can see them and Esme could see them . . ." Clara said, and we could practically hear her brain whirring over this new information.

"What's the correlation?" I asked.

"Esme was the youngest," Clara said.

"But I'm not the youngest," I said.

"The youngest of *three*. The third."

"Oh. And I'm the third."

"Could just be a coincidence," Bernadette said.

"Did Persephone have siblings?"

"Almost certainly," Clara said. "Each source says something different."

"So she could conceivably have been the third daughter," I mused.

"Conceivably," Clara allowed.

I took the book from her and thumbed through it. It was written by Edith Hamilton. It had beautiful and scary illustrations. I felt a little bit like I had fallen down a rabbit hole, like Alice, just trying to sulk in peace and ending up in another world altogether. It all felt more real to me in that moment than it ever had before. Persephone. Us. The children of the in-between.

We had always believed the stories, believed Aunt Bea without reservation, but now, when presented with what could potentially be *evidence* of the truth . . .

Well, it was a lot to consider.

We had believed the stories, when we were children, but we had also believed in the Easter Bunny.

I handed the book back to Clara. She set it carefully back on her lap.

"Okay, so I'll, um, just ask a question . . ."

"I hope *tonight,*" Bernadette mumbled.

"Sure, um, well. Put your hands on the planchette." We did. "And, then . . . Hello . . . spirits."

"Hello, spirits," Clara repeated dutifully, her eyes screwed shut.

"We're trying to reach Henry. He lives in our attic. This attic. Well, lived. And we're just trying to reach him. So . . . Henry? Are you there?"

Bernadette had closed her eyes by then, too, so I closed my eyes, and I tried to concentrate on keeping my thoughts pure and empty, but instead I kept remembering that scene in *Practical Magic* where the sisters stand on either side of the dead man, their hands over him much like ours were over the Ouija board now, tiny pins in their fingers as they prepared to pierce his eyeballs and complete the magic spell.

I cracked my eyes open. Nothing was happening with the planchette. The way the candles were flickering made my sisters look ghastly and strange. I felt scared, stupid, incredibly stupid. I closed my eyes again.

"Henry . . . can you hear us? Please let us know if you're there. Please, Henry. Are you there?"

I didn't think I imagined it, the slight tingling in my fingers, the slight *whoosh* of air through the room, the slight increase in light I could sense even behind my closed eyelids, like the candle flames had grown somehow stronger.

I kept my eyes closed. Whatever spell was working, I didn't want to disturb it. I waited for any sense of motion, any scraping noise of the planchette gliding against the board, any gasp from my sisters as their fingers were pushed by some unseen (undead?) force.

After a few moments of nothing else happening, I opened my eyes.

My sisters were sitting so motionless they looked almost like statues, their brows furrowed in concentration. Clara was biting her bottom lip; Bernadette's nose was crinkled.

And beyond them—

Beyond them . . .

My breath hitched in my chest, catching for a moment before dislodging.

There was a . . .

There was *someone.*

Not Henry.

Not the right size or shape . . .

This ghost was smaller, feminine. A Farthing woman, like all the other Farthing ghosts I'd seen in my life. But I'd never seen one inside the house before . . .

The person we call isn't always the person who answers.

I wrenched my hands back from the planchette and immediately the room grew dimmer; the candle flames, which had been too high a moment ago, shrunk back to a normal level. My hands stopped tingling. The ghost disappeared. My sisters opened their eyes.

"Did you feel that?" Clara asked.

"There was someone . . . There was someone *here,*" I said, out of breath, pointing a shaky finger at where the ghost had stood.

Bernadette and Clara both turned to look at the now-empty space.

"Henry?" Clara asked hopefully.

"Not Henry," I said.

"Persephone?" Bernadette asked, her tone somewhere between *hopeful* and *mocking*.

"No. I don't know. I don't *know*." I was getting lightheaded; I leaned over and put my head between my knees—there was something I was missing, there was something I wasn't getting. The ghost had looked so *familiar*, the size and shape, the *essence* of the ghost, it was as if I had seen it before. "I think it was a Farthing ghost," I said.

"Well, that makes sense," Bernadette said. "You always see Farthing ghosts."

"But never in the house. The only person who's ever died in this house is Henry. The next closest ghost is a few blocks away."

"And thank goodness for that," Bernie said. "One ghost per brownstone is enough, thank you very much."

"Do you see *that*?" Clara asked suddenly, and I noticed that she was the only one still looking at the board.

"Oh," Bernadette said, glancing down, and I followed her gaze and almost said *oh* myself but then found I couldn't say anything, I could only stare at the planchette, which had been, a few minutes ago, in the middle of the Ouija board and was now, somehow, though none of us had felt it move, firmly pointing to the word *NO*.

Please, Henry. Are you there?

NO

I searched for *mythologists* in New York City and found many incredibly sketchy websites and one potentially promising lead: the

Department of Classical and Oriental Studies at Hunter College. There was a professor of classical mythology listed there: Natalie Beard. I figured it couldn't hurt, so I sent her a quick *hey, how ya doing, do you know anything about contacting ghosts?* email, then set off on another nighttime walk.

This time I had a destination, and I headed to Trinity Churchyard, a twenty-minute subway journey I spent hovering somewhere above my body, thinking of the planchette, thinking of Henry, thinking of Evelyn, thinking of the ghost in the corner of the room. Had I called it with the Ouija board? Was it (hopefully) gone for good now?

Trinity Churchyard was attached to Trinity Church, which at one point held the title of tallest building in the United States but was now dwarfed by all the skyscrapers in the Financial District. The churchyard, a burial ground, was the final resting place of a handful of early Americans, including Elizabeth Schuyler Hamilton, Alexander Hamilton, Hercules Mulligan, and Richard Churcher, a child whose grave boasts the oldest carved gravestone in the city. ("Do you know the difference between a cemetery and a graveyard and a churchyard, kids?" my father would have said. I'll save you the trouble of googling: a graveyard is generally attached to a church, and a cemetery isn't. And a churchyard doesn't have to have any graves at all, but it often does.)

Of course both the church and the churchyard were closed for the day, but I pressed my face against the metal gates and stared inside.

There were no ghosts around, which was a bit unusual. I guess the Farthings never had a chance to be buried down here. We preferred unmarked graves.

I closed my eyes. The metal bars of the gates were freezing against my cheeks.

I couldn't stop thinking of the third daughter thing.

A whole lifetime of Aunt Bea's stories about the Farthing girls being descended from Persephone and now I had to confront the fact that it might actually be *true,* not just some story she had made up to keep us entertained as children.

I don't know how long I stood there with my eyes closed, but when I opened them, there was a face just a few feet away from my face, and I screamed and fell backward, hard, landing on my butt on the sidewalk.

"I wasn't grave robbing!" I shouted, immediately unsure why that was where my mind went.

"Pretty hard to grave rob from outside the graveyard, I would imagine," the priest said, for I guess that's what he was, as he had the collar thing and he wore all black, like me. "Are you all right?" he added, as I scrambled to get back to my feet.

The priest took a big set of keys from his pocket, on a big rusty metal key chain, and unlocked a door in the gate. Obviously I thought of *Fleabag* as he pulled the door open and motioned with his head for me to come in. He was about my parents' age and not unpleasant to look at, with a killer smile and really kind eyes.

"Thank you," I said, slipping through.

"*Hamilton* fan?" he guessed.

"Sorry?"

He started to quietly rap the first few bars from the musical, which is when I remembered that Hamilton's grave was just beyond the gates, and I'm sure attracted many musical theater-obsessed fans.

"Oh," I said. "No, nothing weird like that. I'm just trying to commune with a ghost."

What was . . . wrong with me? I thought maybe I had stayed out in the cold so long that my brain had partially frozen, leaving the place that formed coherent language sluggish and strange, causing me to spew absolute nonsense at this poor (hot) priest.

But to his credit, he kept smiling. "What's your plan, then?"

I sort of shrugged a little (not sure my shoulder movement was detectable underneath my enormous coat) and flapped my arms once, like a baby bird.

"I just lost someone close to me. Well. Two people, really. But one of them is dead. Actually, they've been dead a long time. But I really need to talk to them. I have a question for them. And I thought a cemetery, maybe—sorry, graveyard—I thought maybe this would be a place that's, I don't know . . . closer? To them? I don't know where he's actually buried, or else I would have gone there. But anyway. I came here. Does that make sense?"

"It makes perfect sense," the priest said.

"Really?"

"No. But you seem harmless. So have at it."

There was a bench nearby, and the priest gestured to it now, so I went and sat down. The stone was cold under my legs. I remembered all the superstitions around graveyards—hold your breath as you drove by one, be careful not to walk over any graves, never leave a new grave open overnight. We were squeamish about the dead, us humans. All these hang-ups and fears and mythologies around something that was inevitable. One thing all humans had in common: one day we'd all be dead.

Dressed in black sitting in the middle of a graveyard in the dead of winter, in the dead of night, thinking about death.

This was dramatic even by Farthing sister standards.

I was trying to center myself. I was thinking about the planchette again, how it had moved without us feeling anything, how it had pointed to NO and then flatly refused to answer any of our follow-up questions (*okay wait is this actually Henry though, if you're not Henry, do you KNOW Henry, who was that other ghost that just appeared for a minute, what is it like to be dead*) (this last one was from Clara, who sort of hijacked the session by the end of it and went on a long tangent I won't bother repeating here).

The priest had wandered away but was still in view, and every once in a while, he glanced back at me, making sure I wasn't vandalizing headstones or taking any unauthorized stone rubbings (legal in most states but assuredly not allowed here, where the repeated motion of the rubbing could damage the delicate old stone).

He was out of earshot but I whispered anyway, releasing my words into the frigid air, hoping they would freeze into icicles and cut into the earth, wriggling their way like snakes into the ground, ending up wherever Henry was.

"I think you're mad at me," I began. "And I get that, I really do. I said some very fucked-up things and I'm truly sorry. But now Evelyn is gone and everything is so much more fucked up. I just need to know I didn't ruin everything. I just need to know she's okay. I have . . . this feeling? I have this feeling you're together somewhere, and you can't keep being together without at least letting me know she's okay. It's not fair if you don't tell me if she's okay. Whatever I did, however wrong it was, you have to tell me if she's okay, Henry."

After a few minutes, the priest came back over and sat down on the bench next to me.

"Did it work?" he asked. "Have you gotten your answer?"

"No," I said miserably, feeling cold and embarrassed and sad.

"Might I offer some advice?"

"Sure."

"The people in our lives, the ones who have passed on, they're all around us. They're here and there and everywhere. But they don't often respond to demands for performance. They have more important things to do. A whole eternity of important things to do. Down here . . . we're a blip in time. A mere second in an endless expanse of hours. Whatever you said to this soul, it might not reach them for another thousand years. And by that time, you'll be with them again, able to ask them right to their face. Does that make sense?"

"It makes sense, but it's not super helpful for me *now,*" I said.

The priest chuckled. "Indeed not, I admit."

"Can I ask you something else?"

"Anything."

"Do you actually believe in an afterlife? In a Heaven or a Hell or a Purgatory or, like, a Dante's *Inferno* situation?"

"I do," he replied. "I'm not sure I would use any of that exact language to describe it, but I believe there is a place for all our souls, and I believe it is beautiful and will offer unending peace and comfort and love."

"Right. So obviously he won't answer me right away, if he's surrounded by all that."

"Maybe you already have your answer," the priest said. "Maybe it's just something you aren't ready to admit to yourself."

He was cute, that priest, but in that moment, he couldn't have been more wrong.

I didn't have the answer at all. I didn't have *any* answers. Not a single solitary one.

I stopped at Dark Magic again on my way home.

"What even are your hours?" I asked the girl behind the counter, who looked slightly less bored tonight.

She shrugged and picked at her cuticles. "I guess, like, whenever I want. How did your little séance go?"

"I don't know. I mean, it didn't work. Or maybe it did work. Something answered, maybe, or maybe one of my sisters was just fucking with me and is too afraid to admit it now and I potentially saw a ghost, but that's also not *that* unusual for me, so, it's ultimately hard to say."

"How many sisters do you have?"

"Three," I said.

"I'm an only child."

"How's that?"

"It's okay, until I want somebody to use the Ouija board with me. What do you mean it's not unusual for you to see ghosts?"

Never in my life had I been as forthcoming with people I had just met, but something about the priest and now this girl behind the counter made me either 1) trust them implicitly or 2) not give a shit about what they might think of me.

"I might be descended from gods," I said. "And I think something about that gives me the ability to see ghosts. Only ones I'm related to. Well—mostly. And only women. Well—mostly. There's one outlier."

"What gods?"

"Persephone."

"Well, that makes sense. She's the Queen of the Underworld. You'd have a direct connection with the dead, if you were her descendant. And you'd also have a direct connection to her daughter—"

"Melinoë," I interrupted. "I know."

"She's a cool god," she said. "Goddess of nightmares, goddess of ghosts . . ."

"And madness, unfortunately. Look, do you know any other ways? To, like . . ."

"Contact the dead?" she guessed. "Sure. You could try scrying."

"Scrying?"

"Nostradamus used a bowl of water. He predicted his own death, you know."

"He did?"

"Yup. He was big into the occult, too. So maybe he had tapped into something."

"A bowl of water."

"Might as well give it a try."

"Are there any risks?"

"If you pass out and hit your head and land face down in the bowl, you could drown," she said thoughtfully. "Or more likely, you could lose your way in the labyrinthine maze of the eternal abyss."

"When you say *more likely,* exactly *how* likely do you mean?"

"With your skill level, I'd say not very. Ironically, the more practice you have, the more dangerous it becomes."

"Do I need anything to do this?"

"We sell scrying bowls," she said. "But I'm sure you have something in your kitchen already that will work just fine."

"Okay. Um. Thanks."

"Good luck, little god of nightmares!"

I'm sure I don't have to say that scrying out of a vintage Pyrex gooseberry bowl did absolutely nothing except wet the ends of my hair, which I forgot to tie back before dipping my head over the water.

I dumped the water into the kitchen sink and dried the bowl with a dish towel, placing it carefully back in the cabinet before turning back around to the kitchen, which was dark and quiet and empty and—

Not empty.

It was not empty.

The Ouija board ghost was back, standing on the other side of the kitchen island, just next to the kitchen table, just next to the spot on the wall where the full glass of water had shattered after narrowly missing Clara's head.

The ghost was no more distinct than it had been last night, but still I felt that familiarity, that connection . . .

It *was* a Farthing ghost, it had to be, and without really thinking about it, I took a few steps and moved in front of the kitchen island, moved closer to the ghost, which seemed to turn its—her—head to watch me.

I was just a few feet away from it now, and when I paused, it extended its hand out to me, reaching for me . . .

It reached for me.

She reached for me . . .

"Evelyn?" I whispered.

And I swear, I swear, I swear—

She nodded her head *yes*.

The ghost—Evelyn?—disappeared right after it nodded and in the moments directly after, I felt weightless and untethered to reality.

It was my sister. The ghost was my sister. It *was* Evelyn; I knew that down in the very marrow of my bones, I *knew* my sister.

But if my sister was a ghost, did that mean my sister was . . .

Was Evelyn . . .

No.

No. If Evelyn was (I couldn't even say the word, I couldn't even *think* it)—

If something had happened to Evelyn, I would know. I would be able to feel it. I would *know,* in the same way I knew, when I walked in the door of our brownstone, if my sisters were home yet.

And I knew Evelyn wasn't *here* but I knew also, I *knew,* I knew, I knew that she wasn't dead.

Neither Clara nor I went to school on Monday. Bernadette called out sick from the flower shop. We went to a different diner for breakfast, taking a circuitous route to get there, so her boss wouldn't see her.

The professor of classical mythology emailed me back just as my pancakes arrived.

Her response was bemused, indulging, concerned firstly with my well-being (I don't know you, but you sound a little frazzled), and secondly with how she might, if she were so inclined, attempt to communicate with a ghost.

I read it aloud to my sisters:

Bang around the old places.

Visit a temple, if you can (there's a very handy one in the Met).

Scrounge around in some grave soil.

Climb into a coffin (carefully).

Hold an urn in your hands and close your eyes.

Have a séance. Meditate. Light a candle at midnight. Etc., etc.

"The Temple of Dendur," Clara said thoughtfully. "Fascinating."

I made the decision not to tell either of them about Evelyn.

I didn't want to fill them with the same worry, the same dread that I had gone to sleep with, that I had woken up with, that I carried around with me, that I felt settle and resettle in my body with every step I took.

Our parents were due back tomorrow and we would have to tell them that Evelyn had been missing for three days, since Friday night, and we had no idea where she was except I had seen her as a ghost in our house and I couldn't think about what that might mean.

It started snowing while we ate breakfast, a light fall of flakes that lasted throughout the entire morning, resulting in an inch-thick dusting of powder. Everything a pale, soft white. Everything made beautiful and new, sounds muffled, footprints on the sidewalk, air that smelled cold.

New York looks like a postcard, Evelyn would have said, if she were with me as I headed into the Met, because why not, because I might as well explore all my options.

I was quiet as I walked through the lobby, past the Tomb of Perneb, past Egypt under Roman Rule, past the Facsimile Gallery, past Arts under the Ptolemies, past the Ramesside Period. And then, finally, there it was, in all its serious impressiveness: the Temple of Dendur. There was water in front of it, a U-shaped pool that was meant to represent the Nile River. I heard Evelyn's voice in my head, *The ancient Egyptians knew a lot more about death than we do.*

At breakfast, Bernadette had said *But the Temple of Dendur was built for Isis and Osiris. It has nothing to do with death.*

And Clara had answered, *Everything the Egyptians did had to do with death. They were obsessed with it. There was a crypt attached to the temple. It was said to hold the bodies of two boys who drowned in the Nile—Pedesi and Pihor. They were the sons of a Nubian chieftain.*

And I had said, *How do you know that, you're so weird.*

And Clara had taken that as a compliment.

The Met was actually pretty empty, given that it was a Monday and still early. There were about twenty or thirty people wandering around or sitting on benches and staring at their phones or examining the graffiti the temple had become famous for. One of the better-known pieces of graffiti was carved in 1817, which proved that humans had basically been assholes forever, and a young kid with a can of spray paint was nothing new or original.

The temple was actually quite small, once you were inside it. The walls were covered in beautifully carved hieroglyphics. Two massive stone pillars framed the entrance, giving way to a square room. Past that room was a doorway into another chamber, with a single small statue on display in a glass case. Beyond the statue was a third room, but the statue's case blocked the doorway.

There were three people in that second room.

I waited until they were gone, until I was alone, then I closed my eyes.

"Henry," I whispered into the cool, echoing space. "Henry, are you *here*?"

Evelyn's voice again, haunting me:

They understood the changeability of death. The thin veil that separates our world from their world.

"If it's such a thin veil, you could stand to *answer me,* Henry," I said, and I heard a polite throat clearing behind me, some kind stranger letting me know I was no longer alone and I was perhaps scaring them a bit with all my apparent talking to no one.

I opened my eyes, smiled weakly, pointed to earbuds I wasn't actually wearing. "Phone call," I said, relieving the poor woman of her concern.

It hadn't felt right, anyway, being in the Temple of Dendur. Maybe whatever had made it sacred once had been ruined when it was carefully disassembled, shipped over to Manhattan, and pieced back together. No, I'd have to try something else.

I decided to go back to Trinity Churchyard, during the day this time, during actual visiting hours. I let myself in through the front doors just after a family of four, two dads and their bored-looking teenage kids, a boy and a girl, who might have been twins. One of the dads was reading excitedly from a brochure: "This is the third building erected on this site. The very first church built here was lost in the Great Fire of 1776. Man, I would have loved to see that. Huh, guys?" His kids grunted half-heartedly and his partner flashed him an apologetic smile and then they turned a corner and I turned a different corner and almost ran into someone in long, flowing black robes. The priest from last night.

"You again," he said pleasantly. In the daytime he looked a bit less like an ethereal dreamlike figure who'd just departed the page of a Brontë novel (but just a bit).

"Me again."

"I appreciate the newfound adherence to visiting hours, but shouldn't you be in school?"

"Oh, I'm thirty-eight," I said. "I just use very expensive moisturizer."

"Hmm."

"Have you seen the movie *National Treasure*? With Nic Cage?"

A smile quirked at the corner of the priest's mouth. "I have, actually."

"So you know when he comes to the church and he finds the Templar Treasure? I was going to see if I could go there. Down there. To the crypts. There are crypts, right? I know there's not like, a whole underground museum's worth of treasure caves, like in the movie, but there *are* crypts. Where the Bleecker family is buried, right?"

"We don't let people down there."

"Have *you* been down there?"

"I have."

"So you *can* get down there."

"One *can*," the priest replied, still smiling. "If one were allowed."

"And what would one have to do to be allowed?"

"Being a living descendant of the Bleecker family would help."

"Well, aside from being thirty-eight, I also *happen* to be a living descendant of the Bleecker family."

"Oh, really? How fascinating," the priest said. Then, after a moment, "Still trying to get your answer from the other side? Did my rousing speech do nothing for you?"

"I won't touch anything. And I won't be long. And I won't be a bother. I just thought . . . It's sort of *in* the ground, right? We don't have a basement. Maybe if I'm *in* the ground, he'll be able to hear me better."

"And what was your name again?

"Evelyn," I said automatically. "Evelyn Bleecker."

"Well, Evelyn. Right this way."

I followed the priest through a locked door, down a corridor, through another locked door, then down a skinny flight of stairs. The air temperature changed noticeably. We reached another corridor, this one with a low ceiling crowded with pipes, and at the end of that we stepped carefully through what I can best describe as a hole in the wall.

The priest paused halfway through the hole, laid a hand on the wall, and said, "This was built in 1846."

I half expected him to add a *how lucky are we, kids?* but he continued on his way.

We reached the vault a minute later. It didn't disappoint, in terms of vaults. Its walls were laid in brick, there were shelves for ashes and two dozen white, unlit candles, and the small room contained a silence rarely found in New York, one of those silences that almost had its own sound to it, a heavy, thrumming, vibrating silence that felt heavy on my shoulders.

"Wow," I said.

"Wait for it," the priest said, and he removed a matchbook from somewhere in his robes and diligently lit each of the candles, one by one, until the vault was filled with delicate, flickering light.

"Wow," I repeated.

"There are a few other vaults down here, but this is my favorite," he confided.

"It's beautiful."

"I'll give you a few minutes, then," he said. "If you promise not to touch anything or move too much or breathe more than absolutely necessary."

"I'll slow my heartbeat," I promised.

"I'm too kind, that's my problem," he said, shaking his head. "I absolutely *have* to start saying no. I'm going to pray on it."

He left the crypt then, and the silence grew until my ears started buzzing with it. I sat down on the gravel floor.

"Henry, what the *fuck,*" I whispered.

Bernadette, after breakfast, had loudly announced that she was going thrifting. Her anger had grown and grown and grown and then disintegrated, vanishing, leaving a kind of catatonia behind. She had journaled that morning as she ate her omelet, pressing the pen so hard into the paper that she had torn it. She had closed her eyes, sat unmoving for at least three minutes, then carefully shut the journal.

"Henry, I swear to god, to all the gods in the world, if you don't *answer me* I will . . . I will . . ."

I couldn't think of a reasonable threat, something I might actually do that Henry wouldn't want me to do. I thought I might cry, let my tears fall on the tiny stones underneath my butt and consecrate the ground with salty water I had made myself. But I couldn't cry. So I thought I would scream, letting my voice fill up this tiny room, loud enough to wake the dead (or at least one of them). But when I opened my mouth, nothing came out. Then I thought I would take a nap, but that seemed unlikely. I couldn't nap under the best of circumstances, what made me think I'd be able to nap in an underground tomb?

Instead I stayed where I was, uncrying, unscreaming, unsleeping, and I laid my hands flat on the ground and I said, "Henry, please. Please, please, please. Answer me."

I closed my eyes, then closed my hands into fists, scooping up some of the gravel, squeezing it so hard I thought I might have made myself bleed.

"Evelyn? Are you there, can you hear me? I'm so sorry, I'm so *sorry.* Please please please forgive me, if you come back, I promise I'll make everything okay again, okay? Okay? Okay, Evelyn?"

And then someone *did* answer, but it wasn't Evelyn, it was another Farthing sister, it was Clara, and she said, "Oh, Winnie," in a sad, small voice.

She stood in the doorway of the crypt, dressed in layers and layers of warm clothes, just her face visible as she unwound a scarf from her neck.

"Clara," I said. "What are you *doing* here?"

"I have to show you something."

"How did you know where to find me?"

"I tracked you," Clara said, still removing layers, pulling a wool hat from her head and then reaching into her pocket, withdrawing her phone and holding it up a little sheepishly.

"You can track me?"

"I installed an app on both your phones after Evelyn disappeared. I have a new, strict rule about not losing more than one sister per weekend."

"But how did you . . ."

"You were sleeping, and I can be very quiet when I want to be."

"Creepy."

"Look. I finished it," Clara said, and her eyes were flashing, a trick of the light from the many candles behind me. She unlocked her phone, scrolled through a few screens, then handed it to me. It was a photo of her painting.

"It's our—"

"Backyard," she finished. "It's our backyard."

"And what's that—"

"I have no idea," Clara said. "But it doesn't seem good."

The painting showed our backyard in winter, as it was now. You could just see the back of the brownstone, the wide windows and the door to the kitchen. There were the dormant jasmine bushes and the trees behind them. Movement in the branches suggested a strong breeze. The grass was dusted with snow. It could have been today, actually. The amount of snow was right.

"I think it's—"

"Today," Clara interrupted again. "It's today."

The weird thing, the thing Clara had said seemed *not good* was directly above the backyard, in the sky.

The sky itself was a blueish gray and crowded with clouds, except for one dark slash, one blackish smudge, like my sister had taken a paintbrush and swiped it from left to right on the canvas. The mark looked like it had been made carelessly, quickly—but it was the kind of effortless thing that you knew actually took a very long time to get exactly right in paint. Underneath the slash, a sort of shadow. Strange dark shapes bleeding through. But it was hard to focus on the slash. It was hard to make anything coherent out of it. It didn't look like anything real I'd ever seen before. If you stared at it too long, it almost disappeared. It blurred. It could have been a trick of the light. The candles didn't help; maybe outside it would have looked completely different.

"Is it a cloud?" I asked. "Like, a rain cloud?"

"I thought so, at first, something like that," Clara said, shedding her jacket on the gravel floor. "But now I don't think so. I get this, like . . ."

"Bad feeling," I finished.

"A bad feeling," Clara confirmed. "And look."

Underneath the black mark, in the middle of the backyard, a small figure was sitting on a bench. She had her back toward us, but I could tell in the shape of her shoulders, in the tilt of her neck, it was Evelyn.

I tapped the screen of Clara's phone to see what time it was, then handed it back to her.

"Text Bernadette," I said. "Tell her to meet us at home."

I didn't think the priest was ultimately sad to see us go, but I made a mental note to bring him a thank-you card. Something along the lines of: *I appreciate you for bringing me down into a private underground crypt and then letting my sister come, too!*

Clara and I took the C from Fulton Street up to Eighty-First Street, then power walked the rest of the way to home. We didn't know what we would find. We kept looking up at the sky nervously, scanning for an unnatural black slash.

Bernadette was waiting for us outside, like maybe she was too scared to go into the house by herself. She looked slightly more animated than she had that morning, fresh from thrifting and smelling like a mix of roses and lilac (even though she had called out of work).

"What are we doing here?" she asked, in lieu of *hello* or *it's so nice to see you both* or *why do you smell like hundred-year-old bones?* Clara had texted only *meet us at home* and Bernadette had given it a thumbs-up.

Clara had already pulled up the painting, and she showed it to Bernadette now. Her eyes narrowed as she looked at it.

"What's the thing in the sky?" she asked.

"We don't know," Clara said.

"Okay," Bernadette said. "Let's go in."

The house was oddly cold, as if someone had turned the heat down, as if the winter chill had found its way inside. There was a breeze, too, like—

"Is the back door open?" Clara asked, brushing past me, hurrying through the living room and into the kitchen, us following closely behind.

And, yes, the door was open. The kitchen door that led down to the backyard was open, letting in so much cold air, letting in the wind; there was mail strewn all over the floor, some leftover fall leaves that hadn't yet been buried by the snow.

"What the fuck?" Bernadette said.

We walked closer to the back of the house, to the wide windows, and Clara put a hand on my arm and said, "Evelyn," and for a moment I thought she had called me by the wrong name but then I saw her, our sister, sitting on a bench in the middle of the yard, facing the wall of dormant jasmine bushes, sitting unmoving in the snow, which had just begun to fall again.

It was Clara's painting come to life. It was so beautiful and so *creepy* and so impossible.

Clara took off running down the stairs. We'd all been so shocked at the cold air in the house that we hadn't taken our shoes off, we'd have to vacuum before Mom got home—

"We have to vacuum," I said weakly, but Bernadette didn't answer; she pushed past me and followed Clara down the back stairs. My heart was racing, beating far too fast to be healthy, pounding in my chest so hard it *hurt,* and I wondered if I was having a heart attack.

Clara reached Evelyn first, of course, and dove into her arms, collapsing on the bench beside her and hugging her so tightly I felt phantom arms around my own body.

Bernadette and I didn't hug her, just came up to the front of the bench and stopped, staring at her, perhaps not looking the friendliest. I felt happy to see her, of course, relieved, of course, but also deeply, profoundly enraged.

Evelyn looked different.

Her hair was longer? Or shinier? Her eyes were different. Darker. Her skin was clear, porcelain doll skin, unblemished and smooth. She was sitting very straight, hugging Clara back somewhat noncommittedly, an expression of . . . I couldn't decipher it. What was she feeling, my prodigal sister? I couldn't begin to guess. But also, I was so *relieved*. She had been a ghost and now she was here, now she was back and everything would be okay.

"Evelyn," Bernadette said finally, as Clara pulled away, wiping tears from her cheeks, her shoulders bouncing up and down with tiny sobs of happiness. "Where *were* you?"

And Evelyn took a deep breath, and there was something in the way she breathed that was different, there was something about *her* that was different, she was my sister but also I felt like I hardly knew her. I kept thinking that to myself, over and over, *I hardly know you, I hardly know you, I hardly know you . . .*

She shifted a little, on the bench, folding her hands on her lap. She was wearing clothes I didn't recognize. A dark green linen dress, long sleeved and buttoned up to the Peter Pan collar. Flakes of snow were starting to collect on her shoulders; the flakes were so thick and fat that I could make out their details. A memory of sitting in front of the fireplace cutting snowflakes out of folded pieces of paper, my sisters close to me, the smell of hot chocolate, my father dolloping whipped cream on top. She must have been so cold, she didn't have a coat—

"Evelyn, are you cold?"

"Evelyn," Bernadette said, louder than me, so loud in the quiet of the snowfall as she said again, *"Where were you?"*

Evelyn looked up at her then, at both of us, but her eyes took a moment to focus. "I went to find him," she said finally, and not to beat a dead horse, but her voice was different, too, everything about her was *different,* almost . . . changed? And it was like she was coming out of a dream, maybe, or a trance, she kept blinking her eyes over and over, her movements slow and strange and lethargic, like she was moving through something thick and tangible.

"Henry," Clara said. "Is he here?"

"Henry," Evelyn replied, moving her head to look around her. "Where am I?"

"Our backyard," Bernadette said. "You're in our backyard, Evie."

"We tried to come back . . . He was with me . . . He was right . . ."

She tried to stand up, but her legs buckled, she fell sideways, and I caught her. She melted into my arms like she had no strength left.

"He was with me," she whispered into my hair.

"Where?" I asked, holding her tightly. "Where were you, Evelyn?"

"I went to find him. I went to bring him back, but . . . I don't know where he is now. We were together, he was *right there,* but he didn't make it back . . ."

She pulled away from me. She was very pale and shaking a little.

"You went to find him," Clara repeated. "Evelyn, do you mean, like . . ."

"In the Underworld," Evelyn said.

"In the Underworld," I repeated, trying incredibly hard to keep my voice completely devoid of emotion.

"I was there for three years," Evelyn said. "Has it been three years?"

"Three days," Bernadette said. "You've been gone for three days."

"We tried to come back," Evelyn said, and her voice was so quiet we all had to lean in to hear her. "We tried to come back, we tried so hard to come back, we kept trying and trying and trying and then . . . And now I'm back and . . . He was with me. He was with me and now he's not here. He's not here he's not here he's not here . . ."

And she leaned into my arms again, and she buried her face in my neck, and she kept saying it over and over and over:

He's not here

He's not here

He's not here

And I did my best to hold onto her, but she was shaking so much I had to let go.

VI

There have always been accounts of people traveling from one world to another. The Pevensie children stepped through a wardrobe and into the snow-covered wonderland of Narnia. Alice fell down a rabbit hole and ended up in Wonderland. Dante Alighieri wrote an incredibly detailed account of Virgil guiding him into Hell. And Persephone herself spent half the year in our world and half the year under it, ruling over the dead. So it doesn't seem so unreasonable, really, that a Farthing girl, a girl descended from Persephone herself, might be able to discover the secret of making such a journey.

Evelyn had been gone for three nights and claimed she'd been away for three years. I'd read as much Narnia as the next introverted nerd; I knew about fantasy world time distortion.

"The camera didn't show you leaving the house," Clara said later, when we'd convinced Evelyn to come in from the snow and change into more reasonable clothes. Bernadette had put on a fire and I had made us grilled cheeses that I personally wasn't eating so much as tearing into tinier and tinier pieces.

I paused now, mid-tear, because something Evelyn had said to me outside the Met came flooding back:

They say she came to Manhattan before it was even Manhattan. That she planted a jasmine bush on a plot of bare land. They say her descendants would forever be drawn to it, like moths to a flame. They say that her footsteps left fragile places in the earth, places you could crawl from one world to another . . .

"Persephone's footsteps," I said.

Evelyn looked up at me and blinked. She was still moving slowly and blinking a lot, but she had wolfed down her own sandwich and the food had seemed to help; she wasn't shaking anymore.

"Yes," she said.

"The camera didn't show you leaving the house because you *didn't* leave the house. You got to the Underworld from here. From inside."

"The old story," Evelyn said, her voice raspy as if she hadn't used it in a long time. "Years and years ago, Persephone came to Manhattan and ushered in the spring. She planted a jasmine tree. Her descendants were bound to tend to it forever, drawn to it always. Wherever she stepped, her footsteps—"

"Left fragile places in the earth," Bernadette finished. "We've all heard this one, Evie. It's just a bedtime story for weird sisters."

"No, Bernie," Evelyn said. "It's true. It's all true. Everything Aunt Bea told us."

"Did you meet her?" Clara asked, wide eyed. "Persephone?"

"No," Evelyn said. "She wasn't where I was."

"And you got to the Underworld from *here*?" Clara pressed. "From inside the house?"

"It's all kind of fuzzy now," Evelyn said. "But I think so . . . I remember looking and looking and trying to find a way to get to Henry . . . and then I found it. I found him. But we couldn't get back and . . . And I don't know. We spent three years together and . . . Some of it was nice. I won't lie about that; some of it was really, really beautiful, but we also kept looking for a way to come back . . ."

"What was it like?" Clara asked. "What did it look like?"

"The sky is a dark aubergine. And the trees were fuller. It's almost a copy of our world, but . . . Different. Deeper. Darker. Oh, in Grand Central they have these columns, and the ceiling is alive, the stars twinkle and comets shoot by overhead and . . . There was dancing. A lot of dancing." She looked faraway and dreamy when she said this; she looked like our Evelyn but she didn't talk like our Evelyn and she didn't smell like our Evelyn and her eyes looked two shades darker and her skin looked two shades paler, as if she hadn't seen the sun in quite some time. And her hair was longer. Three years longer.

"I have to get back," she said now. "I have to get back to him . . ."

"You can't go back," I said. "You just said you almost didn't make it home."

"But Henry's still there," she said, her eyes brimming with tears.

"Let's say we did try and go back," Bernadette said. "Do you think it would work again? The . . . portal? Are we calling it a portal?"

"A doorway," Evelyn said. "It's more like a doorway. And I don't know if it would work again. Henry said those doors, they're tricky to figure out. Sometimes they'll only work once. And I can't *remember . . .*"

"In the story, the thing about the jasmine bushes . . ." Clara began slowly. "That Farthings will always be drawn to the jasmine bushes because Persephone planted them. Is that why Henry *smells* like jasmine? But he's not a Farthing."

"He's not a Farthing, but he lived here," Evelyn said. "In this house. And he died here. I think that's why he never left. Why he became a ghost."

"Because he died in the house," Bernie said, catching on.

"And the house is magic," I finished.

"Magic is such a simple way of putting it," Evelyn said. "But, yes. The house is magic. The land is magic. Farthings have always been here, lived here, *breathed* in it."

"Of course Henry became a ghost," Clara whispered. "He was drenched in that energy every day he lived in this house. *Our* energy."

"But what about the others?" Bernie asked. "What about the other Farthing ghosts, the ones Winnie can see?"

"They've never been as real as Henry," Evelyn said. "You've always said that, Winnie, about the other ghosts. They're just copies."

At the mention of other Farthing ghosts, I remembered *Evelyn's* ghost, standing next to the Ouija board, standing in the kitchen, the way I knew the shape and size of her, how she had held her hand out to me, reaching for me, how I had let go of her in the backyard because of how much she was shaking, how Bernadette had stepped in and pulled her close, pulled her inside, turned on the fire and tried to bring some warmth back into the house.

I had seen Evelyn's ghost because she had been in the Underworld. I had seen her because she *had,* sort of, been dead. Or at least more dead, technically, during those three days, than she had been *alive*.

"Persephone could come and go from the Underworld," Clara said. "It must be like that, for us, sort of. Our . . . *energy,* maybe. It's *there* but it's also *here.* The children of the in-between, like Aunt Bea says."

"This is giving me a headache," Bernie said, at the same time I said, "I saw you, Evelyn."

Evelyn looked up at me and her eyes were, for a moment, unrecognizable. A full shade lighter than they had been three days ago. I wanted to scream. I wanted to pull her hair. I wanted to push her over and hold her down and tell her how sorry I was.

"I remember . . ." she said.

"Saw her when?" Clara asked.

"When she was down there . . . She was a ghost . . ."

"You didn't tell us," Bernadette said.

"Because I didn't know if that meant she was . . ."

"I was," Evelyn said. "Kind of."

A moment of quiet, and then Clara said, a bit too loudly, "Doesn't it kind of feel sometimes like we're *all* ghosts? You know?"

Evelyn blinked, blinked, blinked, then said, "I think I need to lie down for a while."

She got up and brought her plate into the kitchen, then walked silently past us and went up to her room.

"Okay, so, either Evelyn has completely lost it or we've *all* completely lost it or *none* of us have lost it, and I'm really trying to figure out which one it is," Clara said that night, the three of us crammed into her small bedroom, Bernadette on the bed with Clara, me on the floor, rocking back and forth, unable to be still. Evelyn had gone to bed and not gotten up again and we'd all gone in to check on her at various points, finding her stripped down to her underwear underneath the covers of her bed, sleeping so soundly and so deeply it gave us the feeling that we couldn't wake her even if we'd tried.

"*Something* happened to her," Bernadette said thoughtfully. "She was gone for three days. Clearly she went *somewhere*."

"And the cameras . . ." Clara said.

"And Evelyn doesn't lie," I said.

"Mom and Dad come back tomorrow," Clara said. "What are we going to tell them?"

"Nothing," Bernadette and I said at the same time.

"Are we supposed to just go to *school* tomorrow?" Clara asked.

"Yes," I said. "I think we have to."

"I think it's all true," Bernadette declared. "Don't you think it must all be true? Everything she told us? Maybe we should call Aunt Bea."

"Aunt Bea will tell Mom," I reasoned. "Like, *immediately*."

"She wants to go back," Clara said. "She's going to insist on going back for him."

"Well, obviously we can't let that happen," Bernie said.

"Maybe we should all go?" Clara proposed. "You know, just to check it out."

"No," Bernadette and I said at the same time (again).

"Aubergine skies," Clara mumbled.

"We have to figure out how to get Henry back *here*," I said. "If Henry comes back here, Evelyn has no reason to leave again."

"No reason to leave *ever* again," Bernadette said. "We'd be right back where we started. She would never leave this house again."

"I don't think we can worry about that right now," I said. "I think all we can worry about is making sure she doesn't go back to the Underworld and get trapped there again."

"Great, I'll go to the library tomorrow and check out all the books I can on how to resurrect a ghost and we'll wrap this up by the weekend," Bernadette said with an eye roll, lying back on the bed with a huff.

"I know someone I could ask," I said, and my sisters both shot me a look like, *Who??* "Just someone I know. She works in a store. It's fine."

"This is all *very* weird," Clara said.

"Yes," Bernadette said. "And I can't even talk about it in therapy. Who would believe me?"

We did go to school on Tuesday. Mom and Dad hadn't made it back yet; they'd hit traffic halfway to the city and sent us many apology texts for being absent parents. Bernadette had the day off but got up early and made everyone chocolate-chip pancakes, something she hadn't done in years. They were Evelyn's favorite, and she ate them ravenously, going back for seconds.

"Do they not have chocolate-chip pancakes in the Underworld?" Clara asked, her wide-eyed innocence successfully removing any trace of snark from her words.

"No," Evelyn said. "But there are a lot of pomegranates."

Evelyn and I walked across the park.

We had walked across the park together only a few days before, but it felt like a lifetime ago. She did not ask to veer toward the reservoir. We took the most direct route available to us. She was quiet. She stood up very straight. Shoulders back. Chin up. Steps light. Face smooth and impassive. Distant. If I spoke to her, it took a moment for my words to register. We hadn't been alone together since she had come back, and I hadn't expected the silence between us to feel so awkward. But maybe I *should* have. There were, as it stood, about a million things I didn't want to talk about with her, starting with what I had said to Henry, how I had sent him away, how I had lied to her, how all of this was my fault, etc., etc.

"Do you believe me?" she asked suddenly, startling me. "I can't decide if you all believe me or you think I'm lying or making it up or crazy or . . ."

"We grew up with a ghost in our attic, Evelyn," I said. "We believe you."

"He forgives you," she said. "He wanted me to tell you that."

"Forgives me for what?" I said too quickly. "I didn't do anything. Did he tell you I did something?"

"And I know *why* you did it," she continued. "And it upsets me, but I love you, and I know you were just doing what you thought was right, and I forgive you. You're my sister. I'll love you forever."

I scratched the insides of my wrists. I didn't know how to respond to any of that, so I just mumbled that I loved her, too, and then I said, feeling like I had to say *something* or else lapse back into uncomfortable silence, "So the Underworld, is it, like . . ." I pointed down, toward the earth.

"No," Evelyn said. "Not really. It's more like . . ."

She moved her hands in a wide circle, indicating everything all around us. Then she smiled and took my hands, holding them in her hands, which seemed just a little colder than I remembered.

"I'm sorry," she said, looking so deeply into my eyes that I felt penetrated, violated, itchy all over. "I'm sorry for leaving and not telling you where I was going. I'm sorry for not trying to understand why you did what you did. I'm sorry for pretending that I was completely blameless in this. I'm sorry for falling in love with a ghost. I'm sorry that I have to go back and find him. Even if that means . . . Even if that means never coming back *here*. I'm sorry."

I wasn't going to cry, I *wasn't,* and so I took two very deep breaths before I responded to her.

"I'm sorry, too," I said. "I'm sorry for not coming to you first, for not talking to you about my concerns. I'm sorry for thinking I knew what's best for you. I'm sorry for going to Vermont without telling you."

I'm sorry for what I said to Henry. I'm sorry for sending him away.

But I couldn't say that yet.

Evelyn was still holding my hands, gripping them so hard, as if I was the one who'd disappeared, not her. And then she let them go, and I felt a phantom pressure where her fingers had dug into my skin.

"You don't have to go," I said. "We're going to find a way to bring him back."

"I tried everything," she replied. "I don't think he *can* come back."

Her eyes were getting wet. We were in the middle of the Great Lawn. I could see the Museum of Natural History in the distance, peeking out from behind a cluster of trees. It was a mild day, a brief respite from the bitter cold. The sky was clear and blue and cloudless above us.

And that was when I saw it.

We were facing each other, and I was facing west, and there it was, over Evelyn's head, back toward our house.

"Oh," I said, and Evelyn turned around to look where I was looking, following my gaze up and up and up until she finally saw it, too.

The faint black smear across the sky.

The faint black smear that we could tell, even from here, was directly over our house.

It could have been a leftover exhale of exhaust from a plane or a distant smokestack.

A shadow, a rain cloud, a trick of the light.

But it wasn't. It wasn't any of those things. Because it was the thing from Clara's painting: a clean slash through blue, a delicate line of black.

Evelyn tilted her head to the side, still looking at it.

"What is that?" she said.

"I don't know, I don't . . ."

My chest was filling with a cold, icy sort of panic.

Looking at the mark directly didn't quite work; it faded into the brilliant blue of the sky around it. You had to look just to the left or just to the right, and then it leapt into stark clarity, became something huge and enormous and unmissable.

A man walked by in a rumpled business suit, his head down, his hands stuffed into his pockets.

"Sir! Sir!" I yelped before I could stop myself. Miraculously, he turned around (I would estimate about 90 percent of New Yorkers ignore any and all attempts to get their attention). "Do you *see* that?" I said, as soon as our eyes met, pointing urgently into the sky, toward the mark.

He lifted up his chin, followed my finger, squinted into the brightness of the winter sky.

"See what?" he asked after a minute, his voice already impatient, his feet inching forward to continue their stomp across the park.

"That mark! That black slash! That thing in the sky! Right there!"

I kept pointing. The man made a face *(I don't have fucking time for this)* but looked up again, giving it one more try. He shrugged and when he turned back, his expression was a mixture of apologetic and annoyance.

"I don't see anything," he said. Then, as an afterthought, already pedaling away, hands back in pockets, he added, "Sorry, kid."

When I pulled out my phone to text Clara and Bernadette, Clara had already texted our three-person group chat (No Ghost Lovers Allowed), a cell phone picture of a perfectly unblemished sky.

Clara:

It doesn't show up in pictures.

Bernadette:

What doesn't?

Clara:

The mark.

Bernadette:

What mark?

Clara:

From my painting.

Bernadette:

Holy shit. I just went outside.
Wtf is it?

Clara:

I don't know.

Me:

A man in the park
couldn't see it either.

Bernadette:

I don't know what it is but why do I
have this feeling like we're fucked.

Clara:

same lol

Same lol

Same lol

Same lol

Clara's text became something of a mantra as I made it through the school day, stumbling from class to class to class to lunch to class to class to class to class, taking every available opportunity to look out the window, confirming that the mark was still there, still the same size, still in the same spot, very obviously not a wisp of smoke or exhaust or cloud.

I asked five people throughout the day if they could see it and each of them did the same squint and shrug move. And all of them said no. And one girl apologized again, just like the man in the park, a soft-spoken, sweet girl I'd always liked. Her name is Jackie. When she apologized I felt, for five crushing, expansive seconds, the most alone I'd ever felt in my entire life.

"There has to be a reasonable explanation for it," Evelyn said in the hallway between fourth and fifth period. Our lockers were next to each other (Farthing, Farthing) and though we shared no classes, we met multiple times throughout the day, putting books away, taking books out, hyperventilating into the small metal box we were allotted to hold our things, including our secrets, including our tears, including the whispered screams we poured into them when we had no one else to tell.

"Like *what*?" I asked.

"Like . . . atmospheric pressure . . . conditions . . ."

"Atmospheric pressure conditions," I deadpanned back at her, my words coming out more rudely than I had meant them to.

"I don't know, Winnie, I'm not a weatherman," she said, her voice withering, her expression withering. They must teach you how to be 24/7 withering in the Underworld. It must be one of the perks they offer, besides nonstop dancing and a different dead girl braiding your hair every morning (something Evelyn had told us and that Clara had later said, her voice dripping with jealousy, *Damn, that sounds so nice*).

"Clearly," I said, too late, an already weak comeback becoming weaker, as I wasn't even sure Evelyn had heard it; she had closed her locker and was turning to leave, walking to her next class, leaving me alone.

I turned and whisper-screamed into my locker, sticking my head as far into the metal cage as I could, really letting go.

That night we ate Chinese takeout because our parents were too tired to cook.

"Best Chinese food in New York City and we can just call up and have it delivered to our door," Dad said happily. "How lucky are we, kids?"

"Pretty lucky," Clara said, scooping up another spring roll, dunking it in two different sauces and eating it in two big bites.

"What did you get up to while we were gone?" Mom asked.

"We mostly just sat around and stared at each other," Bernadette said.

"Same," Dad said.

"Anything more interesting to report?" Mom pressed. She was slightly obsessed with fried rice and was steadily making her way through a mountain of it.

"No," I said firmly. "It was a very boring weekend."

"Same," Dad said.

"Oh, stop it," Mom said, ignoring me, hitting Dad playfully on the arm. "We had a lovely time. We went snowshoeing!"

"Same," Evelyn said.

"Did you?" Dad said, perking up.

"No," Evelyn said, apologetically.

"Ah," he said. "I love snowshoeing. What a workout! Right, honey?"

Mom made a sound of agreement through a mouthful of fried rice. We slipped back into amiable silence.

Later, we brought bowls of green tea ice cream to the attic and sat eating it, some of us on the couch, some of us on the floor, Evelyn on her piano bench, legs crossed primly, every inch of her an undead queen.

It felt weird without Henry there.

Usually Henry would join us, pretend to eat, pantomime the actions of being alive, sometimes stare at our food mournfully.

(*Do you miss eating?* Clara had asked him once. *Clara,* he had replied, *I miss* everything.)

"Do you know how you're going to do it? How you're going to try and bring Henry back?" Evelyn asked quietly, tentatively. She had finished her ice cream and was holding the bowl almost reverently, staring into its depths like trying to see something beyond its ceramic glaze (if it was scrying she was after, she needn't have wasted her time; the leftover dairy would have made everything cloudy and unclear).

"No," Clara admitted.

"But we *will* bring him back," Bernadette said. "We'll figure it out."

We sat in silence for a while. I thought of the Pevensie children, opening a wardrobe and stepping through to a snow-covered wonderland. I thought of Alice, stumbling down a rabbit hole. I thought about the girl in Dark Magic. I didn't know her name. I kind of wanted to ask her on a date. Either that or become her best friend. Either that or make a concerted effort never to see her again (I contained multitudes).

"I'm sure you will," Evelyn said finally, with no conviction in her voice whatsoever. "I'll take these bowls downstairs." She got up and collected the bowls and started down the stairs, her footsteps getting quieter and quieter until we couldn't hear them anymore.

Clara got up from the floor then; her left foot was asleep and she sort of half-hopped over to the window, pulling the curtain aside, craning her neck to look up at the sky.

"It's still there," she said. "It kind of glows a little, in the moonlight."

"What do you think it *is*?" I asked.

"Well, it showed up when Evelyn came back," Bernie said.

"And it's right above our house," I added. "So maybe something happened when she went through the doorway the second time? Like she . . . broke something?"

"Broke the sky?" Bernadette asked.

"I don't know. Maybe? If there are these doorways between universes, Persephone's footsteps, you know, and we're not really supposed to *use* them, then maybe it was like . . . like she forced her way through an entrance that wasn't big enough for her. It widened it, warped it. She went there and came back and pushed her way through, and now this doorway has been *opened,* really . . . I don't know; this is stupid . . ."

"No, no," she said. "I think that actually makes sense . . ."

"A tear," Clara said slowly. "Between the universes." She was still at the window, still looking up at the sky, at the black mark. "It's like . . . pulsing."

"Pulsing?"

"Or shimmering. Or *breathing*."

"Breathing?"

"I don't know," Clara said, and pulled back from the window, shutting the curtain abruptly. "It's creeping me out."

"So what do we *do*?" Bernadette asked. "Is it going to get bigger?"

"Let me just google what happened the last time we had a crack between worlds," I said.

"Guys," Clara said. "Shut up. Stop fighting. If there's a tear in the world, if there's this open doorway between our New York and this *other* New York, this *undead* New York . . ."

"Maybe it means other things can get through . . ." Bernadette said.

"It means *who knows* what's about to happen," Clara said. "But it doesn't feel like anything good."

VII

Of course, if you were descended from Persephone, you were also descended from her daughter, Melinoë, and if you were descended from Melinoë, you might find yourself blaming her for any ill fortune that befell you, such as madness, ghostly communication, nightmares . . . You might call any bad dreams messages; *you might wonder what she was trying to tell you . . .*

That night I dreamed about zombies.

A bit on the nose, sure, but it was fucking terrifying, and when I woke up, Clara was sitting on the edge of my bed, that book in her hands, *Mythology* by Edith Hamilton. I checked my phone; it was four in the morning. She had a little book light attached to the hardcover and she didn't look up when I moved.

"You were groaning," she said.

"A step up from neighing," I replied.

"A message from Melinoë?"

"You know, I'd really love being related to a nice goddess. A goddess of, like, bunnies. Or rainbows. Or hugs."

"Hestia," Clara said, turning pages in her book until she found what she was looking for, reading aloud: "'Hestia, the goddess of hearth and home, known to be kind and forgiving, the perfect hostess and a protector for all of her followers.'"

"Yes, that's what I want," I said. "I want a protector. Not a harbinger of nightmares."

"You said you had someone you could ask," Clara said. "Someone who might know how to bring Henry back. She works in a store? What store?"

"You wouldn't know it."

"Dark Magic? That place on Columbus?"

"How do you know it?"

"Where else are you going to get a Ouija board at ten o'clock on a Saturday night? And who else would have told you to try scrying alone on the kitchen floor?"

"How did you know I tried to scry?"

"It's dangerous. It's not something you should mess around with. You could have—"

"Lost my way in the labyrinthine maze of the eternal abyss?" I guessed. "Yeah, I know. But here I am."

"This is so messed up," Clara said.

"I know."

"It feels creepy that I painted it. Like it got inside my head or something."

"And nobody else can see it. Just us. Why is that?"

"Not even Mom and Dad," Clara confirmed. "I asked them earlier."

I pulled up a photo of the painting that I'd taken on my phone. It really *was* beautiful. Maybe the best thing Clara had ever done.

Never mind I couldn't look at it for more than a few seconds without feeling a chill roll down my spine.

We looked at it for a few moments together, then Clara said, "Go talk to that cute girl at the store. Maybe she'll have some insight."

"I didn't say it was a cute girl."

"Sometimes I just know things," Clara said. "I think I get it from Aunt Bea. Or Persephone."

"Good night," I said.

"Good night. Aim for the head."

More surreal than perhaps anything in this absolute mess of surrealness was the action of going to school. Eating breakfast (Dad had made frittatas), walking across the park with Evelyn, sitting through classes, walking back through the park, getting home, changing into something a little nicer (the Dark Magic girl *was* cute, okay), setting off outside again. The normal rote actions of everyday life seemed absolutely hysterical. I laughed out loud in history class, and there is so rarely an appropriate time to laugh out loud during a history lesson ("Sorry, I was . . . thinking of something else," I mumbled weakly).

I left the house for Dark Magic feeling marginally more normal, breathing deep, refreshing lungfuls of the chilly air.

I saw Bernadette outside the flower shop and crossed the street to say hi.

"Where are you going?" she asked. She was wrestling a big, unruly bouquet of lilies into a tall black bucket.

"To talk to a girl about summoning a ghost who's actively refusing to be summoned."

"Oh, the cute girl. Nice. What's her name?"

"I don't know, actually."

"Very on brand for you."

"What do you mean—"

"It's just like, the most obvious question to ask a cute girl. But it escapes you. Will you help me with this?"

I squeezed the stems of the lilies together and helped guide them into the bucket. Bernadette kissed me on the cheek and refused to answer any more questions about what my *brand* was.

I hadn't been to Dark Magic in the daytime yet and the outside of the store looked significantly more normal in the rush of late-afternoon crowds. I had never had a job before, but I could see myself working in a place like this, donning black clothing as a sort of uniform, braiding my hair out of my face, adopting an expression of pointed disinterest.

I pushed into the space and the inside looked different, too. It was brighter, for one thing; the sunlight filtered through the store windows and washed everything in a thin, winter glow. The person standing behind the register was, unfortunately, not the cute girl. It was a very tall man with soft pink hair and a lime-green jumpsuit. He didn't quite fit into the aesthetic of the store but he also *did* look strange enough (in a good way) to be here. He smiled when he saw me. He was much more smiley than the girl had been.

"Hey, there. Welcome to Dark Magic. What brings you in today? Horoscope book? Tarot cards? Crystal collection?"

"Oh, no, I actually was, um, this is weird, but there was this, I was wondering if you could—"

"Maybe," the man said, his smile getting wider.

"Sorry?"

"Maybe," the man said. "Her name. Maybe. Like—*maybe* you didn't come in here to ask about the cute girl who works nights, but I have a feeling you did, and her name is Maybe."

"Maybe," I repeated, feeling a slight rush of warmth around my neck area (pale skin, easy blushers, curse of the Farthings). "I mean. I was, yeah. Asking about her. Going to ask about her. She helped me and I wanted to say, um . . . thanks. So, um. You know. Thanks. Thanks also to you. Thanks to both of you."

"She's on at seven most nights, goes to school during the day. She's one of the coolest people I've ever met, but don't you *dare* tell her I said that. I'm Jon. Can I help you with something? I know I'm not as sultry and attractive as our dear Maybe, but I still know which crystals will dispel bad dreams. Have you been having bad dreams? Sorry for presuming, I just get the feeling. Also don't tell her I said that, the sultry and attractive bit."

I laughed—half nervous, half genuine. "I *do* have bad dreams, actually, but I have another question, sort of a weird question. I don't really know if—"

"Try me. I've worked here for a while. The dress code hasn't worn off on me, but I do know a lot about weird shit."

"I mean, this is going to sound very strange . . ."

"We sell antique Victorian baby teeth on eighteen-karat gold necklaces," Jon deadpanned.

"Let's just say, hypothetically, there was, like, a place where . . . you go. After you die." To Jon's credit, he wasn't smiling anymore, he was listening carefully, nodding his head slightly, no indication that he was internally making fun of me at all. "And in this place, there's a . . . spirit. A ghost. And you want the ghost to come back, you know. You have to . . . talk to it. This person. You have to. It's imperative. Anyway. How might you . . . do that?"

"You want to summon the dead," Jon said, putting it far more succinctly than I had. "Look, people have been summoning the dead for ages. You're not asking to reinvent the wheel here."

"I'm not?"

"Definitely not. People are fascinated with death. They want to understand it. They want to talk to their loved ones who've passed. In my case, I wanted to find out where my grandmother hid her *very* expensive emerald-and-diamond necklace." He paused, considering. "I also wanted to say *hi,* of course. But the necklace was very important to me, and she'd hidden it *very* well."

"Did you find it?"

"In a can of garbanzo beans, beans still in there, can resealed. Don't know how she managed it."

"You contacted your grandmother from beyond the grave and she told you where to find her necklace?"

"No," Jon admitted. "I just got hungry one day. But anyway. What you're asking isn't impossible."

"Okay . . ."

"It isn't *easy* or even *likely,* but it's not impossible."

"Okay . . ."

"You'll need a medium. A good one. Not a hack Instagrammer who's directly responsible for the overharvesting of California white sage."

"Right. So how do I—"

"Obviously, I know one. She might be down. She's particular about what cases she accepts."

"All right. How do I contact her?"

"She's here most nights at seven."

"Maybe," I said.

"Maybe," he confirmed.

"All right. I guess I'll come back."

"Here," he said, reaching under the counter, withdrawing two small bundles. "Cedar," he said, putting the first one down, a small pallet of three-inch long sticks, tied together with twine. "For protection." He put the second bundle on the table. This one I knew was lavender, a dried smudging bundle of it, greenery mixed with delicate purple flowers. "For the invitation of spirits. And also, they both smell lovely." I started to take my wallet out of my bag, but he waved his hand at me. "No charge. Any friend of Maybe gets the smudging sticks for free."

"Oh, well, we're not really *friends*—"

"You will be," he said, with a simple conviction that mirrored Clara's, whenever she said things that weren't true yet but that we knew would become true eventually.

Walking home, still early evening but also quickly getting darker (East Coast winters), I stared at the dark slice in the sky. I should have asked Jon if he could see it. I'd ask Maybe, maybe. And was it . . . getting bigger?

I stopped on our front stairs, halfway up, staring at it, directly above our home.

Above the slash, the moon was bright, its own crescent slice in the darkness. Next to the moon, there was one bright star.

"Mars," Dad said, suddenly behind me. I'd been so engrossed in my skygazing I hadn't heard him approach.

"What?" I said, jumping a little.

"Is that what you're looking at? Mars?"

"The planet?"

"The planet, yes, my love. That little bright thing next to the moon."

"That's *Mars*?"

"Indeed. Isn't it almost impossible to comprehend? We're here, on this planet, going about our days, going to work, going to school, living our lives, and there, in the sky, there's just this *other* planet. Another *planet*. How wild is that?"

"Wild," I agreed.

"Is that what you were looking at? You seemed pretty intensely observant."

"Well, I didn't know it was Mars. But yes."

"Right on."

"Do you see anything else?" I asked cautiously.

"What do you mean?"

"Any other . . . things in the sky?"

"Well, the moon's a lovely little crescent tonight. I've always loved a crescent moon. It looks like the blade of an axe, ready to strike, doesn't it?"

"Sure. And anything else?"

"Not quite dark enough for any stars yet. Is that what you mean?"

"Or just . . . anything . . . else?"

Dad shifted his gaze from the sky to my face, his expression bemused and adoring (in a house full of Farthing women, this was

Dad's default expression). I knew Clara had already asked our parents if they could see the black slice in the sky, but I thought, if it really was getting bigger, it was worth checking again. But clearly it was still only visible to us, for some reason I didn't understand and didn't want to think too much about.

"I thought I saw a shooting star," I said weakly, by way of an explanation.

"Ah," Dad said, touching his finger to my nose. "I hope you made a wish."

He started up the stairs to our front door and I followed him, tearing my gaze away from the sky, forcing myself to move.

"It's getting bigger," Clara said that night. Attic, all four of us, after dinner.

"I noticed, too," Evelyn said.

"I found a medium," I said. "This weekend we can try to contact Henry, and we can ask him if he has any ideas on how to get him home, and we can ask him about the black mark."

"I think I know why he couldn't come back with me," Evelyn said. "I think it's because he's dead. And if you're dead and you go to the Underworld, you don't get to come back."

"Otherwise we'd have a lot of zombies on our hands," Clara said, shooting me a knowing look.

"Well, we're going to try," Bernadette said decisively. She had a journal open on her lap and was scrawling so quickly her hand was almost a blur. She had the uncanny ability to journal and talk at the same time, never missing a beat.

"When will Mom and Dad be out of the house next?" I asked Clara, who somehow always knew their schedules. "We need to have a séance."

"Saturday," Clara said. "Dinner party downtown. At least four hours of parent-free house."

"Perfect. I'll see if she can do it then," I said.

"The cute girl?" Evelyn asked.

"I wish, for *once,* there wasn't a collective pool of sister gossip here," I said.

"Well, that ship has sailed," Bernadette said.

I threw a pillow at her head. Clara started babbling about some TV show she was trying to convince us all to watch. Bernadette put the journal away and started playing with Evelyn's hair, twisting it and braiding it, undoing it and starting over again.

Gradually, the energy in the room shifted: Evelyn was quiet and almost happy, Bernadette was focused and calm, Clara was silly and lighthearted. I was caught up in the moment, so content just to be in a room full of my sisters. The black tear wasn't more than a distant thought on the horizon, a fly in the room that had momentarily stopped buzzing, resting on the windowsill, lulling us into a peaceful state of forgetting that it was there.

But it was there, all right.

It was there and we were right: it was getting bigger.

The good energy lasted throughout the night, the next morning. Evelyn and I set off across the park for school and I thought, in that early morning stillness, that we might not all be doomed. That we might, maybe, be okay.

Which is funny, really, in hindsight.

Because halfway across the park, Evelyn turned to me and said, "January first."

"What's happening on January first?" I asked.

"If we can't figure out how to get Henry home by then, I'm going back. I would rather live there with him than—"

"Here with all of us?"

"That wasn't what I was going to say," she protested.

"But that's the gist of it, right?"

"Winnie, he's all alone . . ."

"He has a lot of other ghosts he can make friends with," I said, and Evelyn didn't answer that, just sighed and smiled in such a sad, apologetic way. "And January first is less than a month away."

"I know," she said. And then, as an afterthought, she took my hand, squeezed it, and said, "I'm sorry."

VIII

Construction on the Farthing family brownstone was completed in 1894 by Blanche Farthing and her husband, Herman.

The house had always belonged to Farthings, would always belong to Farthings.

Blanche and Herman left it to their children, who left it to their children, etc., etc., until it reached four strange sisters with a ghost in their attic.

The ghost, Henry, was not *a Farthing, rather he was an anomaly, taken in by Farthings when his own family had died. You might say he was adopted by Farthings, adopted by the house, and you might also say he was adopted by* Persephone, *loved as if he were one of her very own.*

The Farthing house was built on a very special piece of land, directly in one of Persephone's footsteps. It was a house of the in-between, just like the Farthings were children of the in-between. It was a bit magical, that house, just like the Farthings were a bit magical.

And you might say that is why, when Henry died in the Farthing house, he never left, as if the house itself could not bear to let him go.

I took Clara with me to Dark Magic on Friday evening. I didn't want to go by myself again and Clara wanted to see what the cute girl looked like, so it killed two birds with one stone.

The weather had turned in the last few days. It was cold, yes, obviously, it was winter in New York and it wasn't a stretch to be cold, but there was something *behind* the cold. Something *in addition* to the cold. It was a very specific type of cold, a different kind of cold. It made everything feel a bit . . . hopeless. Quiet. Terrible.

"Does everything feel a bit—"

"Yes," Clara said, interrupting me. We were paused at an intersection, waiting for a walk signal as cars zipped by. "It's the tear."

"The tear?"

"Yes," she confirmed. "There's something coming out of it. A coldness, a darkness . . . I think that's the reason it's getting bigger, actually. Things are like . . ." She made a slow movement with her hands, bringing them together and then sort of expanding them outward, stretching an invisible tear in the sky.

"Oh, well, I don't like that at all."

"This coldness, it's sort of localized to the house. Once we get another block or so away, you'll see what I mean."

"Things are coming out of it?"

"Look," she said, pointing. We were only two blocks away from the brownstone. The sky was a dark gray, and the black tear stood out among the clouds as a dark, smeary shadow. I watched as something—a darker shadow—emerged from the tear, pushing its way through, into our world. It dissipated almost instantly, blending in with the clouds around the tear, becoming mist.

"Well I *really* don't like that . . ."

"I know," Clara said. "Come on; we have a walk signal."

I let Clara drag me across the street, but I couldn't seem to take my eyes off the tear in the sky.

"What was it?"

"I don't know," Clara said. "I'm not an expert on interuniverse travel."

"You don't think it's, like . . ."

"Zombies? I don't know, Winnie. I really don't know."

"Is that why it's so gray? Is that why it's so cold?"

"Again, I don't know, but I think *yes* and *yes*."

"Fuck."

"Also yes."

"Are we all going to die?"

"Ideally, no. And you really need to calm down. Take some deep breaths. People are looking. We're going to figure everything out. We're going to get Henry back up here, and he's going to convince Evelyn not to be such a dramatic idiot and he's going to know what to do about the tear in the sky. Okay?"

"Wait—is this like when you know something? Do you know this? Do you *know* it's going to be all right? Do you know it, Clara? Clara? Do you know it?"

We had reached Dark Magic and we paused outside it, Clara's hand on the doorknob, her face expressionless, her tone light.

"Yes," she said.

A lie so transparent you could call it glass.

I followed her into the store.

Maybe looked somewhat happy to see me (wishful thinking?) and even happier to see Clara.

"One of the infamous three sisters?" she asked.

"Hi," Clara said, nodding. "I'm Clara."

"Maybe. Although I'm sure you already know that; Jon is an oversharer."

"Will you do it, then?" I asked. "Will you be our medium?"

"We were thinking tomorrow night," Clara added.

"I can do tomorrow night. You live around here?"

"Yes!" Clara grabbed a pen and sticky note and wrote down our address.

Maybe took it and nodded. "Not far from my grandma. I'll be there at eleven."

"At *night*?" I said.

"That's perfect," Clara said.

"It's kinda late," I mumbled.

"As close to the witching hour as possible," Maybe said. "Do you have candles? Salt? Olive oil? A Swiffer WetJet?"

"A Swiffer—*what*?"

"Yes," Clara said. "All of the above."

"Perfect. Less for me to carry," Maybe said.

"Do you want, like, money?" I asked.

"The reward of helping a bunch of neighborhood kids summon their first demon is enough," Maybe said. "And also, two hundred dollars."

"Done," Clara said.

"We aren't summoning a *demon,*" I said.

"Hopefully not," Maybe said, flashing a smile so bright I felt exposed by it.

"She *is* cute," Clara said when we'd left, back out into the unnatural cold, scarves wrapped around our necks and half-covering our mouths, so we had to lean in close to hear each other. "Did you see her boots? Original nineties Flower Floral Sienna Miller Docs."

"I don't know what any of those words mean."

"Bernie will," Clara said, spirits undampened.

"Why do you think she needs salt and olive oil?"

"Maybe séances make her hungry."

"Are we sure this is the right thing?"

"You're always so concerned with that, you know. The *right* thing, the *wrong* thing. It's impossible to make that declaration in the moment. You can only do the *best* thing. Make the *best* decision."

"And this is . . ."

"This is the best decision. This is us, trying."

"Trying to bring Henry back."

"Trying to save the world," Clara said, her eyes darting upward, to where the black tear sliced through the gray sky, a tangible portent of doom.

"I'm not feeling great," Mom said later, after dinner. I was helping her clean dishes, rinsing them and slotting them into the dishwasher.

"What's wrong?" I asked.

"I don't know, I just feel this . . . Like a weight, almost."

"A weight . . ."

"Is it strange outside? The cold? I know it's winter. It just feels a little strange."

"Strange . . ."

"I'm sounding silly, I know," she said, taking a sip from her glass of red wine. "I just have the oddest feeling. The oddest sense of . . .

déjà vu, I guess you could call it." She turned to face me, setting her wineglass back on the counter. "Can I ask you something?"

"Sure," I said.

"I don't know why I keep thinking about this," she said, shaking her head, looking past me. "I keep thinking about the day Clara was born. I know you were too young to remember . . ."

I didn't remember, but also, I *did* remember, almost. I shared the memory with Evelyn, with Bernadette. The lollipops, the books, my mother's low, plaintive moans drifting down the staircase. Aunt Bea reading to us, singing to us, braiding our hair, telling us stories about Persephone. Our mother seeing the ghost. Our mother seeing Henry.

"You all had . . . an imaginary friend," Mom said. "Do you remember that? You must have told me about it at some point. I was delirious from the pain, from the water, from the whole experience, and I . . . I guess I would call it a hallucination. But I swear I saw a boy. I swear I talked to him. I swear he told me his name . . ."

Why was she bringing this up now? Was the tear in the sky triggering old memories for her, memories of Henry?

"Henry," Evelyn said from the doorway, standing as still as a statue, her eyes wide and unblinking. "His name is Henry."

"Whatever happened to him? You stopped talking about him," Mom said. "He was an imaginary friend, right? He must have been. And one of you told me about him and I just . . . But he seemed so *real.*" She laughed softly, took another sip of her wine and pointed her glass at me. "Childbirth is a trip. When I was pregnant with you, I kept hearing music. Frank Sinatra. As clear as if someone had put a radio on. But nothing was on, there was no music, your father checked everywhere . . ."

"He wasn't imaginary," Evelyn said softly. "And he wasn't a friend."

"Right," Mom said. "That's right. He was a ghost."

Another sip of wine, emptying the glass, then a rinse and the dishwasher and a kiss on my temple as she slipped past me, leaving Evelyn and me alone together.

"Is she acting weirder than usual lately?" Evelyn asked, and it took everything in my power not to reply, *Pretty rich, coming from you, captain of the weird.*

"She said she's not feeling great. That things seem strange."

"The tear . . ."

"I think so."

"Well maybe tomorrow night we'll figure everything out," Evie said after a moment.

"Yup."

She leaned her head against the doorway and closed her eyes. I watched her chest rise and fall with her breathing.

"I hope we do," she said.

Then, forgetting whatever it was she had come into the kitchen for, she turned around and left.

Maybe was prompt, ringing the doorbell at eleven the next night, dressed in all black, with a long wool coat, a hood pulled down low over her face.

"It's me," she said when I opened the door. "Your friendly neighborhood ghost whisperer."

"Have you ever seen a ghost before?" I asked her in the entranceway, as she unlaced her floral something something boots and shrugged out of her coat.

"I've had unexplainable experiences," she said.

I thought about Henry helping me with my seventh-grade history project, Henry patiently showing me how to fold a paper airplane, Henry making goofy faces when I'd woken up from a nightmare once, our parents hosting a dinner party downstairs, feeling all alone until he'd materialized at the end of my bed.

"Me, too," I said. "I've had a couple unexplainable experiences, as well."

"This is a cool house," Maybe said. "Have you lived here your whole life?"

"My whole life," I repeated. "My ancestors built it, actually. A long time ago."

Maybe smiled. "That sounds so nerdy. *Ancestors.*"

"Just more succinct than saying my great-great-great-great-grandmother."

"What was her name?"

"Blanche."

"Well, I'll tell Blanche she did a great job, if she pops up tonight."

My sisters came around the corner from the kitchen, and Clara gave a little wave. "Hi, Maybe!"

"Hi," Maybe said. "We should do this in the hearth of the home. Usually that's the kitchen or the living room."

"The attic," Bernadette said without hesitation. "For us, it's the attic."

"Right on," Maybe said. "I like your hair."

Bernadette, who'd spent not a single moment of her life flustered, looked a bit flustered now. Her hand fluttered up to the nape of her neck and she stammered a thanks as Maybe looked up the first flight of stairs.

"Shall we?" Maybe said.

Evelyn raised the Swiffer WetJet she was holding. "Let's do this."

Clara led the way, followed by Maybe, then Evelyn, then me, then Bernadette.

"Dang," Bernie whispered.

"Kindly shut up," I whispered back.

In the attic, Maybe dropped a big black tote bag on the hardwood floor and said, "There's definitely some energy here."

(Teaching Henry how to play Miss Mary Mack, reading *Alice in Wonderland* side by side on the couch, watching endless reruns of *Bewitched* and *I Dream of Genie* and *MASH* on late-night cable. Yes: some energy indeed.)

We had already set up a folding table with five chairs and brought up all of Maybe's requested items. She withdrew a bundle of small, neatly cut sticks from her bag, then a metal lighter. The aroma of cedar filled the room as the sticks caught and started to burn. She handed the bundle to Clara.

"First we cleanse," she said.

Clara's face settled itself into an expression of utmost sincerity. She walked around the perimeter of the room slowly, letting the smoke rise up from her hands.

Next, Maybe withdrew a corked glass bottle from her bag. She carefully poured the concoction into the Swiffer and handed it back to Evelyn.

"Open the windows," she instructed. "Clean."

Evelyn did as she was told.

Maybe tossed the lighter to Bernadette. We'd put a dozen or so candles on the table already. Maybe nodded her head toward them, and Bernadette began lighting.

Maybe picked up the olive oil next, said something softly over it, moved her hand, then handed the bottle to me.

"Anoint the open windows," she said, "then close them again."

The whole thing might have had the danger of veering into the corny, but Maybe prevented that from happening. She was serious and stoic, calm and precise, and under her direction, we felt protected. Confident. Like maybe this would . . . work.

When Clara was done with the cedar, Maybe went over the space again with palo santo, which had a deep, woody smell with a hint of something sweet underneath it, like black licorice. Then she stepped back, considered everything, and nodded her head.

"Take your seats, please," she said.

Maybe sat at one of the ends of the table, Bernadette and I sat on one long side, and Clara and Evelyn sat on the other. Evelyn was across from me. She was doing better, blinking less, less slow with her reaction times. I had found the dress she'd returned in shoved into the back of her closet, crinkled into a tight ball. She was quiet now, and I knew she was trying so hard not to get her hopes up. We were all trying so, so hard not to get our hopes up.

I thought of the priest, suddenly, and the quiet, full silence of the Bleecker crypt, lit by candles, like the attic playroom was now. I thought of the gravel floor, of pleading with Henry to answer me, of saying Evelyn's name like an invocation. I thought of sending Henry away. I thought of a morning last year when Evelyn and I had walked across the park in springtime and she had stopped to pick up a dandelion, closing her eyes so tightly as she made her wish, scattered the seeds with her breath. I knew what she had wished for then and I knew what she would wish for now, had she found another dandelion in the frozen ground. I would wish for the same thing.

"Are we all settled?" Maybe asked, and her voice had shifted, from shopgirl to séance leader. "Clear your minds," she continued, and I squeezed my eyes shut tightly, very aware that there was no way in hell I was going to be able to clear my mind. I was always thinking of at least ten useless things at a time. But I tried. I really tried.

I opened my eyes again when I heard shuffling. Maybe had taken a small handmade contraption out of her tote bag and was assembling it on the table. It was made of wood and looked almost like (morbid, but) a miniature gallows. From the top of the device, Maybe hung a thin, braided piece of rope with a crystal attached. She placed her hands on either side of the device.

"My left hand is *no,*" she said. "My right hand is *yes*. We are contacting the spirit world tonight in an attempt to reach someone very close to us." She looked toward me, expectantly.

"Henry," I said. "We're trying to reach our . . . our Henry."

"Henry, if you are with us tonight, we implore you to make yourself known."

I looked around the table. Bernadette's face was impassive, unreadable. Clara looked a little scared. Evelyn looked sad. I thought I probably looked annoyed. I felt annoyed, and I couldn't say exactly why. Was I annoyed at Henry, for being so hard to reach? Was I annoyed at Evelyn, for being so melodramatic as to fall in love with a ghost? Was I annoyed at myself (always)?

Just then, a gentle breeze blew through the room. One of the pillar candles flickered and extinguished. A trail of smoke traced its way up to the ceiling.

"We welcome you," Maybe said.

Clara looked even more scared now. Bernadette a little less impassive. Evelyn more alert, sitting up straighter in her chair.

"We have questions for you," Maybe said. "But first, will you confirm for us: Is this Henry? Are you here?"

The crystal, hanging from Maybe's little gallows-like contraption, twitched. We all saw it. It caught the light of the candles (the ones that still burned) and threw thousands of little pinpricks of light all across the room. A miniature disco ball. It was beautiful. I would have spent more time in awe of it had I not been absolutely paralyzed with fear, because the crystal was still twitching, the crystal was *moving,* the crystal was *definitely, unquestionably moving,* right toward Maybe's calm, cool, still right hand. The right hand of *yes.*

"Thank you," Maybe said. "We're so happy you could join us, Henry. Are you safe?"

The crystal twitched back to center, twitched back again to point at Maybe's right hand.

"We want you to come back," I said, interjecting before I could stop myself, my voice hitching on the word *back.* "Can you come back, Henry?"

The crystal returned to center and made a sort of circular movement. Maybe looked confused for a moment, then let out a soft chuckle. "I think that means *maybe,*" she said. Then, to me: "Also, no more interrupting."

She returned her attention to the crystal, closed her eyes, took a deep breath.

Across from me, Evelyn shifted in her seat. She was biting her bottom lip so hard I was worried she'd draw blood.

"Henry, will you *try* to come back?" Maybe said.

The crystal made its lackluster, noncommittal circle again, and Clara let out a noise of deep irritation and said, "Henry, seriously! If Evelyn could do it, you can do it! Persephone's footsteps made a doorway; you just have to *find* it."

Maybe made a little face, like *what have I gotten myself into with this family.*

The crystal moved to *yes.*

If I could, for a moment, anthropomorphize the crystal, I would say that the crystal moved to yes rather cheekily, and Clara, mollified, sat back in her chair.

"Maybe he didn't know about the doorway," she said reasonably.

"What doorway?" Maybe asked.

"Nothing," Bernadette said, at the same time Clara responded, "Oh, a long time ago Persephone came to New York to welcome back the spring and wherever she went, her footsteps left weak spots between here and the Underworld, so our sister found one and went down there to find her ghost boyfriend and they got stuck there for three years and then she finally found her way back but Henry didn't so we're worried he's stuck. He's a ghost who lives in our attic and then Evelyn fell in love with him and then Winnie banished him. And also there's this hole in the sky now, can you see it?"

A moment of silence and then Bernadette repeated, rather weakly, "Like I said: nothing."

"A hole in the sky," Maybe said. "No, I haven't seen it."

"That's what I figured," Clara said. "Only we can see it, because we're descended from Persephone."

"Are you stuck, Henry?" Evelyn asked quietly, looking at the crystal. "Are you stuck down there?"

The crystal moved to *yes* (anthropomorphizing again: rather despondently).

"Huh," Maybe said. "You're all very weird."

"Yes, well," Clara said.

"And what's the hole in the sky?" Maybe asked.

"One of Persephone's footsteps, the weak spots. We think when Evelyn came back, it sort of ripped it open," Clara said.

"Right."

"Maybe if Henry came back—*maybe if you would just come back now, Henry!*—he would know how to fix it," Clara said.

"But he can't come back," Evelyn said, still staring at the crystal. "We *tried*."

"You really went to the Underworld?" Maybe asked.

"Yes."

"What was it like?"

Evelyn tore her gaze away from the crystal and looked at Maybe. "Horrible. Beautiful. Miserable. Wonderful. Very overwhelming. If I'm being perfectly candid, I tried to get back last night, and it wouldn't let me through."

"You tried to WHAT?" Bernadette said loudly.

"The doorway is closed to me now," Evelyn said.

"You tried to *go back*?" Bernadette said.

"I can't leave him alone," Evelyn said. "You don't understand—"

"I don't understand? I DON'T UNDERSTAND?"

"Bernadette, *please*—"

"I thought you said January first," I said, and Evelyn looked at me, caught. "You told me January first."

"She told you what?" Bernadette said, glaring at me. "You told her *what*? You were really going to go back? You want to *go back*?"

Evelyn ignored her and turned to me. "I know I told you January first, Winnie, but you don't understand, I can't *sleep*, he doesn't have anybody, he shouldn't be alone down there!"

"No wonder you fell in love with him; you're both *insufferable*," Bernadette said to Evelyn, pushing back from the table so abruptly that she knocked a taper candle over. It fell, harmlessly, toward the center of the table, extinguishing itself on the way down.

"I'm *insufferable*?" Evelyn said, her mouth tight, her eyebrows slanting dangerously downward.

"You're insufferable and inconsiderate and you only think about yourself!"

"We should all try to remain calm," Maybe said. "Did I not say that at the beginning of this? I need to add that to my introductions. Aggression, anger, negative emotions . . . They can all attract things we don't want here."

"The only thing I don't want here is *her*," Bernadette said, spitting her words at Evelyn.

"FINE," Evelyn said, jumping to her feet, storming across the room, stomping her way downstairs.

"Can we talk to John Singer Sargent next?" Clara asked, as if she had not witnessed a single part of the last two minutes. "If nobody has anything else for Henry? No offense, Hen, I've just always wanted to talk to him."

I had never once heard Clara call Henry *Hen*, but I found it not necessary to bring up at the moment. Plus, Clara's request had the added benefit of immediately removing all the tension from the room, which, knowing her, might have been her intention all along. (Or, knowing her, she might have just actually wanted to speak to John Singer Sargent. It was a bit of a toss-up.)

"All right," Maybe said. "I would guess everyone is thoroughly séance'd out. What do you say we close the portal?"

"Sure," Bernadette said, falling back into her seat. "Fine. Whatever."

"Henry, thank you very much for joining us," Maybe said. "Our safe space here, our portal, it will remain open to you, and you only. If you have anything further to tell us, you can send us a message however you are able. Tonight, we'll all leave paper and pencils on our bedside tables. You are free to speak with us there."

"Can he really do that?" I asked.

"Maybe," Maybe said. "For anyone else who may be listening or watching, I now say goodbye to you. May you rest peacefully and easily."

Maybe stood up and, one by one, blew out each of the candles on the table. Then she opened each of the windows. Then she turned to face us, pulled a business card out of her back pocket, tossed it on the table and said to me, "My Venmo's on there. Walk me out?"

We packed up her tote bag and headed downstairs.

"Your family is something else," she said.

"That's a genuinely very kind way of putting it."

"But cool. I like how you all just yell at each other and then get over it."

Because a few moments ago, Bernadette and Evelyn had walked by, holding mugs of tea, talking about their feelings. I heard Bernadette apologize for shouting at Evelyn. I heard Evelyn apologize for trying to go through the doorway again without telling us. I heard Clara (unrelated) listening to a YouTube video about John Singer Sargent, top volume, at the kitchen table. It felt suddenly too hot in the house. I grabbed the closest jacket from a hook on the wall—an old wool Pendleton of my father's—and slipped past Maybe, opening the door.

The night air was frigid. I hadn't felt air that cold in a long time. Had it gotten this cold last winter? Had it ever gotten this cold before? Had it gotten this cold when Henry was alive, before global warming, before we'd burned a hole in the ozone layer (then, okay, mostly repaired it)?

Maybe followed me. Her breath came out in a misty, gray fog. She shut the door behind her and pulled her hood over her head.

"You can tell that something isn't quite right out here," she said quietly. "Where is the hole?"

"Above us," I said, pointing.

She looked up, then nodded her head slowly, as if digesting all the information she'd learned in the past hour.

"Is there really a ghost?" she said finally, turning back to me.

"Henry," I said. "He's always been here."

"Do you have any . . . proof?"

"What kind of proof?"

"Video evidence, sound recordings . . . have you thought about letting anyone come in and look around?"

"Like . . . are you talking about, like . . . *ghost hunters*?"

Maybe shrugged. "Well, yeah. But I probably would have called them something more professional, like paranormal investigators."

"Why would you need a ghost hunter if the ghost doesn't need to be hunted? Because it's sitting on your sofa watching your sister play the piano, and later you're all going to have a game of Monopoly?"

"Could he . . . move the pieces?"

"Most nights, yes. Sometimes he was less solid. And he could only ever touch Evelyn. We were never sure why."

"And you don't want to have proof of this? This could . . . I mean, if what you're saying is *true,* this could change everything . . . Everything we know about science, about life, about death . . ."

"He asked us not to tell anyone," I said. And it sounded simple, it sounded like a cop-out answer, almost, but it was also the truth. He had asked us not to tell anyone and so we hadn't.

"Can your parents see him?"

"Once," I said. "Our mother saw him once."

"So it's just the four of you," she said. "You must be born under full moons or something." This last part, I thought, was a joke, because she smiled afterward, but her smile quickly turned into a sort of grimace. "*Fuck* it's cold. What was that thing about Persephone's footsteps?"

"Oh, right. Um. Nothing."

"No, I'm remembering now . . . you said something to me in Dark Magic. About being descended from the gods. I thought you were just referring to your incredible cheekbones, but now I'm thinking there's something more there . . ."

I touched my face. "Do I really have—"

"Yes. Persephone? Really?"

"I mean, sure. It's just a story, probably."

"Do you really believe that? That it's just a story?"

"No," I admitted. "I mean, not anymore. I used to. But it does appear to be the truth."

"And what about Henry? What's his deal?"

"The Persephone footstep thing. I think she like, essentially blessed this house or the land or something. My family has always lived here. Henry was sort of adopted by Farthings. He moved in and died in the house and then . . . never left."

"Magic," Maybe said.

"I guess, yeah. Magic."

"I'm gonna go. I have a lot to think about."

"Do you want me to call you a car?"

"No, I'll walk," Maybe said. "It's nice to walk, after one of these. I need to clear my head."

"But are you sure, it's late and—"

Maybe withdrew a slim canister from her coat pocket. It was the same brand of pepper spray I had. I had no doubt that, with Maybe wielding it, it would actually work as a self-defense tool.

"Well, thanks," I said. What did you say to someone after they performed a séance in your attic? "I'll, um, Venmo you."

"You better," she said brightly. "I know where you live." She got serious, then, and for a moment bit at her lower lip, then stopped, then looking up at the sky again, her face clouding over with worry. "John Singer Sargent," she said.

"What about him?"

"You're like that painting. The four of you. *The Daughters of Edward Darley Boit.*"

"I've never heard of it."

"Ask Clara to show you." She looked down at me again, her expression still worried. "You'll keep me posted? On everything?"

"Oh, yeah," I promised. "I'll text you."

"Great. See you, ghost girl."

She skipped down the stairs, blending into the darkness, starting off down the street without so much as a final look back at me.

I was freezing but I found I couldn't move right away. Instead I stood there, letting the cold rush over me, my own thoughts growing darker and darker with each degree my skin dropped. If I stayed out there long enough, unmoving, would I become a human statue? Would I—as my father said whenever one of us pulled a funny face—stay stuck like that forever?

I would never know, as the door opened a moment later and Bernadette popped her head out, wrinkling her nose at the temperature.

"Will you get your ass inside?" she said. "Your face is blue. Like *literally* blue."

"Something is seriously wrong with our family," I said.

"Yes," she agreed. "I'll make you some tea."

I did ask Clara to show me the painting later, while she was brushing her teeth. She pulled it up on her phone and turned the screen around.

"Oh," I said.

"I know," she said around a mouthful of toothpaste. "That's part of the reason I wanted to talk to him."

The next morning I found Evelyn sitting in front of the piano bench, not playing, staring down at her hands resting on the keys. We had all decided to go to Todd's for breakfast and I had been sent up to fetch her. She had been sleeping later than she usually did, these days. In truth, we all had, and I had the sneaking suspicion it was due to the tear in the sky, that it was somehow leaching our energy from us . . .

"Evie?" I said, standing behind her in the attic.

"Can you come here?" she said softly, not turning around. "Will you sit next to me?"

She slid over to make room for me, and I sat next to her on the piano bench. She folded her hands on her lap.

"What's wrong?" I asked.

"Will you play something?"

"I don't know how to play anything."

"'Chopsticks,'" she said. "You know how to play 'Chopsticks.'"

I wanted to question her, but I also wanted breakfast, and I sensed the fastest way to the latter was to skip the former.

I played "Chopsticks."

I was far from musically inclined, and even the simple, staccato melody of "Chopsticks" came out rough underneath my fingers.

When I was done I looked at her and said, "Okay?"

"I thought it might be broken," she said.

"What do you mean?"

"I thought maybe there was something wrong with the piano, because . . . I can't play."

"There's nothing wrong with the piano."

"But I can't play," she repeated.

"I don't understand."

"There's either something wrong with the piano or something wrong with *me*."

"You're not making any sense, Evelyn."

"Watch."

She put her hands back on the keys and began to play . . .

But no sound came out.

The keys moved as they should, and I could hear the heavy, muted *thunk* of each one dipping down and popping back up, but the piano itself remained silent.

After a few moments of this, Evelyn removed her hands and looked at me, her eyes wide and fearful.

"It's the tear," she said. "It's whatever's coming out of the tear, Winnie. It's doing something to me. And Mom, the other night, talking about Henry. I think it's doing something to her, too."

"We don't know that . . ."

"I know that. I *feel* this . . . heaviness . . . This *lethargy*. Do you feel it, too?"

"I just feel cold," I said. "And tired, I guess."

"It's the tear. It's all the tear."

She turned back to the piano, gave the keys a few more noiseless taps. "This is how I got in," she whispered.

"To the Underworld?"

"I played this song. A secret song. I don't even really know how I knew it, it just came to me . . . And when I tried to play it again, the other night, I couldn't remember it. And then I couldn't play *anything*."

"We're going to figure this out, Evelyn," I said, and she turned her body toward me and looked into my eyes, her own eyes wide and frightened.

"Are you sure? Are you *sure*?"

And I wasn't, of course, but I lied to her again.

I was getting so good at lying.

IX

If you were liked by a god, favored by a god, related to a god, the great-great-great-great-great-great-great-granddaughter of Persephone, for example, the daughter of a daughter of a daughter

of a daughter

of a daughter

of a daughter

of someone with great, mythical power—

She might bestow a gift upon you.

She might bless you with the craft of weaving, making your fingers long and bendy and untiring, making your eyesight good enough to see all the little stitches in your work.

She might kiss your forehead and leave you with the power of foresight, women's intuition, a prescience that is never quite explainable.

She might give you the power of opening up a doorway, of closing one again, of sending someone through…

We did all sleep with paper and pencils next to our beds, but Henry didn't write any magical messages from beyond the grave, not the night of the séance or the morning I sat with Evelyn at her piano or any other night that week.

The tear in the sky was still getting bigger and it sort of shimmered around the edges, catching the light in strange ways. I had started to think of it as a black hole, or maybe a reverse black hole, spitting things out of it instead of drawing things into it. But if it got bigger, would there be a reversal? Would it magnetize, turning on like a vacuum, sucking us all in, body by body, depositing us unceremoniously in the Underworld, pulling us in and spitting us out, from one universe to the next?

Evelyn was right; it was affecting all of us.

It was hard to sleep, hard to concentrate. We felt like we were walking through thick fog. I kept finding our mother staring out windows at nothing. She still couldn't see it, but I knew she felt its presence just like we did. The only one who seemed blissfully unbothered was our father, and I knew it was because he didn't have any Farthing blood—any *god* blood—running through his veins.

Bernadette, too, was on edge. I kept peeking over her shoulder to find her on her phone, frantically searching for new information on Melinoë. Her obsession with the goddess of madness had been rekindled, and she had taken to spitting out random facts with a fevered intensity.

Did you know some people thought she could shape-shift?

Did you know the ancient Greeks used to perform rituals in order to protect themselves from her nightmares?

Some people confuse her with Hecate, who was the goddess of magic, ghosts, and necromancy. But they were different people. Maybe they were friends, though? I'm going to see if I can find anything about them being friends.

Clara had started slipping into my bed at night; we'd browse through her mythology book together or talk or not talk. I sometimes was able to fall asleep with her beside me, but she was always gone when I woke up.

"Are you worried that Evelyn can't play the piano anymore?" I asked her one night.

"I'm worried about a lot of things," Clara said simply. "I'd like to just, like . . . go shopping. You know?"

"God, I'd really love that," I agreed.

She snuggled into my side, pressing her cold nose against my shoulder. She was wearing a flannel nightgown, somewhat old-fashioned, a gift from Aunt Bea last Christmas. We'd all gotten matching ones. Black Watch, that was the name of the tartan pattern. It had a bib collar with delicate lace. Bernadette had declared it *very punk*. Evelyn had cooed over its softness. I had never worn mine.

"Since when do you call him *Hen*?" I asked.

"Just sometimes, late at night, when he used to watch me paint," she said.

"Could you ever imagine . . ."

"Kissing him?" she guessed. "God no. How gross."

"Yeah, I just don't get it."

"But love is weird like that. You know? It doesn't make sense to question it."

"I guess so."

She wriggled closer to me, burrowing into the blankets.

Sometimes Clara was wise beyond her years and sometimes, now, she was exactly fourteen, younger, even, a little girl in a flannel nightgown who was, maybe, just as scared as I was.

"I think I might actually sleep tonight," she said.

"I think I might actually go for a walk."

"Are you sure? It's getting late."

"I'll bring the pepper spray."

"Are you going back to the crypts?"

"I think my crypt-dwelling days are behind me."

"Good. It was creepy down there. Keep me posted?"

"I'll text you every five blocks."

Outside, the tear in the sky glowed and pulsed and spewed freezing air over our house.

I walked quickly, trying to get away from it, feeling its presence like a physical thing, like it had its own gravity, its own magnetic pull. I knew it had done something to Evelyn, taken her music away from her, and I was worried it would do something to me next, or to one of my sisters. I was worried it wouldn't stop getting bigger. I was worried it would swallow all of us up.

I was on autopilot, not making any conscious decisions about where I was walking but also completely unsurprised when I ended up at Dark Magic, pulling the door open and letting myself inside, immediately calmed by its now-familiar scent of lavender and sage.

"Welcome to Dark Magic; we're having a buy one, get one sale on pocket crystals," said a girl with platinum-blond hair and an eyebrow piercing.

"What's a pocket crystal?" I asked.

"It's a crystal that can fit in your pocket," she said, and managed to not make me feel silly for asking such an obvious question.

"It's okay, Gillian, she's not an actual customer," Maybe said, coming around a corner. My stomach did a little flip-flop that I tried my best to ignore.

"I actually am, if you'll remember," I said. "I bought that Ouija board."

"Ouija boards are fun," Gillian announced. "I swear one time I talked to Elvis."

"What brings you to our fine establishment on such a cold and blustery night?" Maybe asked me.

"I thought maybe you wanted to go for a walk?"

Maybe considered this, looked around the store for a moment, noting the number of customers (a young girl checking out said pocket crystals, two men browsing a table of books).

"Gillian, keep an eye on things?"

"I've never met a friend of Maybe's before," Gillian said, leaning against a cabinet. "What's she like outside of the store?"

"You don't have to answer that," Maybe said.

"She's pretty cool," I said. "She did a séance for us."

"Oh, you're the séance girl. Jon was telling me about you."

"There are no secrets in the workplace," Maybe said dryly.

"Well," Gillian said, "not *this* workplace. Maybe other ones."

"I'm going to get my coat. Text me if you need anything," Maybe said.

"I will hold down the proverbial fort," Gillian said.

Maybe wore her long coat with the hood again, and if we weren't in the middle of Manhattan I would have said she was more suited for Middle Earth, a strange creature on a quest to destroy a ring. Her skin was very pale and her cheeks got red quickly and I found it was easier to not look at her. Looking at her was too distracting.

"I take it he hasn't come back?" she asked after we'd walked a bit in silence. My phone was buzzing in my pocket and I knew it was Clara, admonishing me for not texting her yet, but I ignored it. It was too cold to take my hands out of my pockets and type a response.

"Nope. Do you know anything about people losing their, like . . . abilities?"

"Abilities?" she questioned.

"Evelyn can't play the piano anymore. I think it has something to do with the tear in the sky."

"Huh. Like it's . . ."

"I don't know. Maybe . . . sucking something out of her?"

"Her life force?"

"Her soul?"

"Her youth?"

"No. Maybe. I don't know," I said.

"Maybe she's just stressed. It seems like you're all pretty stressed?"

"When she presses the keys, no sound comes out."

"That *does* feel like something more than stress."

"Yeah . . ."

"What about Clara? Has she started painting anything else?"

"No, nothing."

"That makes sense; she's probably worried about painting any more prophecies. What about Bernadette? Is the medication still working out?"

"How do you know so much about my family?"

"When I like someone, I pay attention," Maybe said simply, and I tried to ignore my itchy palms, the blush I knew was crawling up my neck (but, thankfully, hidden by my jacket).

We had, at that point, walked in a big square and ended up back in front of Dark Magic.

"Thanks for the walk," I said.

"Of course. But I'm not counting this as a date, just so you know."

"Oh, I wasn't . . . I mean I didn't . . ."

"A walk around the block is nice, and I'm down for it pretty much any time, but if I'm clocked in at work, I can't *also* be on a date. That defies the logical rules of space and time."

"No, no, you don't have to—"

"Catch you later!"

Maybe walked back in the store without waiting for me to finish my sentence (which was probably a good thing, since I had no idea what the end of my sentence would have been).

My phone buzzed in my pocket again. The most recent of seven texts from Clara read *Date over already?* Judging from the other six messages, she had been closely tracking my walk around the block and obviously figured out that it both started and ended at Dark Magic.

I typed a quick response and started walking home: It wasn't a date and aren't you supposed to be sleeping?

We can sleep when we're dead, she wrote, and then, a few minutes later, when I hadn't responded: which might be sooner rather than later!!!

She included an assortment of goofy-faced emojis and I couldn't help—even as I got closer to home and the black mark in the sky grew heavier and heavier—but smile.

When I got home, everyone was up and sitting around the attic, waiting for me.

"Clara's had a feeling," Bernadette said, yawning.

"Remember when I said I thought I might actually sleep tonight?" Clara said. "Well, I was clearly wrong about that. Because I was *about* to go to sleep and then my brain started whirring and I kept thinking, I mean I kept having this feeling, well, really I've been having it the last few days, and right now specifically—"

"Spit it out, Clara," Bernie said gently.

"My painting came to me in a dream, right?" Clara continued. "In a *nightmare*. So many of my paintings do . . . And Melinöe is the goddess of nightmares. And we've always said, right, I mean maybe we were mostly joking but we've always *said* our nightmares were a message from her. And maybe that's actually true? And maybe if you're a god, or you're related to a god, those things you do, like painting, like music, they become kind of magic? Because they're sort of *from* the gods or messages from gods, maybe? Or *gifts* from them."

"What are you getting at?" I asked.

Clara turned to Evelyn and said, "You said you used the piano to open the doorway, right? That you played some song, and that's how you got in?"

"Yes . . ." Evelyn said. "I don't know how I knew what to play, it just came to me . . ."

"Like a message," Clara said excitedly. "That's your gift, Evie, *music,* and it's magical."

"But now you can't play anything," I said.

"It feels like something was *taken* from me," Evelyn whispered. "Like this black mark, this tear . . . like it's doing something to us . . ."

"I've felt really tired," Bernadette said, thinking. "And like . . .

almost like . . . *nothing.* I've felt nothing. I tried to write in my journal last night before bed, and I just kept staring at the empty page. Like before I had all this *anger* and these *emotions* and now I'm just . . . empty."

Sometimes Clara just knew things; she had always, always just known things.

"You think you can use your painting to open the doorway," I said slowly, processing, trying to understand.

"Like maybe we were given these gifts, or . . . or . . . *inherited* these gifts," Clara said, getting more animated as she struggled to find the right words. "Gifts handed down to us right from Persephone, from Melinöe. Gifts that can *do* things. Open a doorway. Like Evelyn's music, like my painting . . ."

"I'm worried our family has jumped right off the deep end," Bernadette said, mostly to herself, but I saw Evelyn almost crack a smile in response (and these days, Evelyn *almost* cracking a smile was a little bit of a miracle).

"But it makes sense, too, right?" Clara said.

"It does, Cece. It really does."

And it did make sense.

It did.

But what I found myself fixating on, what I wanted to say was . . .

What's my *gift*?

But maybe I was scared of the answer.

Because I didn't say that.

I said, "So how do you do it?"

And in the end it wasn't an incantation or a ritual or a big dramatic bloodletting—it was a quiet offering, a meditation, a promise that you were willing to give up the thing you most loved to get something even greater, to *go* somewhere greater (or, in our case, to call someone home).

And Clara gave up her painting.

We did it in the attic, of course, candles lit, Clara standing by her painting while the rest of us sat in a semicircle on the floor. It felt very witchlike, very *The Craft,* very *Charmed,* which was fitting, because there were four girls in each of those (even if they had to kill off Prue to bring the fourth sister in).

"I think you all should close your eyes," Clara said.

"What? No. Don't be ridiculous." Bernadette.

"Can you stop stalling, *please*?" Evelyn.

"Why do you want us to do that, Clara?" Me.

"It just feels a little personal," Clara said. "I don't know. You're all just sitting there *watching* me. It's distracting. It's weird. I wish I were an only child."

"I *was* an only child," Bernie said. "For two whole years. It was delightful."

"Oh, you don't remember anything from before I was born, don't be a dweeb," Evelyn said. "We'll close our eyes, Clara, okay? Will you hurry up now?"

"Yes," Clara agreed. "Thank you."

My sisters closed their eyes and I mostly closed my eyes, watching Clara through a blur of eyelashes as she turned to her painting. She took a breath so deep I heard it and saw it, her tiny shoulders rising and falling at least two inches.

And I will never be able to accurately describe what happened next.

In the flicker of the candlelight it was magical, incredible . . .

Clara reached a hand out and suddenly her painting was *opening,* the canvas swinging toward her like an actual door, and a light so enormous and bright was coming out of it; I had to actually close my eyes, and turn my face away, and shield my face with my arm, and even then the light was painful and hot and I thought I heard Clara yelp and I sort of groped around for her, trying to help her, but of course I couldn't see anything, I could barely even move . . .

And then I smelled it.

And then I smelled *him*.

The familiar, missed, welcome smell of jasmine.

Then his voice: "Oh, Clara. Your painting."

And it was Henry.

It was Henry.

Henry, Henry, Henry.

Henry was back.

X

Melinöe was born in the Underworld, amongst the dead things and the demons and the flaming blood rivers that boil souls. Amongst the world her mother had been stolen into but grew to love, amongst the souls who spent their eternal rest in the Elysian Fields. She was made the goddess of ghosts and it was fitting, for her, because she loved the ghosts, she loved them deeply, and she swore to always protect them and care for them and look after them.

Of course sometimes, rarely, a ghost wouldn't make it to the Underworld. A ghost would get stuck behind, trapped in our world, where Melinöe could not reach them. For even though her mother spent half her year walking on our soil, Melinöe herself was eternally imprisoned below.

Did she miss them, then, these ghosts she could not reach, these souls she was forced to live without?

Yes. Yes, I think she missed them. I think she pined for them. I think she hated every moment they were forced to be apart…

The five of us sat on the floor, our witchy circle expanded.

The five of us, again:

Girl, girl, girl, girl, ghost.

As it always had been.

Henry held Evelyn's hand in his lap.

It had been a bit of a shock.

It had been a *lot* of a shock.

He looked . . .

Alive.

More alive than I had ever seen him.

When he'd come through the doorway, when he'd come through Clara's painting, there had been a sound. A loud sound, a ripping sound. When we looked through the window, we could see that the tear in the sky had gotten bigger.

A lot bigger.

"Right," Henry said. "We'll deal with that in a moment."

And he'd hugged Evelyn, who'd risen to meet him, a long hug that made me uncomfortable, unsure of where to look. And then he'd hugged me, and it was such a shock that I actually forgot to breathe for a moment, and when he pulled away I started choking, and Bernadette had to slap me on the back to get my lungs started up again.

"You touched her? You hugged her? You can touch her?" Clara had said, blinking rapidly like the light had hurt her eyes and she was still recovering, and then Henry had hugged *her* and then Bernadette and then we had all sat down and been mostly speechless, just processing, just trying to understand.

"How are you this solid?" I asked finally.

"I don't know," Henry said. "Something about the doorway?"

"How come you couldn't follow me through?" Evelyn asked, and I saw him squeeze her hand tighter.

"I don't know that, either," Henry said. "But I *think* it's because of the tear in the sky. I sort of . . . *fit* now. And I didn't before."

I couldn't stop shivering, but I wasn't cold.

Henry had hugged me. Henry had *touched* me. For our entire lives, the only one he'd been able to touch was Evelyn. I felt like my brain was short-circuiting. I couldn't even look him in the eyes, I just kept remembering how horrible I'd been when I last saw him.

"I called to you," I said, staring at my hands in my lap, twisting a ring around and around my pointer finger. "We used the Ouija board, we left paper and pens by our bedside . . ."

"I heard everything," Henry said. "The crypt, the temple, the closet . . . It *killed* me that I couldn't find a way to answer."

"No pun intended," Clara said, and giggled at her own joke.

"Can you see it in the Underworld?" Bernadette asked. From her place on the floor, she could see out the window, and she looked out it now, up at the black mark.

"Yes," Henry said. "It's affecting things there, too."

"It's affecting *us,*" Clara said. "Evelyn can't play the piano anymore. Gosh, I probably can't paint anymore. I didn't even think of that. Did you guys think of that?"

"Deep breaths, Cece," Bernadette said, turning back to the room. "Obviously, we're going to have to figure out what to do about the tear. But maybe not tonight, you know? Maybe tonight we can just be happy that Henry's back."

"*I'm* happy that Henry's back," Clara said.

"I'm so happy," Evelyn said, and truly, she was glowing.

And I was happy, of course I was so, so happy, but I still couldn't make myself look at him.

Our mother woke up crying in the middle of the night. I knew because Clara was still awake, and still sleeping in my room, and she nudged me until I woke up, too. We could hear her through the vent (old house, old vents, and in certain places you could play telephone with other people, whispering into the grates, hearing each other perfectly).

Did she have a nightmare? Had Melinoë delivered a message to her, whispering into her ear as she tried to sleep?

Our father was awake, too, comforting her, saying low, soothing words too quiet to catch. Clara and I looked at each other scared and wide-eyed until, finally, our mother stopped crying. The house fell silent again. Clara fell asleep. It was three in the morning. I was utterly, devastatingly, awake.

I stared at the ceiling as if, with enough concentration, I could burn a hole into Evelyn's room and see her curled up with Henry, sleeping soundly.

Next to me, Clara was breathing heavily, twitching a little, fully immersed in dreamland.

I texted Maybe. She would want to know that Henry was back. After a solid six minutes of trying to come up with a witty or clever way of saying it, I settled on: Hi. Henry's back. (Neither witty *nor* clever—perfect.)

I didn't know if I really expected her to be awake or not, but she responded less than a minute later. My heart did a little flutter kick when I saw her start to type back, those three dots of infinite potential.

Damn, that's great! How did you
manage it?

Clara had to sacrifice her painting. It was a whole thing.

Aw, man. Poor Clara.

The tear in the sky also got bigger. When he came back.

A bit of a good news, bad news, situation then.

Maybe one day I'll only have good news for you.

I will be waiting patiently. Now get some sleep, ghost girl. It's late. xx

I fell asleep warm and quickly and buzzing with those two little letters: xx.

In the morning, I caught Mom alone in the kitchen, sipping from a mug of coffee, staring out the window at the jasmine bushes that lined our backyard, dead-like and bare in the winter. They would return with a vengeance in spring; no matter how aggressively Dad cut them back, they'd blossom and explode all over again.

She turned, then, sensing me behind her. She still looked so sad. Her face was red and puffy and it scared me, how dark her eyes were.

"Good morning, third daughter," she said.

"Hi, Mom."

"I didn't sleep that great. Did you?"

"Not really, no."

"Why do you think that is?"

"I'm not sure."

"Your aunt isn't sure, either. We're both a little out of sorts, it seems, but neither of us knows why."

Was the tear in the sky affecting Aunt Bea in Vermont?

Did my mother and aunt have gifts, too, that were being taken away from them?

Should I tell my mother everything, every single that had ever happened, starting from the very first time I could remember Henry, making funny faces at me over the railing of my crib?

Should I tell her about the tear in the sky and ask her how to fix it, beg her to fix it, pray that she knew how to fix it?

I wanted to, part of me desperately, desperately wanted to, but another part of me wouldn't allow it, wouldn't allow myself to admit just how much I had fucked up, didn't want her to know what I had said to Henry, how I had sent him away, how Evelyn had followed him, how we had dragged her back again, how the sky had split open.

No, I couldn't. I couldn't. I—

"There are downsides to this Persephone thing, aren't there?" she said, interrupting my spiraling thoughts, smiling almost sadly at me, like she knew there was so much I wasn't telling her but also knew you couldn't make a Farthing girl tell you anything she didn't want to.

"Every so often," I replied.

And she turned back to the windows, back to the jasmine bushes, and I watched her gaze move upward, up up up to the tear in the sky, which was only getting bigger.

Henry and Evelyn had so far spent the entire morning curled up on the attic couch, arms around each other, whispering and giggling.

"Barf," Bernadette announced around ten, when she finally pulled herself out of bed and found Clara and me in the kitchen. "Barf, barf, barf."

"Give them a break, Bernie, he's just come back from the dead," I said.

"Still dead, actually," Clara said. "Although he does *seem* more solid, right?"

"And he can touch us, now," Bernadette said. "That's just weird. You can't just *touch* someone after twenty years of not touching them. Where are Mom and Dad?"

"Brunch and tennis with the Zimmermans," Clara recited automatically. "Not expected back until after two. I've compiled a list of questions for Henry."

"Let's hear 'em," Bernie said, pouring herself a glass of water.

Clara took a neatly folded piece of paper from her mythology book, which was closed on the counter in front of her, cleared her throat, and started reading. "Can we all go and see the Underworld? Do you know how to fix the hole in the sky? Is the Underworld anything like Dante's *Inferno*? Did you meet any famous dead people? Do you have to get a job in the Underworld? Are dead girls better at braiding hair than living girls? Is there a river you have to pay a token to be ferried across? Are you sure we can't go and see it? Oh, that last one is assuming that he said no to the first one."

"What circle of Hell would you want to live on?" Bernadette asked. "If you, like, had to."

"Limbo, obviously," I said. "Nothing ever happens there."

"Heresy," Clara replied. "I'd like to be trapped in the flaming tombs. I'm always cold."

"Avarice," Bernadette said. "It's basically a big workout class." Then, to me: "Of course *you* would pick the place where nothing ever happens. Boring."

"Sorry if I don't want to be burned alive," I mumbled.

We heard the footsteps on the stairs at the same time. Two sets of footsteps. Did Henry have footsteps before he went to the Underworld? I genuinely couldn't remember.

They came into the kitchen holding hands. Henry was as bright and solid down here as he had been upstairs. He seemed to be in an excellent mood. Evelyn went to pour herself some coffee and he sat down next to Clara and tapped her book.

"Nothing in there is accurate," he said, picking up the book, scanning through it briefly. He smirked at something, then bit his lower lip and said, "All right—*hardly* anything in here is accurate. There *is* a flaming blood river that boils souls. But this makes it sound much more dramatic than it actually is."

"Phlegethon," Clara whispered reverently.

"Bless you," Bernadette replied.

"I just have a few dozen questions, actually, if you're available," Clara said, rustling her paper, which I saw now was absolutely covered in writing.

"Maybe later," Henry said. "I'm still sort of adjusting. I thought we could go for a walk or something?"

"But you can't go for walks," Bernadette said.

"It's different now," Henry said. "I'm not tied to the attic anymore."

"How do you know?" Bernie pressed.

"I just know, I guess."

This was interesting. This was something none of us had considered.

Would he be able to . . . stay here now? Go to college with Evelyn? She would become the weird loner kid who actively refused to make any friends, join any study groups, trudge across campus with anyone to the school cafeteria. People would whisper about her. *What's with that girl who always looks like she'd holding hands with the air?*

Would he age now, too? Or would Evelyn celebrate birthday after birthday, blooming, blossoming. She'd graduate college and Henry would still be seventeen. She'd turn thirty, thirty-five, forty. And Henry would still be a teenager, still invisible, still as dead then as he was now, even if he didn't really look dead, not to us, not at all. There was even color in his cheeks, as if somewhere in the Underworld, he had found a good supply of blood to inject into his veins.

He looked in my direction now. He had a shy smile on his face. "You're staring at me, Winnie."

"What? No? I wasn't?"

"You were," my sisters said at the exact same time. A chorus of annoyance.

"Well, I *wasn't*."

"I think maybe we should talk?" Henry said. "Alone?"

"Whatever. Not now. Sure. I don't care."

"Who is Maybe? I heard her come through very strongly during the séance. Very funny, by the way, that you all had a séance. Well—sort of funny, sort of dangerous. You could have summoned a demon."

"There are really *demons*?" Clara said, picking up a pencil and scribbling more questions on her list.

"There was already a hole in the sky at that point," Bernadette pointed out. "Can't get much worse than that."

"And now you're back, so we can get everything sorted out," Clara said. "Fix the tear in the sky, repair whatever's going on between you and Winnie, get back to life."

"There's nothing going on between us," I said, trying to keep my voice light and airy but managing, I was sure, the exact opposite.

"Maybe's a cute girl who works at a magic shop," Clara said.

"Not, like, card tricks," Bernie clarified.

"They probably do have card tricks," Clara said. "It's a really big store."

"I think I hear my phone ringing," I said, leaving the kitchen even as Clara said, "I don't hear anything."

I was already dressed, so I pulled on a pair of Bernadette's boots (closest to the door), a jacket, a hat, and pushed out into the cold air before I (or my sisters) could change my mind.

The tear in the sky was—I couldn't think of a better way to describe it—*writhing*. Pulsating. No longer just shimmering around the edges but actually moving, the black perimeter changing shape, coming together then wriggling apart again. It was about the size of a plane on its descent, taking up a fair amount of sky over our brownstone, looking exactly like it might land on top of us.

I tried not to look at it.

I needed to walk, and I kept my head down as I set off toward Central Park, letting my feet lead the way while trying to keep every and any thought from entering my consciousness.

The farther I got from the brownstone, the better I felt. I hadn't realized how *heavy* my body had become until that heaviness dissipated. To get out from underneath the black tear was like breaking through the surface of a great body of water, taking a breath after years of not breathing, feeling the pressure on my skin lessen and lessen until I felt so light I might float away.

With my head mostly down (just aware enough to avoid crashing into anything), I didn't realize where I was going until I got there, out of breath and slightly sweaty even in the frigid winter air.

The reservoir.

Of course.

I had maybe seen enough of the reservoir to last me a good lifetime or two, but my directional subconscious apparently had other ideas.

It was gray, very cold, and when the wind blew it felt like a personal attack. I pulled the collar of my coat as high as it would go and sat down on a bench that, I quickly realized, was covered in a thin sheet of ice.

The reservoir was frozen over.

If Evelyn were here, she would have said something poetic and sweet like, *It looks like a postcard.*

If Bernadette were here, she would have said something witty and dark like, *I wonder how many dead bodies are in there.*

If Clara were here, she would have said something innocent and completely random like, *Do you know Dante Alighieri dedicated most of his poetry to a girl named Beatrice? Like Aunt Bea! Isn't that a weird coincidence?*

But I was alone.

Or—I *was* alone.

Because just then, Henry sat down beside me, cracking the ice on the bench, bringing with him the faint but beautiful smell of jasmine.

It was so strange to see him here, so far from the attic. For a long time I just looked at him, trying to process the fact of his existence. I reached out and poked his arm. He smiled, then shrugged.

"I know, it's hard to believe."

"But *how*?" I asked. "How are you *here*?"

"I don't think any ghost has gone there and come back again," Henry said. "I imagine there will be some . . . side effects?"

"And this is one of them?"

He shrugged again, then turned toward the reservoir. The expression on his face was hard to read.

"I thought I'd never see this place again," he said after a long silence. "We used to go ice-skating here," Henry said. "My sisters and me."

You weren't allowed to ice-skate here anymore. Instead, everyone crowded into Rockefeller Center and rented cheap ice skates and hoped not to fall on their ass.

More importantly, though: Henry had sisters. Henry had *sisters*.

It was the first new piece of knowledge I'd learned about Henry in years. Henry, who was so careful and so private and so reserved.

Henry had sisters.

"You had sisters," I whispered, and he nodded slightly.

"Three of them. Just like you."

"Will you tell me about them?"

He smiled, and I knew, as he looked out at the reservoir, that he was remembering them. That maybe he was *letting* himself remember them, for the first time in a long time.

"Emma, Lucy, and Olive. We were all very close in age. I was the oldest, Lucy and Olive were the youngest—they were twins—and Emma was in the middle. Our father was a doctor. Our mother was an expert embroiderer. She had years-long commission waits for her work. Pillows, chairs, curtains, she did everything. We had a dog. Aramis."

"*The Three Musketeers*," I said.

Henry laughed. "We were obsessed with it. And obsessed with that dog; we took him everywhere with us. He'd slip and slide all around us while we skated. Emma was the best. She looked like a ballerina out there, which was ironic, because on dry land, she was quite clumsy."

He paused, lost in thought. I elbowed him gently.

"I know you all want to know how I died," he said. "And I didn't want to tell you because . . . it's sad. It's terrible. It's . . . private, I guess. But that's silly. It was a lifetime ago. Literally. A hundred years ago. I was born in 1901. Emma in 1903. The twins in 1906. And everything was pretty quiet. Everything was nice. My childhood was . . . peaceful. And then right around 1918 . . ."

"Oh," I said.

"My father was a doctor," Henry continued. "He brought it home early. We all got sick. My parents died first, then my sisters . . . They say thirty thousand people died in New York, but now they think that number is so much higher . . . The Farthings took me in. Our neighbors. Even though . . . Even though I was sick, too. They were taking a big risk. I stayed in the attic, away from them. They gave me a safe place to die, a quiet place . . . I'll always love them for that. I'll always love all the Farthings."

He smiled at me, his eyes watery.

"Henry . . ." I whispered.

"By then, the city was already running out of graves. There were mass graves, illegal graves, a panicked disposal of the dead. The Farthings didn't want that for me. They dug a place for me in the backyard, by the jasmine bushes. They put my body inside it as the first light of dawn was spreading across the sky."

"The jasmine bushes," I said, realizing.

Henry was buried beneath the jasmine bushes in our backyard.

Henry, who always smelled like jasmine, even now, even in the freezing cold.

Henry, whose bones were underneath the dirt where my sisters and I had sat and played dolls, sat and played Matchbox cars, sat and fought and loved each other and cried and laughed.

Had he looked out of the attic windows and watched us, so close to his remains?

I felt how I felt after a glass of wine, drunk quickly and secretively on Christmas Eve, hiding in a closet with Bernadette. Lightheaded and giddy, like my head could detach from my body and float upward like a balloon. Never had Henry volunteered so much information about his life. Never had we even thought to ask.

"It's not a very noteworthy death," Henry said a moment later, when it became clear that I was too stunned to speak. "A lot of people died. I wasn't anything special. Later, years later, they made up a skipping song about it. Jump rope. I would watch them in the street outside my window." He cleared his throat and recited:

I had a little bird
And its name was Enza
I opened the window
And in-flew-Enza

"What is *wrong* with people?" I whispered.

"No, no, it wasn't like that . . . It was a way to talk about the impossible," he explained. "We're always trying to find ways to talk about the impossible."

I felt the wine I hadn't actually drunk sloshing around in my stomach, turning sour. I worried for a moment that I might be sick. I wanted to hug Henry forever. I wanted to skate away across the frozen reservoir and never come back. I wanted to disappear. I wanted to be a ghost myself, done with this mortal life and free to roam around forever, clanking chains and jumping out at people, saying *boo*.

"I'm so sorry for what I said to you," I managed. "The most horrible, awful—"

"Winnie, no. *I'm* sorry. I wasn't able to see past my own selfishness. I should have talked to her, I never should have . . ." He shook his head, trailing off. "I was letting myself live in a fantasy. Just for a little while. I know now, obviously, how wrong that was."

A cold wind cut through the park then, slicing through our clothes and making us shiver.

"Do you feel that?" I asked him. "The wind?"

"I do," he said, smiling. "It's so nice, actually."

I thought of Pinocchio, so insistent on becoming a real boy. Had Henry become a real boy? I could almost see his pulse through the pale skin of his neck as he sat beside me, closing his eyes, turning his face into the wind. But it might not have been his pulse at all. A trick of the light. Wishful thinking. My own beating heart, obscuring my vision, causing the corners of my eyes to waver slightly with each thrum of blood sent pumping through my veins.

"What's going to happen?" I asked—or more accurately, I begged, I pleaded. *Please tell me we aren't all going to die because it will sort of be my fault and I don't think I could recover from the guilt of killing absolutely everyone in the world, but I'd be dead myself at that point, and I don't think you can heal from trauma if you're dead yourself.*

"It will be okay," Henry said.

"But how do you know that?"

"Because I know," Henry said. "Because I can fix it."

"You know how to fix it?"

"I do. And you can't tell them, okay? You can't tell them."

"I promise," I said, aware that my promises weren't worth

much to anyone these days, were really just the ghosts of promises, maybe, which is why only Henry took a chance with them. A ghost for a ghost. An eye for an eye.

"It will keep getting bigger and bigger," Henry said. "Eventually, it will get so big that it will reach the house. The house is magic, the land . . . Persephone's footsteps. The tear is drawn to it. Drawn to *you.*"

"And what will happen then?"

"Nothing will happen. Because I can fix it."

"How?"

"It's complicated. Just trust me."

"No way. No, you have to tell me. You have to tell me what will happen and you have to tell me what you're going to do to stop it."

He nodded. "Okay. Fine. The tear will sort of . . . *merge* with the house. It was Persephone's domain, down there, for a long time, and she's the one who planted the jasmine bushes, and she's your relative and . . . Those things are trying to get back together now. To come back together."

"Okay. So what does that *mean*?"

"It means . . . the two points, here and there . . . the Underworld is sort of like a mirror image of our world. And those two points would come together. Like I said—*merge*. Like a . . . oh what's that famous painting. M. C. Escher. With the stairs, you know. A sort of . . . paradox. You'd all be trapped inside this infinite loop. In between worlds."

"I understand why you didn't want to tell me," I said. "Because it's terrifying."

"It's a bit terrifying, yes," Henry agreed.

"I guess we could leave, though? We could all leave before that happened?"

"I've thought about that. And I think it would pull you back in. I don't think any of you—as Farthings—would be able to get away."

"Great. That's really great. So how are you going to stop it?"

"I'm going to patch the hole."

"Oh. Okay. That's easier than I thought it would be . . ."

"It sounds easy, yes," Henry said, and he smiled sadly. "How do I explain it . . . So basically. I lived *here,* right. When I was alive, and then after I'd died. And then, more recently, I lived *there.* For quite a long time."

"Evelyn said three years . . ."

"Ah, but I got there before her. So I was *there,* and I was *here* . . . and now I'm back here again."

"Okay?"

"And I don't really have a body, you know. Not like you. I'm just made up of . . . like . . . *spirit.* And that spirit sort of holds me all together. And that spirit has been here, has been there . . . And if it holds *me* together, you could think of it as being, almost . . . sticky. I could patch up the hole in the sky. As in—*I* could."

It made no sense but it made all the sense, and I reached out to touch Henry now, to poke his arm, as if I might find him, in this moment, a little tacky, a little gluey, a little gloopy.

"Spirit glue," I whispered before I could stop myself, and for one moment Henry and I looked at each other with wide, frightened eyes, and then, in the next moment, we fell into absolutely unhinged, hysterical laughter.

Anyone looking would have thought I was laughing by myself, holding on to the arm of nothing, beginning to cry even as I was struggling to catch my breath, laughing, laughing, laughing until I really was sobbing, sobbing and laughing and laughing and sobbing and holding on to the arm of a ghost who would save us all.

XI

Persephone spent the spring and summer months aboveground, tending to her beloved flowers, visiting with her beloved mother, Demeter, goddess of the harvest. But because Persephone had eaten one single pomegranate seed while in the Underworld, she was bound to return there every autumn and winter. Her departure from her mother was bittersweet, for Persephone hated to leave her, but she had also grown to love her husband, had grown to love her home amongst the dead.

For Demeter, saying goodbye to her daughter each year caused the harvests to die, the plants to go dormant, the earth to grow cold. Whenever you feel the sharp, biting breeze of a winter's day, know that this is Demeter, yearning for Persephone, and in her deep, deep sorrow, keeping everything cold until spring.

Clara had a dream of a new painting but when she stood at her easel and tried to start it, nothing would transfer from the brush to the canvas. I watched her that afternoon, over and over, dipping her paintbrush into vivid oil colors that seemed to evaporate into thin air in the journey from the palette to the creamy stretch of canvas.

"I don't like this at all," she said after it became clear that it wasn't working, after Bernadette took the brush herself and of course managed to paint a tiny swath of color in the bottom left-hand corner. It sat there like an accusatory brand, that little spot of paint. Eventually Clara removed it with paint thinner and an old, stained rag.

"And it wasn't even a nightmare this time," she said. "It was just a dream. A really nice dream, actually."

If everything Henry had said was true, it would seem like the black tear was already devouring the Farthing girls.

We called Aunt Bea, up in Vermont, just to see how she was faring. She seemed less affected by the black tear because there were so many miles between her and it, but at the same time, she expressed a feeling of unease that followed her throughout her days.

"Like I've forgotten an important meeting and someone is *just* about to call me and tell me I'm in deep shit for it," she explained. "Or like I've left the stove on."

Our mother was still sad and lifeless, drifting in and out of rooms with a strange, vacant expression on her face, pausing like she had momentarily forgotten where she was or what she was doing.

Our father, on the other hand, was absolutely fine. He had made carrot cake that afternoon because *Everyone seems a bit glum around here lately, huh? Must be that time of year. What do they call it, honey? SAD. Right. Anyway. It's potentially a little burnt. But I am almost positive it's still edible.*

We ate the carrot cake if only to appease him, to not cause him any more worry. It was mostly tasteless in our mouths.

"When can I see that new painting you've been hiding away in the attic, Clara?" Dad asked, trying so desperately to start a conversation with any of the women in the room.

"Oh," Clara said. "I destroyed it."

"You—what?"

"Yeah. I realized it didn't fit my vision. It wasn't serving me. As an artist, you know. So I destroyed it."

"It wasn't serving you . . ." Dad repeated slowly. "I really don't know what to say to that one. Honey?"

He turned to Mom, who took a deep breath, as if willing herself to be present, to engage.

"Sweetheart, I think that's wonderful," she said finally.

"You think it's wonderful that Clara destroyed her painting?" Dad asked.

"Clara has always known what she wants," Mom said.

Dad did not know how to respond to that, so he resumed eating and let it go.

I tried to slip out that night for another long, solo walk, but Mom was waiting for me, already dressed in her coat and winter boots, standing on the front porch staring up at the sky.

"Oh," I said. "Are you going somewhere?"

"I'm going with you," she said, lowering her face to look at me, smiling and tucking me underneath her arm.

"How did you know I was going out?"

"Because you're always where you're supposed to be," she replied. "And tonight I just knew you were supposed to be with me."

"Where should we go?"

"You lead the way. I'd follow you anywhere."

It was too late for any museums, we'd already had dinner and dessert, and I wasn't about to take my mother to Dark Magic, so an aimless walk around the block it was (my favorite). She kept her arm looped through mine and we didn't talk for the first ten minutes or so. It was cold but manageably so, as in, my face didn't feel like it was going to freeze solid.

I still wasn't used to the feeling of getting farther away from the tear, how much better I felt even half a mile away from it.

"So strange," Mom said, as if reading my mind. "I've had such a terrible headache all day, and now I feel perfectly fine."

"Maybe you just needed some fresh air."

"Some fresh air, some ibuprofen, and some you time. The perfect combination." She let me go and stretched her arms over her head, taking a deep breath. "Short school week for you girls, huh? I know you must be happy about that."

"It is? Why?"

"Christmas, silly. Aunt Bea is driving down on Wednesday. It's supposed to snow again, too. They're predicting lots and lots."

"I completely forgot about Christmas," I admitted.

"Well, it's that time of year. Yesterday I couldn't find my favorite hair pin, the whole morning I spent looking for it."

"It was in your hair?"

"It was in my hair," she confirmed. "That's still not as bad as talking on your cell phone while looking for your cell phone. Which I have also done, many times."

"When is the snow supposed to start?"

"Thursday. We'll have to pick up lots of wood and have fires. Remember that Christmas we all read *Little Women*?"

Of course I remembered. It had snowed so much we hardly left the house for a week. Clara had been four, me six, Evelyn and

Bernadette eight and ten. The electricity kept going in and out and we'd toasted marshmallows on the fire and Mom had read a couple chapters every night, holding all of us in rapt attention, even our father, who had at first hung around near the doorway, downplaying his interest, but by the third night was sitting cross-legged on the floor with us, Clara on his lap, their eyes wide as they waited to hear whether Amy would die after falling through the ice.

"We all loved that book so much," I said.

"I loved it, too. It was a secret thrill, having four girls. I tried to get you all to call me *Marmee* but it never stuck."

"Well, Bernie cut off all her hair. That must count for something."

"She's my Jo, for sure. Always has been."

"You know, Louisa May Alcott based that scene on her own life. She caught typhoid pneumonia during the Civil War and the doctors cut off all her hair while she was delirious."

"And she had three sisters, too. One of them died. One of them got married. She wasn't really subtle with the parallels."

"Do the rest of us," I prodded. "Who's Clara?"

"Amy. Although less frivolous. But still underestimated."

"Evelyn?"

"Meg. Sweet, reliable, stalwart."

"And that leaves me as Beth," I said. "Which is sort of depressing, as she's nobody's favorite sister, and all she does of interest is die."

"I don't think that's true, at all, that she's nobody's favorite sister," Mom said. "She's *my* favorite sister. She was the kindest and the most decent. And the most altruistic."

"What does *altruistic* mean again?"

"It means you care about other people. And you need to study more SAT words."

"I don't know about that. I feel pretty selfish."

"Don't be ridiculous. You're anything but selfish. You care so much about your sisters, about this family. You're always exactly where you're supposed to be. And you keep everyone together."

She kissed my temple as we continued to walk, as we looped around and headed back toward home, every step feeling heavier and heavier, Mom's headache, I knew, coming back, by the way she rubbed at her forehead absentmindedly.

"Just like Beth," she said a full minute later.

By then, we were underneath the black tear again, in front of the brownstone, the house Persephone had blessed, the house the Farthings had built and then lived in forever, the house where Henry had died and been buried underneath the jasmine bushes.

I couldn't let anything happen to this house. I couldn't let anything happen to my family. I wouldn't.

"Come on, kiddo," Mom said. "I think it's time for all good godlings to be in bed."

I had a dream about the night Clara ran away from home.

She'd been eight and absolutely obsessed with Bernadette, who was fourteen and incredibly unpredictable; sometimes kind and loving, sometimes cruel and distant. I couldn't remember the details now, but Bernadette had said something to Clara after dinner, and I'd watched Clara's eyes close into slits, resolution spreading across her face.

As a family of girls, we were no strangers to running away. Bernadette had done it, even Evelyn had done it, and now Clara would do it. Only I seemed unwilling to leave the family home; my long walks always led me straight back to our front door.

Clara waited until everyone had gone to sleep (even then, at eight, she was a little night owl) and I waited to hear the telltale signs of a suitcase being packed.

At least it was summer, and a soft, mild night, and I slipped into flip-flops to follow Clara out the front door, dragging her small Muppets suitcase behind her noisily (the dream stuck very close to what had actually happened; both then and now I thought to myself, *How is nobody hearing this??*).

I walked behind her for half a block and in that time her stride went from determined to unsure before stopping altogether. I let her stand there for a moment and then I walked up beside her, making plenty of noise, clearing my throat so I wouldn't scare her.

"Going somewhere?"

"Winnie! What are you doing out here?"

"What are *you* doing out here?"

She struggled to make herself seem tough and sure of herself.

"Don't try and talk me out of it," she said.

"I would never."

"I'm running away from home."

"Cool. Where are you gonna go?"

"To the bus station. I'll go stay with Aunt Bea for a while, until I figure some things out."

"Not a bad plan," I said. "You have the money for the ticket?"

She patted the pocket of her shorts. "From my piggy bank."

"And you've checked the schedule?"

"Of course. I'll have to spend the night at the station, but the first bus leaves in the morning."

It was just like Clara to check bus schedules, bring money; I was sure if I peeked in her suitcase I would find snacks and a water bottle.

"I'll miss you," I said, and I saw a flicker of doubt flash across her face. She had been expecting me to talk her out of it.

"Bernie is *so mean,*" she said.

"I know. She definitely can be."

"I'm sick of it."

"Me, too!"

"She can't talk to people like that."

"I agree."

Clara's eyes were filling up with tears. "I don't even love her."

"I think you do love her," I said. "Otherwise she wouldn't be able to upset you this much."

Clara didn't know what to do with that truth bomb, and for a moment she just glared at me and continued to produce tears that didn't quite spill onto her cheeks.

"Just go home, Winnie," she said. "Mind your own business."

"You *are* my business, Clara. And I'm not going home without you."

Here is where the dream departed from real life, because in the dream it started snowing, but the snow wasn't snow, it was jasmine petals, and everything smelled beautiful and hypnotizing. I caught a petal on my palm and closed my fingers around it. I looked up and noticed, for the first time, a long, deep gash in the sky. The petals were spilling out of the gash, floating down around us, quickly covering the street in a fragrant blanket of white.

"This is weird," Clara said, sniffling.

"Come home, Clara," I said, holding my hand out to her. "I can't do this without you."

"Do what?"

"I can't fix this," I said, pointing upward.

"But I don't care about this," she argued. "I care about Bernadette being a jerk."

"She doesn't mean to be," I said. "She'll apologize."

"Will she never do it again?"

I thought of the glass slamming into the wall a few years from now, shattering into a million pieces, missing Clara's head by such a slim margin.

"She'll do it again," I said. "She will definitely do it again."

"Then why would I come home with you?"

"Because you love her. And she loves you. And we have to get home before this stuff drowns us, okay?"

Because the jasmine petals were up to our knees now, because I took a step toward Clara and it was hard to get my leg over it. Her suitcase was completely buried. She let it go and nodded.

"Okay, fine," she said. "But I'm not talking to her for at least a week."

"Very fair," I said. "Make it two weeks."

The petals were too high for Clara to wade through; I turned around and she climbed on piggyback.

It was ten times harder to move like this, but step by step we got closer to the house, step by step we got closer to home. The petals kept falling and the black tear kept getting bigger but I never stopped moving, not until we pulled open the front door and slipped inside.

Aunt Bea arrived late on Wednesday, and it started snowing sometime that night.

The walk with my mother, our conversation, and the dream with Clara stuck with me. I kept seeing echoes of jasmine petals threatening to swallow us whole.

On Thursday Aunt Bea slept late and the snow fell so quickly and so heavily that by midday, it was at two feet and quickly accumulating. We spent hours sprawled around the living room, tending the fire, playing board games, drinking coffee and tea and hot chocolate and some truly disgusting smoothie Bernadette whipped up. ("Oh, right, we have a *blender,*" Mom said, sounding genuinely surprised.)

In the evening Dad cooked dinner and Mom and Aunt Bea drank glasses of wine and occasionally "helped" (passed him the salt or refilled his glass). In the living room, it was the five of us as it always had been: Bernie, Evelyn, me, Clara, Henry. Girl, girl, girl, girl, ghost. If Mom and Dad and Bea noticed the five game pieces on the board, they didn't mention it. If they noticed the way one of the pieces (the hat) sometimes seemed to move of its own volition, they didn't say anything. If they noticed how one of us would occasionally talk to the empty space between Clara and Evelyn, wait for a response that never came, then burst into peals of laughter, they didn't say anything. But it was Christmas break and snowing and they were happy and preoccupied so most likely, they didn't notice any of these things.

"Do you miss food?" Clara asked (she was currently dominating the game, owning multiple properties on every side of the board and occasionally counting her money aloud in a booming, irritating voice). "What was your favorite thing to eat?"

"Lasagna," he said. "My mother made an excellent lasagna."

"Did you have electricity?" she continued. It was her turn, and she was taking a very long time deciding whether she wanted to buy another railroad (she owned two already and I owned a third; it had almost put me into bankruptcy but I was determined to stop her from becoming too powerful over our public transportation).

"Just missed it," Henry said.

"What about toilets?"

"Yes, Clara," Henry said with a smile. "We had toilets."

"Thank god for that, at least."

Bernadette's phone chimed: a timer she had set for Clara's move.

"I'll buy it," Clara announced. "I might as well. It's becoming hard to find places to store all my money."

"You are infuriating," Evelyn declared.

"It's all part of my strategy," Clara said. "I'm embodying my role. I mean, did you ever meet a real estate tycoon who *wasn't* infuriating?"

"Sustained," Bernadette said, and handed Clara the card for Reading Railroad.

It was so normal.

It had been my entire life.

The five of us playing the same worn out, dingy board games.

The five of us being silly, being here, being together.

The five of us.

But soon . . .

"Are you not having fun?" Bernadette said, angling toward me.

It was my turn, and I hadn't moved a muscle. "Is it because you're losing very terribly?"

"Is it because I've monopolized almost all forms of transportation?" Clara.

"Is it because you have to read *Wuthering Heights* for English over break and it's the worst book ever written?" Evelyn.

"Is it because you thought I didn't have toilets?" Henry.

"I liked *Wuthering Heights,*" Bernadette said, then tapped on her phone a few times. A moment later, "Wuthering Heights" by Kate Bush started playing on the stereo speakers.

Dad poked his head into the living room. "I love Kate Bush! Right on!"

Out the windows, I could still see the snow falling against the deep-blue blackness of the winter night.

On the stereo speakers, Kate Bush sang about wandering the moors at night.

Aunt Bea came into the living room then and I thought of Esme, all alone in Vermont, playing with her dolls in front of an unlit fireplace.

"Gosh, this *snow,*" Aunt Bea said, pausing by the wide front windows.

"And it's not supposed to stop for days," Dad replied, emerging from the kitchen looking slightly flushed now, from the heat or from the wine or both.

"Is the food ready yet, chef?" Aunt Bea asked, and Dad did a little flourish and bow and swept his arms toward the kitchen.

"Dinner is served," he said dramatically, just as the lights flickered out.

Clara screamed, Evelyn gasped, Bernadette swore, and Aunt Bea drew in a sharp intake of breath. Mom came out from the kitchen a moment later, holding a candle in front of her face, shielding the flame with her hand.

"Be prepared," she sang.

"Are there more of those?" Aunt Bea asked.

"A lot more," Mom said. She brought the candle over to me as everyone else pushed into the kitchen, desperate for light. "Guard this flame well, for it is our only hope," she said (she was a little drunk).

"What happens if it goes out?" I asked, taking it from her, playing along.

"Oh, gosh. We don't want to think about that."

She slipped back into the kitchen, leaving just Henry and me in the living room.

I could hear matches striking, the delicate *whoosh* of tiny flames catching. The kitchen glowed brighter and brighter with candlelight, and I moved to the window where Aunt Bea had just stood.

"I guess the game is over," Henry said, a little sadly.

"Clara was crushing us, anyway."

I moved the candle away from the window so I could see out and up. It was dark out, but the tear in the sky was darker, a clear outline against the sky. It was so big now that its edges almost reached the horizon. I was no expert on tears in the fabric of reality, but that didn't seem good.

Henry moved to stand next to me. For a moment, the smell of jasmine was overwhelming. I closed my eyes and breathed it in.

With my eyes still closed, I said, "When are you going to do it?"

"I just want a little more time," he said.

"I wish you didn't have to."

"I know."

"We could find another way."

"There's no other way," he said. Then, an afterthought: "I'm sorry."

"When are you going to tell them?"

"Soon."

I opened my eyes and turned around.

Aunt Bea was standing in the doorway of the room, holding a pillar candle, staring at me curiously.

"Talking to myself," I said, a little too loudly.

"Sounded like a fascinating conversation," she replied.

"Oh, you know."

"I think maybe I don't know," she said, and I swore her eyes flickered over to Henry, and something flashed across her face—a memory, maybe, or some sort of recognition, or some sort of understanding.

"Come on," I said. "Let's go eat."

"You would tell me, right?" she asked as I walked closer to her. "If something was really wrong? If you were in trouble? If you needed help?"

"Totally," I said. "Of course."

"The worst liar of the bunch," she said, and gave a weary look into the living room before turning around and going back into the kitchen.

After dessert (Aunt Bea and Mom made sticky toffee pudding that was somehow both a little burnt and a little underdone) I was crawling out of my skin. All I wanted to do was go for a nice, long, cold walk, but the snow was at least four feet high and still falling. The farthest I got was the front door, pulling it open to let a sizable heap of snow fall in, soaking my feet and the stone tiles of the entryway.

My phone buzzed and I pulled it out of my pocket, thrilled to see it was a text from Maybe:

My grandma just said "Where do they think we're going to put it all?"

I smiled. I wanted to meet her grandmother. I wanted to see where Maybe lived. I wanted this whole nightmare to be over.

I wrote her a reply:

Please tell her I will write a letter to the city weather committee immediately and bring her concerns to their attention.

Thank you. That's a relief. Hope you're having a good night, weather girl.

You too xx.

I closed the door and turned back to the living room.

Clara was reading her mythology book. Bernadette was nodding off in an armchair. Mom was putting away the abandoned board game. Aunt Bea was sitting on the floor in front of the fire, patiently waiting while our father showed her a very elaborate card trick.

"Oh, that's not right," he said. "Let me start over."

Only Evelyn and Henry weren't there, and I started the long journey upstairs to look for them, not liking how it felt to be apart from them. If I could lock everyone in a room, I would. If I could keep an eye on everyone forever, I would.

I found Evelyn in her bedroom. She had a small suitcase open on the floor and there were three piles on her bed, various clothes and belongings and knickknacks. She didn't hear me coming, and I stood in her doorway for a moment, watching her. Henry wasn't there, but I smelled jasmine, like I had just missed him.

"Marie Kondo?" I guessed, and she jumped a little and turned around.

"I didn't hear you come up," she said.

"Are you going somewhere?" I asked, nodding my head toward the suitcase.

She lowered her head and said, without looking at me, "No. I mean . . . No. This is just in case. Just in case we can't fix it, and he can't stay here, and I have to go back with him."

"How does that make any sense, Evelyn? You went through twice and you ripped a hole in the sky. What would happen if you did it again? You'd destroy the entire city, probably."

"I'm just planning for everything, okay?" she said. And it was so like her, so like my sister, to make sure she was ready for any possible outcome, even if one of the possible outcomes was leaving us forever.

"Where is he?"

"He went out. He doesn't know I'm doing this."

It was strange, that he could go out now. He could leave the house that had been his home-slash-prison-slash-afterlife for so many years.

I took a step into the room. The suitcase only had a few things in it. She had just started packing.

"Let me guess," I said, pointing at the smallest pile on her bed (old paperback copy of *Pride and Prejudice,* dark-green clothbound journal, fancy fountain pen that had belonged to our grandmother). "Yes." I pointed to the next pile (small handwoven purse she'd bought in Mexico, collection of folded notes, hat our mother had knit for her). "Maybe." I pointed to the last pile, the biggest (selection of European coins, set of colored pencils and sketchpad, chunky plastic watch she had worn every day of third grade). "No."

"I just don't know what else to *do,* Winnie. We're all just sitting around and waiting and meanwhile the tear is only getting bigger and nobody is coming up with any ideas of how to fix it."

I know how to fix it, I wanted to say.

Henry told me how to fix it, and you're not going to like it one bit.

"You told me you wouldn't lie to me again," she said, her voice quieter now, my own silence spreading out and filling up the room.

I didn't answer. I couldn't answer, I couldn't think of anything else to say.

Eventually, she picked up a small stuffed animal from her bed. It was Roo, from *Winnie the Pooh,* complete with a powder-blue knit sweater that had his name embroidered on it in darker blue thread.

"Do you remember when we got this?" she asked.

"Of course. Disneyland."

"You got Piglet. With the little scarf around his neck. Do you still have it?"

"Somewhere, sure."

She held the small Roo tightly to her chest, closing her eyes, concentrating.

"What color was the scarf?" she asked, and I had to admit I didn't remember.

She set Roo carefully down in the *no* pile, and that tiny action made me feel like when all of this was said and done, no matter where Evelyn ended up, we had really lost her for good.

XII

And what about now? Does Persephone still wander the earth for half the year, does she still perform her seasonal tasks, or is she able to instead rest, to recede into the background, to retire comfortably in the halls of the dead, where aubergine skies spread out above you and in Grand Central there is endless, fevered dancing under the twinkling lights of a thousand real stars . . . ?

I like to think that she visits us, yes, but not because she has to anymore, rather, because she wants *to, because she misses the feel of the grass and the scent of the jasmine and the places she once wandered. I like to think that she retraces her steps, placing her feet in the same spaces she once stood. Her footsteps deepening, widening, remaining . . .*

It stopped snowing, but it was so cold outside that the world remained covered up in a white, unmelting blanket all week.

The city seemed paused; time seemed to stand still. We had fires, watched movies, read books.

It was easy to forget about the tear in the sky, even as it continued to get bigger, even as it continued to weigh more heavily upon our shoulders.

Aunt Bea paused one morning before Christmas (who knew what day it was, all days melting together in that no-man's-land of snow), and smelled at the air near the front door, her nose crinkling in sensory concentration.

"Do you smell something . . . floral?" she asked my father, who happened to be closest, dusting the mantelpiece (boredom leading to household chores; he'd finished three books in three days and didn't know what to do with himself anymore).

"Floral?" he questioned. "I sprayed some Fabulosa earlier."

"No, it's definitely not that," she said. "It's flowers, a specific flower, a creamy, rich, heady, earthy—Bernadette, what am I thinking of, you're the flower expert." Because Bernadette had just come down the stairs to the first floor and even though I was there, I was practicing not moving, the art of becoming invisible in clear view of others.

Bernadette hesitated a moment, shot a look at me (invisibility cloaks rarely worked on sisters), weighed the pros and cons, decided it was harmless to tell her—

"It's jasmine," she said.

"Jasmine! That's it!" said Aunt Bea. "But where is it coming from?"

"It's Evelyn's perfume," Bernadette said, and this made me snort, and this made my father look over at me, his eyes widening in pleasant surprise.

"Oh, I didn't know you were here," he said.

That was the point, I wanted to say, but instead I said, "Ta-da," rather lackluster.

"It doesn't *smell* like perfume," Aunt Bea persisted. "It doesn't smell artificial at all."

"It's a very expensive perfume," Bernadette said. "Like, you know. An essential oil."

"I mean, okay," Aunt Bea said, very obviously not convinced. "If you say so."

Henry himself didn't materialize all that much, but I smelled jasmine everywhere, so he was a constant presence, anyway. I did catch him once, the night before Christmas, sitting by himself at the kitchen table in the middle of the night. I'd woken up to Clara elbowing me in the ribs (Aunt Bea was sleeping in her bed) and I'd gone downstairs for a glass of water. When I turned the kitchen light on, it took everything in me not to scream out in fright.

"Henry, holy crap, what are you doing sitting here in the dark?" I hiss-whispered.

"You don't really notice it," he said in this super dramatic, low voice. "The dark, the light. It makes no difference when you're dead."

"Okay," I said, my heart still beating like a timpani drum. "Creepy."

"I'm sorry," he said. "I'm glad it's you. Your aunt came down a little while ago and just stood here in the dark, sniffing."

"She has a great sense of smell, apparently."

"I used to love the smell of jasmine. I can't smell it anymore."

"You can't?"

"I can't smell anything," Henry admitted sadly.

"They're my favorite flower. All my life, walking into a room, I'd know if you were there or if I'd just missed you or if you hadn't been around in a while."

"If I wasn't a ghost, your favorite flower might have been . . . I don't know. Lilies. Bluebells. Amaranthus."

"Sure, maybe? What's going on?"

"The tear is too big now. If I wait any longer . . . I won't be strong enough to close it. And I still haven't told her. I'm scared to tell her. And now it's here. It has to happen tomorrow. I've waited too long already; I can't wait any longer."

"But tomorrow's Christmas," I said.

"Is it?" he asked. "I'd lost track."

"Oh, Henry," I said. "I wish there was another way."

"I know," he replied, not looking at me, looking out the dark windows to the backyard instead. "Me, too."

The next morning—Christmas morning—it snowed again.

We woke up early, thanks to Clara, who hadn't yet outgrown the urgency of Christmas morning, the anticipation of the presents under the tree.

"It's just like Narnia," she breathed, standing in thick wool socks, peering out the front windows of the house at the street beyond.

"It's been like this all week," Evelyn said.

"Right, but in Narnia, it's never Christmas and then it *is* Christmas," Clara argued. "And now it's Christmas!"

It was too snowy, too gray, to see the tear in the sky, but I felt it deep inside me. It had a heavy pulse to it, like listening to music with the bass turned up too high.

No one else was up yet, just us, not our parents, not Aunt Bea.

Bernadette made hot chocolates, carried them into the living room balanced carefully on a tray. She took the mug with the chip on the rim and faded photos of puppies. She'd made whipped cream the old-fashioned way, with heavy cream and our mother's older-than-us hand blender.

"What are you watching?" she asked, sitting on the couch as the three of us remained by the window, looking out.

"The snow," Clara said.

Evelyn went and sat next to Bernadette. I couldn't look at Evie, couldn't bear to see her face. I didn't know where Henry was but I knew today was the day and that secret felt too heavy to carry by myself.

Clara took a mug of hot chocolate and sat down, and I followed her so I wouldn't be the only one left at the window. I stared at the floor as Bernadette tapped her phone and started Harry Connick Jr. on the speakers. *Let it snow, let it snow, let it snow.*

"It *is* snowing," Clara said, her voice filled with so much wonder and happiness that it made us all laugh.

Then Evelyn said, "I have something for you all," and from her thick, plush robe, she pulled out three identically sized boxes. She handed one to each of us.

"It's not much," she said, but we knew even as we were peeling off the wrapping paper, opening the boxes, that it would be the most thoughtful and meaningful presents we would receive all day because Evelyn had always been, this will surprise no one, the best at gifts. She saved up her money all year, whatever she got from the few long-term piano students she tutored during summer afternoons, from the music lessons she gave on weekends in the spring and summer, from saving pennies and hoarding dimes, she would buy us each a gift that was guaranteed to make at least one of us cry.

Clara, who had no money to her name at all, usually made us

something homemade and personal and sweet, coming in second place in the unspoken Farthing sister gift contest.

Bernadette, who had a job but saved everything until last minute, usually got us something we wanted but which wasn't a surprise (because she asked us): an expensive sweater, new paints, a vintage cashmere scarf.

And I, having sometimes money from various allowances and odd jobs and birthdays, and sometimes good ideas, usually got my sisters books. Books I had loved, books I knew they would love, books I thought might be meaningful to them in whatever their current struggle was.

The three of us took care to unwrap Evelyn's gifts at the exact same speed, so no one would spoil it for anyone else. Under the paper was a small cardboard box and inside that was a beautiful evergreen velvet jewelry box.

We opened it together, our movements in near unison. Clara gasped, Bernadette sucked in a sharp breath, and I was silent as we pulled the necklaces out.

They were gold, twinkling, circular discs set on delicate gold chains. The discs had lines emanating from the middle outward, like the rays of the sun. In the center of the lines was a raised heart. On the other side, in the middle of the disc, were all of our initials: BEWC.

"I thought it would always connect us. Remind us," Evelyn said, moving aside her robe to show us that she had bought one for herself, too.

What I wanted to say was—*I don't need a reminder that I have sisters.*

What I wanted to say was—*This is so, so beautiful.*

What I wanted to say was—*I'm so sorry, Evelyn. I don't deserve this. If I could use this to patch up the hole in the sky, I would. I would in a heartbeat.*

What I *did* say was, "What about the rest of the note? What was it going to say? *I know why you did it and I*—what? You *what,* Evie?"

Evelyn's face was hard to read, and she didn't quite look at me when she replied. "I didn't know you saw that."

"We looked *everywhere* for you, we were *so* nervous," I said. "What was the note going to say?"

She closed her eyes for the length of four heartbeats, one for each of us, then she opened her eyes again and looked at me and said, *". . . and I love you always."*

. . . and I love you always.

And she would always love us, love *me,* no matter what I did, no matter what terrible decisions I made. Wasn't that what it was to be a sister?

"This is too much, Evie," Bernadette said, hooking the necklace around her neck.

Clara held up her own necklace so it caught the weak, gray, morning light from the window, and let the pendant twirl and twirl around. "It's so beautiful, Evelyn," she said, and she caught the still-spinning pendant between two fingers, then brought the whole thing to her chest, hugging it.

Evelyn stood up from her seat on the couch and walked over to me. She took the necklace out of my hands, gently moved my hair aside, and clasped it around my neck.

"Always," she said, then leaned over and hugged me so tightly that I felt suffocated by her, I felt the insides of my wrists itch, I felt safe and happy and protected and exactly where I was supposed to be.

It was—despite everything—a really lovely Christmas.

We wore pajamas until the late afternoon, we ate a hundred pancakes each, we played nonstop Christmas music, we opened presents from our parents and from Aunt Bea and gave presents in return.

We did our best to ignore the heaviness that poured out of the black tear in the sky, even though Mom complained of a persistent headache and Aunt Bea kept pausing and staring out the window, as if she knew *something* was there but couldn't quite tell what it was. Dad remained perfectly fine, remained solidly *Dad,* and by three o'clock he'd dressed in an array of new Christmas gifts (argyle sweater, four pairs of socks, wool scarf, earmuffs Clara insisted were *made for him*) and had settled in to read the book I'd given him (*A Gentleman in Moscow*).

After dinner Mom announced that the neighbors a few houses down had invited them over for a cocktail hour, but "I don't really feel like going, do you, honey?"

"We should go," Dad said. "It's Christmas!"

"How would we even get there?" Mom asked, peering out the window. "The snow is up to my eyeballs."

"We'll tunnel through," Aunt Bea said. "Like squirrels."

"It's only five houses down," Dad said. "It will be a little adventure."

"Do we have to go?" Clara asked.

"No, no," Mom said. "You're not invited."

"Thank god for that," Bernie said.

So the adults got dressed and Dad grabbed a shovel from

somewhere and carried it over his head like a spear or a sword, in the style of someone going off to fight a noble battle.

"Snow is really heavy," he said once he'd made a pathway down exactly two of the brownstone's front steps. "I don't think you girls realize that."

"You're doing an excellent job," Mom said from the doorway. She and Aunt Bea were drinking glasses of white wine and seemed dedicated to either finishing them there or carrying them to the neighbors', whatever came first.

Henry, who up until then had made himself scarce, appeared on the stairs next to me, where I was sitting and watching the entertainment. I smelled jasmine before I saw him, and when his arm touched mine, I got a chill down my spine that had nothing to do with the still-open front door.

"Hi," I whispered, quiet enough that no one else would be able to hear me.

"Hi," he whispered back.

Dad wrestled his way down the remainder of the stairs and Mom and Aunt Bea finished their wine and handed the glasses to Clara, who went and put them in the kitchen. We all called goodbye and Bernadette shut the front door and Clara brought the wineglasses back, each filled to the brim with more chardonnay.

"Cece, honestly," Bernadette said, but took one of the glasses and had a long sip, before turning to Henry and me and saying, "When are you two going to tell us whatever it is you don't want to tell us?"

Evelyn was sitting on the rug in front of the fire, and she turned her face toward us then, and she looked so beautiful with the firelight reflecting on her cheeks, dancing in her eyes, and I knew in that moment that I would have to be the one to tell her. I would have to be the one to tell all of them. It would have to be me.

"I'll make some tea," I said.

What a Farthing thing to do, to make tea when the world was ending.

Nobody argued with me as I went into the kitchen. Nobody followed me as I filled the electric kettle, put it back on its holder and turned it on, got four mugs down from the cabinet and set them in a neat line on the kitchen counter. Nobody was there as I pulled down a half-empty tin of loose-leaf peppermint tea, as I filled four tea strainers and set them into the mugs. Nobody came into the kitchen as I took the honey from the cabinet and put it down, leaving my fingers sticky. Nobody was there as I washed off my hands at the kitchen sink. Nobody was there and then Evelyn was there and she was standing so still and so quietly that I remembered when she was a ghost, when I saw her from beyond the grave, when she reached her hand out to me and I knew that I knew her, I would know her in any dimension, in any universe, in any world.

"I know it's something bad," she said, moving closer to me. "I know I won't be going back. I know he can't stay here. I know you know. Will you tell me now? I can't wait any longer, I have to—" Her voice broke then, snapped in half, and I felt it deep within my chest. "I just have to know now, Winnie. Will you tell me?"

I remembered Henry sitting on the edge of my bed when I was five or six and sick with a stomach bug that just wouldn't quit.

I remembered Henry telling me he loved my hair, when I had to cut it to my shoulders after Clara stuck gum in it (accidentally, she claimed).

Henry was one of my earliest memories. It was my sisters and Henry, always. One of the first faces I saw, after my parents and the doctors and the nurses and the taxi driver who brought us all home from Lenox Hill. It was Henry, waiting inside the house, so happy to meet a new Farthing sister. It was Henry, telling me not to be frightened of the dark, that the scariest thing in this house was him.

But you're not scary at all, Henry.

I know. That's my point, silly goose. You're safe here.

You're safe here.

You're safe here.

You're safe here.

And thanks to Henry, we would continue to be safe here.

The kettle boiled and turned itself off and I ignored it and walked around the kitchen island to stand next to Evelyn, to take her hand and look her in the eyes as I told her what was going to happen.

"I'm so sorry, Evelyn," I said, and then I explained it like Henry had explained it to me, and she was very quiet as she listened to me, and occasionally she nodded her head or made a little sound, cleared her throat or swallowed loudly.

When I tried to apologize again, at the end of it, she shook her head and said, "No, no, Winnie. No more apologies. What has to happen will happen now. We can't help it anymore; this is how it has to be."

Then Clara and Bernadette came into the kitchen and Clara was crying, which is how I knew Henry had told them as I had told Evelyn, and I couldn't help but feel a sense of relief, that I wouldn't have to say it all over again.

Henry came into the kitchen behind them and then it was the five of us.

Girl, girl, girl, girl, ghost.

As it had always been, since we were little, since we were born.

"We have to close the doorway first," Bernadette said. "The one she created all those years ago. The one tied to this house."

"Or else some idiot Farthing years from now will make the same mistakes we did," Evelyn said, nodding. "Okay. How do we do that?"

"You and Clara have both given something up," Bernie said. "It's my turn now."

We followed her upstairs to the attic and sat in a circle on the floor as she went into her bedroom, coming back a moment later with one of her journals. It had a worn, red leather cover and it was so stuffed it didn't close properly anymore. It was one of her journals from Vermont.

"No," Clara said.

"It's okay, Cece," Bernie said. "Everything in here is in here, too." And she pointed at her chest, then smiled at herself. "Man, that was corny. Okay. Here goes nothing."

And just like Clara had used her painting to open the doorway and let Henry through, Bernadette somehow used her journal to find the doorway and then *close* it. And I knew it was closed for good, forever, and I swear I heard a sound like the latching of a lock, the click of a dead bolt, the heavy catch of something solid and unmovable.

The journal was gone from Bernadette's outstretched hands, and I saw her look at her now-empty palms with sadness. I remembered the time I had gone into her room and held her journals. I had wanted so much to be her, to be any of my sisters, to be anything but myself. But of course I had always remained me. The one sister who always played it safe, who hadn't had to make any sacrifices because I had never taken any risks, because you can't get burned if you stay as far away from the fire as you could.

I don't think anyone would have moved if I hadn't moved first. I took Evelyn by the hand and gently nudged Clara's arm and Bernadette let her hands fall to her sides and followed us down the long flights of stairs, all the way to the kitchen, the back door.

The mugs of tea were still on the counter, the water in the kettle was tepid again. The kitchen smelled like peppermint and jasmine.

I got everyone boots and winter coats but when we stepped outside, I discovered it had turned suddenly mild. Snow still fell lightly around us, but just like in my dream, it wasn't snow. It was—

"Jasmine," Evelyn said, holding her hand out, palm outstretched, catching the creamy white flowers as they fell.

"Whoa," Bernadette breathed.

"How is this possible?" Clara asked, patting her pocket vaguely for what I thought must be the mythology book, coming up empty, catching a jasmine petal in her fingers and examining it with big, wild eyes. Then: "I think I had a dream about this . . ."

Which made sense, because sisters shared dreams just like they shared clothes, just like they shared memories, just like they shared ghosts.

I led them down the back stairs to the yard and we stood in a loose circle, Henry following behind us, his eyes trained upward.

The black tear took up the entire sky now. It was blacker than the sky had ever been, and devoid of stars, and echoing and cavernous and horrible. It pulsed down on top of us, sending waves of something we could feel in our fingertips. It would swallow the entire house, just like Henry had said. It would swallow all of us. We couldn't wait any longer.

Henry stepped into the circle and stood before Evelyn.

"No, Henry," she said, her voice a little more than a whisper.

"I'm sorry, Evie," he whispered back, and raised his free hand and brushed her hair with the back of his knuckles. "It's the only way."

"You were mine," she said, her voice small and fragile. "You were *mine*."

"I'm still yours."

Henry dropped her hand, moved to Clara, who was openly weeping, her small shoulders shaking.

"I love you, okay?" he said, and pulled her into a hug.

"I'm going to miss when you would sit and watch me paint," she sobbed.

"I will always watch you paint," he said. "Always."

She pulled away then and looked up at him, her eyes panicked. "But I can't paint anymore. What if I never paint again?"

"When this is over, you'll paint again. As soon as this is over."

"You promise?"

"I promise."

He turned to Bernadette next. She stood tall and unwavering, like a sentinel watching us all, the older sister in her age-old role of strength. She had jasmine flowers caught in her short hair.

"Remember the magpies," he said, a reference I did not get, a secret joke between them.

"I'll always count them," Bernadette said, her words a vow.

They hugged for a long time, and then Henry turned to me, and I tried not to let my knees buckle.

"Are you almost ready?" he asked.

I nodded.

Because somehow, in the shower of the jasmine petals, in the circle with my sisters, somehow, without knowing *how,* I knew what to do. I knew what to sacrifice, what to give up.

I had always been the only one of us who could see the other ghosts.

Sometimes I had liked it, sometimes I had hated it, sometimes it had made me feel alone in a way I couldn't really describe. But it had always been mine. My connection to *her,* to them, to Persephone and Melinöe.

Henry hugged me—still such a new, weird feeling, that he could *hug* us—and the smell of jasmine surrounded me, like a blanket, and the feel of Henry's arms around me, well, they weren't the arms of a dead boy. He had come back to life in that moment. He had come back to life before dying all over again.

When he let me go, I felt colder than I had before, and I couldn't watch as he stepped back to Evelyn again.

The three of us, Clara, Bernadette, and me, we stepped a few feet away from them, so we couldn't hear what they said, so we wouldn't intrude on their privacy.

We held hands.

We put our foreheads together, leaning into each other.

Clara was still crying. We put our arms around her shoulders. We closed our eyes.

Then I felt a hand on my arm and Henry pulled me gently away from my sisters. Bernadette and Clara drew Evelyn in between them.

"I'm not really sure what to do," I said.

"Winnie, you've always known exactly what to do," he replied. "Even if your execution is a bit hit or miss."

He smiled and I smiled and how could I possibly be smiling here, at the end of the world? At the end of *Henry.*

"Will it come back? Like with Clara?" I asked. "Will I see them anymore?"

"No," he said, shaking his head. "No, I don't think so."

My mother's words came back to me then:

You're always exactly where you're supposed to be. And you keep everyone together.

Is that what I had done, with all the Farthing ghosts? Had I kept us all together without even really meaning to?

Would I miss them, the ghostly strangers I passed on my night-time walks, the Farthing women who had come before me?

Would I miss Esme?

"You're releasing them," Henry continued. "All the Farthings. Esme. And *me.* You're releasing all of us."

"And that's okay?" I asked. "You think they will want that?"

"Yes," he said. "I know they will."

"But you?"

"Well, that's a bit more complicated," he said, and his smile turned sad, and he took my hand and held it between us.

"I don't know how," I said.

"You do," he assured me. "You'll find it."

I closed my eyes.

I remembered Henry watching Clara paint on a thousand different nights, listening to Evelyn play the piano, sitting quietly as Bernadette sat and journaled, occasionally showing him something she had written, making him laugh or grow serious or shake his head in disbelief. Henry reciting silly poems to make me laugh. Henry appearing out of nowhere, scaring me to death. Henry, Henry, Henry.

And he was right.

I did find it.

The thing inside of me that let me see them all, the same thing that kept them *here*. And I could release it, release them. I had that power, inside me, that power over them, that power *for* them. I could open a door, raise the curtains, set everything right.

I opened my eyes before I did it. Just to see him one last time, our ghost, our Henry.

Then I let go of his hand and set him free.

The light, when it came, was so bright I couldn't understand it.

It burned through my closed eyes, a hot, warm, bright light that pulsed and thrummed, that contained music and felt like static in my brain. The whole city was going to see that light. The whole city would know about Henry.

I found out later that the light *did* touch everything, sweeping down alleyways and snaking down avenues and crawling through open doorways and windows.

The news would write about it.

MYSTERIOUS LIGHT BAFFLES CITY OFFICIALS

BRIGHT FLASH OF LIGHT LASTS TEN SECONDS BEFORE DISAPPEARING

DID ALIENS VISIT US ON CHRISTMAS?

But the light was Henry, somehow. Henry expanding, Henry releasing.

The light was Henry, growing, stretching, building, soaring, floating, rising.

The light was Henry, and it grew wider and thinned out to cover the tear in the sky perfectly, blending in so seamlessly that no one ever noticed it.

Except us.

We noticed it.

Every time I looked up, I could see it.

The thinnest, subtlest whisper of gold.

Like the Japanese art of kintsugi.

Like anything torn apart and glued carefully, lovingly back together.

Delicate stitches along the seam of a beloved dress.

A stuffed animal hugged every night for years and years until the stuffing starts to leak out of its ear and your mom fixes it, mends it, makes it good as new again.

Your grandmother's gold watch, once shut in a car door, glass replaced, worn forever and ever on the wrists of one sister, then another.

An eye blackened by a fist, hair tangled in gum and cut short to grow again, a broken heart, a broken piano string, a canvas with one black gash across the perfect winter sky, a journal stuffed with so many thoughts, so many words, that it becomes exponentially heavier than when you bought it.

And then Henry.

Henry, above us.

Henry, saving us.

Henry, always, always with us.
The brightest light I had ever seen.
A closet door.
A thousand games of Monopoly.
Our mother, asking who Henry was.
The rich, syrupy smell of jasmine.
And then the light went out.

XIII

Does Persephone know intimately every soul that has ever passed through her kingdom, every baby yet to be born, every old and weary traveler ready for a rest before they are put back in the game?

Did she know us before we were us, *before we were the Farthing sisters, before we were Bernadette and Evelyn and Winnie and Clara?*

Does her daughter, Melinöe, handpick the ghosts that will return to Earth as people, as babies again?

If so, what made her put the four of us together? (Even though I am glad she did, grateful she did, so, so happy she did.)

But was it chance or was it something deeper than that? Something predetermined, something eternal and ageless and immutable?

When I am with my sisters, when we are all together, when the room feels too small to contain all of us—

Well I have to imagine it is the latter.

Our aunt has only seen the ghost once.

On the night I was born, Bernadette was four and Evelyn was two and Clara wasn't even a distant thought on the minds of a single human in the world.

Isn't that weird, how humans don't exist and then do, how life is created out of a few small building blocks, how it grows and grows and grows until it is a full person who likes to make friendship bracelets and paint and dreams of taking a gap year and has more financial stability than most fifty-year-old men I've met?

On the night I was born, my parents didn't see a ghost because they'd gone to a hospital to have me.

And there was no possible way any of us could remember this, certainly not me, just a few minutes old at the time and not even there with my sisters, but anyway, here it is:

Aunt Bea came down from Vermont and stayed with Evelyn and Bernadette in our brownstone. She made omelets for dinner. She let my sisters play in the bathtub until the water was cool and all the bubbles had popped. She dressed them in pajamas and brushed teeth and brought them to Bernadette's bedroom, which back then wasn't in the attic, it was where my future bedroom would be. Evelyn's bedroom was where Clara's would be. Nobody bunked with a ghost then; there would be no closet-knocking for some years, yet.

Evelyn and Bernadette were both tucked into Bernie's bed, a sleepover for a special occasion. Aunt Bea was weaseled into reading far too many books, and when my sisters finally fell asleep, her voice was hoarse and she was tired and all she wanted in the world was a cup of tea. She switched on Bernadette's nightlight and left the door open a crack and walked to the stairs that led down to the second floor.

She paused at the top, her hand on the banister, something making her pause.

She turned around and looked up the stairs that led to the attic, which back then held a guest bedroom and a catchall room—catching everything from a broken sewing machine to a large amount of mostly unused ski equipment to a set of dumbbells to a myriad of board games to an old bike with flat tires and many, many plastic totes full of infant clothes that had once belonged to my sisters and would soon be mine.

And a ghost.

The catchall room had a ghost.

He was a shy ghost, a sweet ghost, a lonely ghost.

He hadn't quite befriended the young souls who lived in the house with him yet, but he watched them from afar as they learned to walk, learned to talk, learned to play, learned to laugh. He watched them from afar as they multiplied. He knew them intimately, and occasionally he would show himself to them and he would wave and he would delight in their manic giggles, in their squeals of happiness. Even then, before they knew his name, they loved him. How could you not love Henry?

But back to Aunt Bea, paused in between stairwells, looking up into the darkness. It was a little creepy, how dark it was on the fourth floor, how the stairs stretched up into nothingness, disappeared into shadow.

But Aunt Bea was a fan of creepy things, and something was telling her to go up there, and something was telling her not to turn on the light, and if there was one thing about our aunt, it was that she always listened to those voices in the back of her head, she always listened to those little instincts that told her what to do, those whispered messages from Persephone (or from her daughter).

So she went up.

It was lighter in the attic; there was a full moon the night I was born, and it shone through the windows, and it lit up the space in a warm, yellow glow, and it wrapped itself around Aunt Bea's body, and it made her feel safe and protected.

Remember, Aunt Bea lived with a ghost, too, and though I don't think she ever saw her little sister the way I did, I knew she sometimes caught movement out of the corner of her eye, I knew she sometimes heard little ghostly footsteps on the hardwood floor, I knew she sometimes *knew*.

"Is someone up here?" she said, quietly, hopefully, and there was the tiniest noise from the doorway of the catchall room, a noise that would have scared the pants off anyone else in the world but which invigorated Aunt Bea, and she turned again, her heart racing, her senses tingling, and there he was—our Henry.

"Oh," she said. "You're something else."

And he was, wasn't he?

He was both something else (unique, unusual, set apart from the crowd) and something *else* (not a human, not alive, not really meant to be here on this celestial plane at all).

"You can see me?" Henry asked—a somewhat stereotypical response for a ghost, but he had never been seen by a grown-up before, and he was very young at this point, just a boy, hardly older than Bernadette herself. He was just getting used to Bernie and Evelyn seeing him, and it thrilled him and scared him all at once, but this, a *grown-up* seeing him, after he had spent so long in this house without anyone at all to watch over him, well . . . This was almost too much.

Aunt Bea, sensing all of this, sensing everything in the entire world, knelt on the floor. She put her hands on her thighs and smiled at the little ghost boy. In that moment, for whatever reason, because of her ancestry, perhaps, because of all of our ancestries, she knew him intimately. She could sense his loneliness. She could see his life with us (maybe not all the details, but the general gist), and, most importantly, she could see the end of it. The end of everything. Henry saving us, saving the world. This was a very important ghost.

"You're so brave," she said to him then, and Henry, having of course no idea what she was talking about, nevertheless liked this *immensely*. A strange lady comes into your attic and calls you brave, well, he about fell in love with her.

He gave a little half-shrug, made a noncommittal sort of grunting sound, then, overwhelmed with happiness and peace and the distinct joy of being perceived, disappeared.

She never saw him again.

And then, Christmas Day, almost seventeen years later.

This is what happened in the immediate aftermath:

Our mother, arriving home just as we were leading Evelyn up the first flight of stairs to our attic respite, each of us holding a different part of her, guiding her forward as gently as we could, said, "Why do I suddenly feel so much *lighter*?"

I made new cups of tea, reheating the water in the kettle, taking the little circular tray down from the cabinet so I could carry them all upstairs at once.

We sat on the floor in the attic, so quiet that we could hear the clock chime midnight all the way downstairs in the living room.

Clara glanced at our grandmother's gold watch and frowned slightly. The time was off. She adjusted the delicate gold crown until she was satisfied, then she stared at it for another moment, unclasped it from her wrist, and turned to Evelyn, who sat close beside her.

Evelyn did not say a word, did not move her eyes to meet Clara's gaze, but she did hold her hand out, and Clara carefully placed the watch back on Evelyn's wrist and clasped it shut.

Evelyn covered the watch with her other hand, holding it, feeling the cool metal against her skin once again.

Aunt Bea came upstairs to say good night.

We hadn't talked for so long, it was startling to hear her voice, even if she did whisper (sensing the mood called for it).

"Everyone still awake up here?"

She walked to the window, which we had opened, despite the cold winter air. To let in the smell of jasmine. As much of it as we could get.

There was no way she could see the once-black-slash-now-mended, but she looked up at the sky for a long time, then turned back to us.

"Good night, my little demigods," she said.

What happened in the days that followed:

Aunt Bea went back to Vermont.

She called me on a Saturday afternoon. I had gone back to the churchyard. I answered the phone amongst the graves.

"It feels like something has happened," she said. "It feels like something is different."

"How do you mean?" I asked. Perhaps if one thing had changed about me in the last few months, it was that I had become a slightly better liar.

"My house feels different," Aunt Bea said. "Your house felt different, too."

"I hadn't noticed."

"Oh, you noticed. All you girls noticed."

"Well, I don't know about that."

"Emptier," Aunt Bea said. "That's what my house feels like. Like it's emptier."

Esme, playing dolls in front of the fireplace.

Henry, introducing himself to our mother.

Every Farthing ghost I had ever seen, gone now, released, never to return.

"Is it okay?" Aunt Bea asked when it became clear I wasn't going to be responding. "Is it going to be okay, Winnie?"

"Yes," I said, and at least I didn't think I was lying now. At least I thought I meant it. "Yes, it's going to be okay."

We hung up. I wandered the paths of the churchyard for a long time.

I saw the priest.

He was walking with a group of other people, some clergy, some not, and when he saw me, he smiled. A really big, genuine smile. And when no one was looking, he raised an index finger to his lips. *Shh.*

It was our little secret, that day in the crypt.

I smiled back at him and nodded.

What happened in the weeks that followed:

Our parents had, of course, noticed a shift in everyone's mood, and while they might have written it off had it been just me or Bernadette or Evelyn, they looked to Clara as their canary in the coal mine, as their truest indicator that something was really, actually wrong.

Not for the first time in our collective lives, they thought maybe we'd had a sort of *folie à deux*, but not madness this time, rather, a seasonal affective depression.

It had been a *very* cold winter.

We were prone to fits of crying, fits of silence, fits of staring off into space at nothing.

I sometimes caught our mother looking at one of us, a perplexed expression on her face, perhaps wondering if Melinoë was exacting some revenge on our family, perhaps wondering why she was being spared.

I wore Bernadette's old college sweatshirt every day.

I spent long hours staring out of windows, watching the snow fall steadily, burying all signs of life.

Sometimes I would smell jasmine, and I would turn around quickly, trying to catch sight of him, convinced he had found his way back to us.

Sometimes I closed my eyes and when I opened them, I would

be, for a moment, among the stars, pinned across the sky like our Henry.

Clara spent hours in front of empty canvasses, holding a brush, never quite managing to paint.

Bernadette had started reading voraciously, an obsessive, frantic hobby. She ate breakfast behind a book, finished the last page of one and transitioned seamlessly into the first page of another, went days without speaking to anyone who wasn't made of ink.

It wasn't unusual to find Evelyn crying in strange places. Standing in the pantry. In the downstairs hallway. In the bathroom, sobbing so hard she made herself dry heave.

"All right," my mother said at dinner, one of our last nights of Christmas break. "*What* is going on? Everyone is walking around like someone died."

It was an unfortunate choice of words.

Evelyn burst into tears at the table. Clara, next to her, eyes widening with sudden fear, unsure of what else to do, wrapped her tiny arms around Evelyn's shoulders. Bernadette covered her face with her hands.

My mother looked to me, and I could practically hear the unspoken question: *Status report?*

How could I possibly begin to sum up what had happened?

What answer could I possibly give that might satisfy them without raising too many questions, without giving too much away?

"Bernadette has decided to go back to school," I finally said, and Bernadette uncovered her face and looked at me. "In Vermont. With Aunt Bea. And we're all just really going to miss her."

"Is that true, Bernie?" Dad said, brightening. "Oh, honey, that's great."

"It's true," Bernadette confirmed.

"And Evelyn has accepted a spot at the music conservatory," I continued. "In Boston. She starts in the fall. And we're really going to miss her, too."

"Evelyn," Mom said. "Oh, sweetheart, that's magnificent."

"I'm not going anywhere," Clara said helpfully.

"Or me," I said. "Not yet."

"It's a lot of changes," Mom said, nodding her head, somehow satisfied with these answers. "It's a lot of changes and you're all just processing."

"Yes," I agreed. "We're processing."

"I think it's fantastic," Dad said, and raised his wineglass. "Cheers to my beautiful, bright young women. I'm so proud of all of you."

"Persephone would be proud, too," Mom added, winking, raising her own wineglass.

What happened in the months that followed:

I turned seventeen.

I blew out birthday candles on cupcakes and Evelyn put on the bravest face she'd managed in months, and all of us tried to be normal, at least for one night.

It was the first day of spring.

Seventeen years ago, on the night I was born, my parents watched the full moon through the hospital window and my mother declared, "For my next one, I'm doing it at home." (Okay, so maybe Clara *had* been a distant thought.)

"Let's focus on this one," my father said.

"Trust me, I'm focused," she replied. "And in a *lot* of pain."

My father brought her more ice chips.

It was the very tail end of winter, and the past two weeks had brought hope that the world would not always remain such a cold, uninhabitable hellscape.

Persephone was returning from the Underworld, ushering in the spring.

In the Brooklyn Botanic Garden, the magnolias were having their moment: Yulan magnolia, saucer magnolia, star magnolia. The hellebore was blooming alongside its unfortunately named cousin, the stinking hellebore. The daffodils, the Korean rhododendron, the Japanese quince.

The winter honeysuckle. The winter aconite. The buttercup winter hazel.

The week before, during a particularly warm afternoon, our parents brought my sisters (and me, technically), to the gardens and our mother noted all the flowers with the word *winter* in their name. It was our grandmother's name, our mother's mother, the original owner of Evelyn's watch. Another Farthing woman; another Farthing ghost. Our father squeezed our mother's hand in front of all these winter flowers and they remembered her.

Then an old lady, passing by, remarked to my mother, "How are you even standing at this point, you're as big as a house!" which kind of dampened the mood, and they all had lunch and went home.

"Remember that *horrible* lady at the gardens," my mother said now, in the hospital, about two hours away from delivery.

"You can't let people like that stay with you," my father said. "Let's remember the flowers, instead."

"You try staying Zen with contractions," she replied sulkily, but even so, she closed her eyes and remembered the flowers and then she knew what they would name me, just moments before my father arrived at the exact same conclusion.

And so I had been born on the vernal equinox and my parents had named me Winter, after a Farthing woman whose ghost I would never see again.

And now winter was officially over, behind us, and I felt a certain sense of relief at that.

It had been a long winter, to say the least.

It had been the longest winter of my life.

And now, on the night of my seventeenth birthday (the age Henry was when he died, the age Evelyn was when she realized she was in love with a ghost), I couldn't sleep.

The moon was big tonight, it would be full in a few days, and the moonlight came through my window at the perfect angle, falling across my pillow, landing squarely in my eyes. No matter how I adjusted the curtains or threw an arm over my face, it somehow reached me, turning impossible corners and penetrating what I swore was, just the other night, light-blocking fabric.

I felt dizzy.

I felt like . . .

Like it was Henry.

The moonlight was Henry.

Coming into my bedroom to wish me a happy birthday, to tell me everything was okay, he was okay, *we* would be okay.

That was perhaps the silliest thought I'd had in a long time, but it was also comforting, and before I knew what I was doing, I got out of bed and tiptoed out of my room, letting the thought guide me. Clara's light was still on, but I was quiet enough as I crept past her door that I didn't think she heard me.

I walked down the stairs to the first floor, navigating my way through the living room back to the kitchen, to the wall of windows and the back door that led to the stairs and the backyard. Despite it being spring now, it was a chilly night, and I was shivering by the time I reached the jasmine bushes, still dormant, but bound to come alive now that Persephone had returned.

I felt closer to Henry here, where his body was buried, somewhere underneath my feet, resting in the cold earth for the past hundred-odd years.

I felt closer to Henry outside, where the gash in the sky above me was covered by him, made of him, *him*.

Outside, here, in the backyard, he was above and below me.

He had never missed one of my birthdays before.

And I knew he was here now, all around me.

I knelt on the ground, putting my hand on the earth and forcing my fingers not to recoil at how cold it was. I thought of Henry's bones, of my own bones, of all the bones that had ever been inside all of the people who had ever lived.

I squeezed my hand into a fist and knocked my knuckles against the ground just like Henry had knocked against the closet door as he fell in love with my sister, night after night after night over the course of her entire, sweet lifetime. That part I understood. It was easy to fall in love with Evelyn.

"Henry," I whispered, directing my words down, down, down, through the ground, through stones and insects and whatever else made up the Manhattan dirt.

Then I pointed my face to the sky and, for good measure, said his name again, this time sending my voice upward, covering all my bases.

"I miss you," I said. "Winter is over."

The days would get warmer now. It wouldn't snow again. We might still have the occasional morning frost, but the sun didn't have to work so hard to come out from behind the clouds, and most days we could get away with a T-shirt or a long skirt, sans tights.

The city would wake up, shake off its winter doldrums, stretch its limbs.

The Farthing girls would continue.

Thanks to Henry.

I was still looking up at the sky.

I could see the outline of the black tear, where it used to be before Henry fixed it.

I would always be able to see it, I knew; my sisters and I would always be able to tell where it was. Where he was.

I stood up again and closed my eyes. I was finally getting tired. I thought I might actually be able to fall asleep.

"Anyway," I said, my eyes still closed, my face still turned up to the sky. "I just wanted to say hi. So—hi."

I opened my eyes.

To the right of the moon, there were two stars.

If I suspended disbelief, if I squinted, if I used all my powers of wishful thinking, I could almost pretend they were Henry's eyes.

And I could almost pretend that one of them winked at me.

That one of them said, "Happy birthday, Winter."

That one of them said, "I miss you, too."

Epilogue

So what, then, becomes of the Farthing sisters?

What becomes of the children of the in-between, of the great-great-great-great-great-great-grandchildren of the gods?

Well, we continue, of course.

We persevere.

We practice our gifts, we find new gifts, we go forth into the world and make a life for ourselves.

In a lot of ways, we are more fortunate than Persephone, because we are bound to no one, to nowhere, to nothing. We can change our minds a hundred times. We can try one college, drop out, try another, move to Vermont, eat croissants every single morning for breakfast, spend hours in coffee shops drinking lattes and missing our sisters and writing down our story while it is still fresh in our memory. We can take art history classes and go to therapy and heal generational trauma from a generation that most people think only existed in myth.

But what is myth, anyway, if not stories?

And what are stories if not recounts of our history? And no matter how embellished, no matter how many times a story is told and retold, there is always truth there. There is always some basis in reality.

So, yes, the Farthing sisters are real.

The Farthing sisters continue.

And we are just fine.

I turned eighteen.

It had been a mild winter, much milder than last winter, and Mom insisted on an afternoon garden party, setting up a long table in the backyard and crossing her fingers that the weather would hold. I submitted my very short guest list. Bernadette and Aunt Bea drove down from Vermont. Evelyn took the train from Boston. Maybe rang the front doorbell around three; she wore a long-sleeved floral dress and her floral Doc Martens Clara loved so much and she had put her hair into twin braids.

"Oh, man," I said when I pulled the door open. "You look so beautiful."

"Happy birthday, ghost girl," she said, and held out a small package, wrapped sloppily but perfectly in dark-purple paper.

"I said if you brought a gift, you wouldn't be allowed inside."

"I'm a rebel. Now open it!" she said, bouncing on her heels in excitement.

It was always best not to argue with Maybe, especially when it came to gift-giving, which she took very seriously and was very good at.

I tore off the paper to reveal a square jewelry box. "Maybe . . . I can already tell that this is too much . . ."

"You can tell nothing of the sort," she said, still bouncing.

I opened the box and actually gasped.

Sitting inside was a beautiful silver cuff bracelet with a quarter-sized blue stone. The stone was a soft, delicate blue-gray and it sparkled in the light of the small foyer chandelier.

"Oh my gosh . . ."

"I had it made for you," she said. "By my friend, the jeweler. I just couldn't find anything that was perfect, and I couldn't find anything that was *you* enough, so I asked her to—"

I cut her off with a kiss, then pulled away and carefully put the bracelet on my wrist. "I love it."

"The stone is celestine," she said. "To strengthen communication with ethereal beings."

"Oh . . ." I said, looking at her, feeling tears well up in my eyes.

"I know how much you talk to him," she said. "I just thought . . . Well, this couldn't hurt, you know? Maybe give things a little boost."

"It's perfect . . ."

"I just love you," she whispered.

It wasn't the first time she had told me she loved me, but each time was a tiny thrill, and each time was unbelievable in its own way, and each time made me pause and close my eyes and wonder how I had gotten so lucky.

"I love you, too," I said. "Thank you."

We held hands as we walked through the house and out to the backyard, where my sisters and parents and Aunt Bea were already sitting around the long table, drinking prosecco (Dad, Mom, Aunt Bea, and finally, to her immense pleasure, Bernadette) and eating finger sandwiches Dad had meticulously put together from classic British recipes.

"Maybe!" Mom exclaimed, standing up when she saw us approaching. "My goodness, you look like a little spring flower."

"Oh, Anastasia," Maybe said with a wave of her hand, affecting an English accent. "This setup is absolutely *divine*."

"You're a nut," Dad said, hugging Maybe. Then, winking at me over her shoulder, he added, "Just like my daughter."

It was so rare, these days, that we were all together. It was all I had wanted for my birthday. It was all I ever wanted.

We ate about a hundred finger sandwiches each, snuck sips of prosecco, laughed, talked, cried happy tears.

The jasmine had bloomed early that year, and every time the wind blew, I smelled Henry.

And every time the wind blew, I caught Evelyn's eye, and she smiled at me so sadly and so sweetly and I knew we were both thinking of him.

After dinner, Mom and Aunt Bea lugged out a cake they had made themselves—well, really, it was two cakes, one in the shape of the number one and the other a number eight. They put the two plates on the table backward and Dad gasped and said, "You're eighty-one?? Man, I feel old."

Then Bernadette laughed and switched the plates and Clara lit the candles, one on each, and everyone instructed me to make a wish.

The obvious choices danced through my head (*I wish Henry was still here, I wish my sisters and I would always be together, I wish Maybe doesn't wake up one day and realize I am not as cool as I've managed to trick her into thinking I am*), but in the end I went with a classic:

I wish I always feel as happy as I do right now.

It was only after I had blown out the candles, after Maybe had rested her hand on my leg, after everyone had eaten their fill of cake and my sisters had begun to clear the dirty plates away, that I realized it was true.

I *was* happy.

We were happy.

Despite everything, we really were.

Once early evening hit, the weather turned chillier, and we moved inside to open presents, spreading ourselves out in the living room.

Aunt Bea and Maybe shared the love seat and I heard Aunt Bea, working on her fourth or fifth glass of prosecco, lean close to Maybe and say, "Have I ever told you that Farthing girls are descended from Persephone?"

"Have I ever told *you* that I once held a séance in this very house?" Maybe countered.

"Gosh, I like you," Aunt Bea said, and wrapped her arm around my very cute girlfriend.

The first present I unwrapped was from Mom, who affected a wise-ass smirk as I pulled a sweatshirt from Hunter College out of the gift bag. It was the school I was attending in the fall. (I had indeed kept in touch with Professor Natalie Beard.)

"You will burn the other one," Mom said, referring to the sweatshirt from Bernadette's old college, which I wasn't currently wearing and—to be fair to me—usually only wore around the house now.

"Point taken," I said, hugging the sweatshirt to my chest.

Dad, notoriously bad at gifts but incredibly well-meaning, had gotten me a gift card to the Hunter College co-op. "For your books," he explained helpfully. "Oh, and this is probably silly, but—" He tossed me a small, unwrapped box: a replica set of the illuminated fifteenth-century playing cards he always went to see at the Cloisters.

"Dad . . . these are perfect," I said.

"Who knows the next time we'll be able to go together," he said, trying to keep his voice light but clearly beginning to tear up. I got up from my seat and went and hugged him.

"I'll be about a twenty-minute bus ride away, Dad," I said.

"I know, I know," he said.

"A forty-minute walk, if it's nice out."

"I do love walking," he said, sniffling loudly in my ear.

"I know you do," I said. "Thank you for the cards. I love them."

"I love *you*. I'm so proud of you."

"Keep it together, waterworks."

I gave him a kiss on the cheek and went back to my seat.

Aunt Bea had gotten me an incredible vintage Coach messenger bag, big enough for my laptop and a few textbooks.

"I picked it out," Bernadette fake-whispered, and Aunt Bea elbowed her in the side and said, "Happy birthday, honey."

Bernadette's present was next, and it made my breath hitch in my throat: it was a red leather journal, just like the one she had used, over a year ago, to close the doorway that Persephone had opened all those years ago.

"It helps," she said. "To write it down. That's what I'm doing, you know?"

Then Evelyn handed me a small, thin box, and I opened it to find a beautiful silver fountain pen. She smiled and tilted her head in Bernadette's direction. "We coordinated," she said.

"This is so lovely," I said, uncapping the pen to reveal a delicate, gold-plated nib.

"There's a bottle of ink upstairs, too," Evelyn said. "I forgot to wrap it."

"It's green," Bernadette added. "Hunter green. Get it?"

"Thank you, guys," I said. "This is really, really nice."

"My turn!" Clara exclaimed, and from behind the couch, she pulled a flat package, about as long as her torso.

I knew what it was before I even touched it. "Clara . . ."

Out of everyone, Clara's ability to paint had taken the longest to come back.

For months, she sat in front of empty canvasses, holding her paintbrush so hopefully, so longingly, but she couldn't make so much as a single stroke.

Evelyn began to play the piano again, Bernadette went back to journaling every morning, but Clara was somehow left behind.

I took the package from Clara when she held it out to me. "Is this . . ."

"The first thing I've actually finished in a year," Clara confirmed. Then, with a wink: "It came to me in a dream."

I took the longest to open Clara's gift, because my fingers were shaking and kept slipping off the wrapping paper. When I finally got the last strip of paper off the canvas, I closed my eyes, waiting a moment before I opened them and looked at the canvas.

The first thing I noticed were the jasmine flowers.

There were hundreds of them, painstakingly rendered with the most delicate of brushes, filling the bottom half of the canvas and practically spilling over its edges. They were so realistic and so beautiful that I swore I could smell them.

It was our backyard, of course, similar in composition to the painting Clara had destroyed but more zoomed in, cutting out the bench and focusing only on the jasmine bushes and the sky above them, where Clara had painted the tear, then painted a shimmer of gold around the edges.

Henry, holding up the universe.

Henry, always above us.

"Clara, it's so . . ."

But I couldn't get the words out.

And that's when I noticed us, the four of us, in the bottom left corner of the canvas, just our hands, peeking through the branches of the jasmine bush, one of us holding a flower, two of us holding hands, one of us wearing a dainty gold wristwatch . . .

The five of us, as we had always been.

Girl, girl, girl, girl, ghost.

Later, we stood in front of the jasmine bushes, just like in Clara's new painting.

Maybe had gone home and Mom and Dad and Aunt Bea were inside, and it was just the four of us, now, just the Farthing girls, and the smell of jasmine all around us and the bones of a boy we had loved below us and a perfect, chilly blue sky above us.

A perfect, chilly blue sky with one almost imperceptible blemish.

We might have been standing in one of Persephone's footsteps even now, in a place she had stood hundreds of years ago, in a place she had knelt down, to strike her shovel against the earth, to plant the jasmine bushes that exploded every spring, announcing her return.

I reached out to touch one of the flowers and it fell off in my hand, a tiny blessing, a tiny hello from a goddess aunt who had really thrown us all for a loop, who had blessed us all, in a way, but also cursed us all in a way, too.

"I wish I could talk to her," Clara said, reaching out to touch the flower in my palm. "Just talk to her. I have so many questions. I have a list of questions. Should I go get it?"

"Not just yet," Evelyn said. "Let's enjoy this moment. Just for a little bit. It's really been such a beautiful day."

Clara let her hand fall and I closed my own fingers in a gentle fist around the flower.

Later, I would put it on my bedside table so I could fall asleep with the smell of jasmine, with the smell of Henry. A talisman for good dreams, I hoped.

We were all quiet now, all reading each other's thoughts, dipping into each other's memories, the shared knowledge of sisters that would forever connect us.

I looked around at them all and smiled and said, "How lucky are we, kids?" and Bernadette laughed, and Clara snorted, and Evelyn took my free hand.

And we were.

I knew that now.

We really, really were.

Acknowledgments

The very first sentence of this book was written on May 15, 2020. I don't think I need to say too much about what was happening around this date, except that I needed a big escape, and *Persephone's Curse* gave that to me. So thank you first and foremost to Lily King and her novel *Writers & Lovers*—without which I might never have looked up the John Singer Sargent painting *The Daughters of Edward Darley Boit* and I might never have had the idea to write about four haunted, haunting sisters and I might never had found this story and this world, which helped me through such a strange, scary time.

I've always referred to this book as "my New York book." In so many ways, it is my love letter to NYC, and to my own time there, as a much younger woman. Every time I've walked through a Central Park tunnel to find a violinist waiting on the other side, I've felt real life magic. If there are truly doorways to other worlds, I'm sure plenty of them can be found there.

Thank you to my very first reader, Mary Clark, for helping me find the confidence to continue working on this. You are one of the only people who saw the very first iteration of this story, and I hope you love where it ended up.

To my editors, Eileen Rothschild and Char Dreyer: When I say I couldn't have done this without you, that isn't merely a platitude. I genuinely could not have finished this book without you. You saw this story so perfectly, and you helped me see it, too, even when I was absolutely certain I couldn't make my way to the ending. Thank you for that and thank you for welcoming me to Wednesday Books and the Macmillan family with such warmth and kindness.

I can't believe my wonderful agent and I have been together for nine books now. You are, as ever, such an important and integral part of my journey. Thank you, Wendy Schmalz.

I was blessed to have such a lovely group of early readers for *Persephone's Curse*. Thank you to Jennifer Niven, Romina Garber, Mackenzi Lee, and Kerry Kletter, for lending your words of support and championing the Farthing girls as hard as you did. Especially to Kerry—your kindness is unparalleled, and I owe you everything.

From the very first sentence to the very last sentence (both revised about a 120 times), the writing of this book spanned four years. Through all of those four years, I received unfaltering support from my family, my friends, and my partner, Shane. Thank you for the good, the bad, and everything in-between.

And I think the Farthing girls would agree: The in-between is where all the important stuff happens.

About the Author

Shane Abrahamovich

KATRINA LENO is the author of seven young adult novels, including *Horrid* and *Summer of Salt,* and the middle grade novel *The Umbrella Maker's Son*. She was born on the East Coast and spent four years in New York City—though never once saw a ghost in her attic. She currently lives in Los Angeles. Still no ghost.